FACE DOWN
IN THE PARK

Also by Leonard Foglia and David Richards

1 Ragged Ridge Road

FACE DOWN IN THE PARK

LEONARD FOGLIA
AND
DAVID RICHARDS

POCKET BOOKS
New York London Toronto Sydney Tokyo Singapore

POCKET BOOKS, a division of Simon & Schuster Inc.
1230 Avenue of the Americas, New York, NY 10020

Library of Congress Cataloging-in-Publication Data

Foglia, Leonard
    Face down in the park / Leonard Foglia and David Richards.
      p.   cm.
    ISBN 0-671-02728-X
    I. Richards, David, 1940–   . II. Title.
    PS3556.036F3   1999
    813'.54—dc21   98-50124
                                                 CIP

First Pocket Books hardcover printing March 1999

10 9 8 7 6 5 4 3 2 1

POCKET and colophon are registered trademarks of
Simon & Schuster Inc.

Printed in the U.S.A.

QBP/✶

For Joanne

1

I was the first thing he saw. The letter *I*. The capital letter.

Was he really seeing it? Or dreaming it?

He wasn't sure. It filled his entire field of vision, a black *I*—floating against a swirling white . . . something. He couldn't make out the background. Didn't want to try for the time being. The *I* was puzzling enough.

What did it mean? Was it a message? God speaking to him in some way? "I am the way, the truth and the life. He who believes in Me will never die."

Maybe he was dead and this was the beginning of the aftermath, the slow sorting out that the priests had told him about as a boy, when his eternal self would emerge from its earthly shell and his true essence would finally shine clear, as the letter was clear. His body felt numb, heavy, as if he would never get up again. His right cheek was cold. So all physical sensation had not left him. He heard a faint voice inside his head, arguing that numbness wasn't death. Not yet anyway. And the isolated patch of cold on his cheek was growing colder. So, no, he couldn't be dead.

It had to be a dream then—the swirling and the heaviness that rooted him to the spot and the stark letter *I* that kept coming toward him, bigger and bigger, like a soldier on the march.

He blinked his eyes and slowly lifted his head. A wave of nausea swept over him, and he quickly put his head back down again. He had the sensation of spinning through space and remembered another time he had fallen down.

He must have been three or four. He had scraped his knees badly on the pavement. As he sat there, stunned, blood had risen to the surface of his skin. Bright, tiny drops at first that formed a trickle, then a ribbon of red that snaked down his leg. He had begun to cry. Someone had picked him up and held him high in his arms.

The image was suspended in his mind, like the letter *I* was suspended in the whiteness. But he couldn't say who the man was or, indeed, if he was even the boy with the tear-stained face in the man's arms. It all looked familiar enough, like a photograph in a family album. But it promptly faded away, and the swirl returned.

He lay there for a while.

The next thing he was aware of was a hand touching the *I*. He assumed it was his. Whose else could it be? The proof would be if he could move the fingers. He concentrated hard. The index fingers rose and fell several times in a faint tapping motion. Aha! It was his hand, after all. He had pretty much concluded beforehand that he wasn't dead, but this confirmed it. He was putting things together, making progress.

He lifted his head a second time, shifted it slightly to the side, and saw two more letters. *G-I-N.* He had an urge to laugh, but that physical reflex didn't seem available to him now, no sound came from his lips. "Gin." He couldn't remember whether he liked gin or not. Had he ever drunk it? It would come back to him when he woke up. Vodka, yes. That much he knew. Gin was clear like vodka, though. Had he gotten the two confused?

Maybe gin was responsible for the dull ache he was starting to feel in the back of his head. He was going to have one hell of a hangover, if that was the case. But something told him it wasn't so simple. That wasn't why he was lying here, his body leaden and his cheek icy cold, with visions of the alphabet passing before him. It was more complicated than just too much liquor and an incipient hangover. There was some other reason for what he was experiencing.

But finding an explanation required too great an effort. It was taking all his strength just to keep his head up. He decided to lie back down. He would puzzle things out later. Tomorrow. Whenever he woke up. Gently, as if he were sinking into a downy pillow, not onto the hardness of stone, he rested his cheek next to the capital *I*.

As he did, his only desire was to be clean. Washed clean in the blood of the lamb. No, that wasn't right. That's what the priests said. A different boyhood image flashed into his mind—the blackboard in his first-grade classroom. If you were good, you got to wipe it with a wet cloth for the teacher. Back and forth, until all the chalk marks were gone. After the water dried, the blackboard looked brand-new.

Yes, that's the answer, he thought, before he lost consciousness and slipped into a tunnel of darkness. I can wipe it all away. I can be clean again. A clean slate.

2

"He is the most popular box office star in the world. She, the highest paid actress ever and, many say, the sexiest. Together, they epitomize Hollywood's new royalty—young, privileged, successful beyond anyone's dreams and very much their own bosses.

"Tonight in a rare television interview, their first as husband and wife, Christopher Knight and Jennifer Osborne on the *Deborah Myers Special*. Join us at nine as we go up close and personal with the new breed of superstars, who are turning the tinsel of tinseltown into solid gold."

Deborah Myers, dressed in a blazing red suit, sat back in the white armchair and wrinkled her brow in displeasure. "Too flat. Let me take it again." She looked over at her producer. "How are we doing for time, Pete?"

"Don't worry. Our time is their time," replied a compact man in a black turtleneck and sports jacket. "If they want to stay upstairs all morning, we are more than happy to wait. Hell, if they want us all to stand on our heads, we'll stand on our heads."

"Don't count on me. My new stylist would never forgive me." But Deborah Myers knew Pete was right. Just getting an interview with the two stars was a big coup. To be able to conduct it in their Malibu beach house, well, she could imagine the ratings already. If this didn't flatten *Emergency Squad*, nothing would.

Behind her, sliding glass doors opened onto a wooden deck on which the set designers had arranged several large pots of pink hibiscus in full flower. The sky was cloudless and glints of sunlight flashed off the flat ocean, like sparks off an anvil. She had to admit it was the perfect backdrop—America's enduring image of all that was desirable about Southern California. In spite of the mud slides and the fires and the earthquakes, people persisted in believing the place was some kind of earthly paradise, populated by the fit and the underdressed. They really believed in stardom, too, as if it were a higher state of existence, with flattering lighting and music playing in the background. Far be it from her to wise anyone up.

Deborah checked her wandering thoughts and prepared to run through the promo again, when the click of footsteps at the top of the stairs stopped her. Jennifer Osborne was putting in an appearance at last. The room fell silent as the crew turned to gawk. Deborah couldn't help noticing that they were like a bunch of high school boys in the presence of the prom queen.

Objectively speaking, Jennifer Osborne was no more beautiful than dozens of Hollywood starlets with well-endowed bodies and blonde hair that fell to their shoulders. The thing is, it was impossible to be objective about her. "Not since Marilyn" was the phrase the columnists had used when she first appeared on the scene in low-budget potboilers and tight sweaters. But she had proved to be Marilyn without the neuroses. She didn't need anyone to reassure her that she was sexy or tell her that she could act. She knew it. Confidence seemed bred into her.

It was said that the camera adored her, but it was really the studio lights that adored her. Where they washed out others and flattened their features, they lent a radiance to her face. Her skin—smooth, unblemished, white as alabaster—was responsible for that. One of the lessons that her mother had drummed into her as a child was never to go outside without a hat, "unless you want to look like that." Since "that" was Aunt Hattie, a flashy widow from Naples, Florida, with cheap jewelry and a leathery tan that aged her a full fifteen years, the lesson had taken.

Jennifer Osborne's outfit was casual, the off-white slacks emphasizing the length of her legs as she came down the stairs, and the matching silk blouse showing off the fullness of her breasts. If she were walking by a construction site, Deborah thought, the wolf whistles would be deafening by now.

"I'm sorry," Jennifer said, looking around. "Am I interrupting?" Her voice was barely a whisper, but in the silence, everyone heard her.

"Of course not." Deborah sprang from the armchair, sidestepped a camera and several reflectors, and went to Jennifer with outstretched hands.

"You look absolutely stunning."

"Not too informal? It isn't every day you bare your soul for forty million television viewers. Christopher should be along in a second. He couldn't decide between two blazers. And they say women take forever to dress! By the way, that's a terrific suit."

"Armani. Just on loan. Thanks for noticing, although how could you not? Back home in Texas, we call this 'chile-pepper-red.' Let's hope Christopher doesn't wear blue or the three of us are going to look like the French flag."

"Actually, he was leaning toward gray," Jennifer said.

"Is there a red, white, and gray flag, Pete? With our luck, it belongs to some Middle Eastern liberation movement, and we'll be flooded with irate letters next week."

She laughed. On the surface, Deborah Myers didn't give the impression of being a tough interviewer, but nobody doubted that she was a canny one. Like most of the celebrities on her specials, she had worked her way up the ladder and knew the costs of success. Her hour-long telecasts were as much a celebration of her own fame as her guests'. She wasn't out to destroy anyone's career, although she was perfectly willing, if the career had fallen apart, to explore the wreckage. Her reputation rode on capturing that "special moment," when her guests divulged an intimate detail about themselves, displayed a flash of temperament, or rarest of all, told the unvarnished truth.

She didn't know what it would be today, but counted upon the easy, free-wheeling approach to work in her favor. You couldn't badger people like Christopher Knight and Jennifer Osborne, but you could sometimes cajole them into a state of relaxation that let them forget the presence of the camera momentarily.

"What's this talk about flags?" Christopher Knight bounded down the stairs and slipped his arm around his wife's waist. He had opted for the gray blazer and a pale yellow shirt, opened at the neck. "Sorry to hold things up, dear. Will this do?"

"Perfect," Jennifer said. "It matches the gray in your eyes." She ran her hand playfully through his jet black hair and gave him a peck on the tip of his nose. Then she turned back to Deborah. "Am I married to the most handsome man in the world or not?"

It wasn't a question that needed answering. Six foot three inches tall, thirty-three years old, Christopher Knight was a Cary Grant for the 1990s—expensively tailored, impressively muscled, exquisitely mannered. "The impeccable hulk," some critic had quipped. He'd started out as a rebellious juvenile on a daytime soap opera but had long since blossomed into a leading man of some versatility. To many, he personified the American heartland and American decency, but he could also project an aura of brooding and danger that his female fans loved. There was something almost tyrannical at times about his good looks, and his most recent screen roles acknowledged the ambiguity of his heroic personality.

He returned Jennifer's kiss. "Ah, flattery, flattery, thy name is woman!"

"It's frailty, darling," she said.

"That, too." He gave her an amused grin.

The crew wasn't even pretending not to stare. A few jaws hung open dumbly. Even Clinton hadn't gotten this kind of reaction, Deborah mused, when she'd snagged that first exclusive interview. It had something to do with secret fantasies. Movie stars triggered them; politicians didn't. Except for Kennedy. And maybe Reagan briefly, when he was younger, before his cheeks got so rosy and he started shellacking his hair. Beyond that, she wasn't able to say why certain people had this power over the imagination of others without doing anything really, just by being.

8

The words ordinarily used to describe the phenomenon—
magnetism, *chemistry*, *charm*—belonged as much to the
vocabulary of sorcery as that of science.

The hush was broken by a middle-aged woman who
slipped into the room as unobtrusively as possible, whispered into Christopher's ear, then stepped back and waited
dutifully. Earlier that morning, the woman had been
introduced to Deborah as the stars' press agent, but
Deborah knew she wasn't the big gun—not the one who
had called her office no fewer than twenty times a day
over the last month in an attempt to regulate every aspect
of this interview. His calls had become so frequent, in fact,
that her secretary began referring to him as "the stalker."

"Stalker, holding on line two."

"Stalker insists you ring him up immediately."

Whenever Deborah eventually got him on the line, she
had trouble keeping the laughter out of her voice.

This woman, altogether more self-effacing, had turned
out to be an assistant from the office, pressed into service at
the last moment. The situation was unorthodox. Stars of
Christopher's and Jennifer's magnitude always had the top
man (or woman) dancing attendance on their every move.

Just as well, Deborah thought now.

In her opinion, most public relations honchos were
overpaid pains in the butt—intent, like the stalker, on
demonstrating their indispensability and proving to their
clients that they had a potentially damaging situation in
hand. In reality, they controlled nothing and made everybody else's job twice as difficult. If this assistant seemed
out of her depth, she was at least conveniently meek and
wouldn't speak up in the middle of the interview, demand-
ing that some juicy tidbit be stricken from the record.

A flicker of annoyance registered on Christopher's face. "Tell him that we're busy," he said to the mousy woman.

"But he's been desperate to talk to you for two days now. Please?"

"Explain to me again why His Lordship isn't here today?"

"Um, personal business, I believe."

"Really? I thought *we* were his personal business."

"Of course, you are—"

Christopher cut her off. "Fine. I'll be right there. Sorry to be a nuisance, Deborah, but could you spare me a second to take a quick phone call?"

"Please. Our time is your time," replied Deborah, who suspected that "His Lordship" referred to the stalker.

A man in a powder blue smock fluttered up to Jennifer Osborne to inspect her makeup for any infinitesimal flaws that might have escaped eyes less practiced than his. Finding one, he emitted little squeaks of disapproval and said, "My, my! Would you mind coming with me for just a teeny, tiny minute, Miss Osborne?" The crew roused itself out of its stupor, and the living room came alive again. There was a growing charge in the air that this wasn't going to be just another show.

Deborah took her position in the armchair, opposite the empty sofa where the stars would sit. "Okay, Pete," she said. "I'll redo the promo afterward. Let's go straight to the intro."

She fixed on the camera lens, as if it were a friendly neighbor who had just dropped by for coffee, and held the expression until the audio man called out, "Tape is rolling."

Her face muscles relaxed.

"Good evening. I'm Deborah Myers. Tonight, the new royalty. Two of the biggest stars in Hollywood. They are powerful, they are self-assured, they are sexy. For one full hour, Christopher Knight and Jennifer Osborne talk about their careers, their marriage, and their biggest gamble yet—the controversial $100 million epic *In the Beginning*, in which they play Adam and Eve. We'll have a preview. Stay with us."

3

The man in the charcoal gray suit, white button-down shirt, and gray and plum striped tie watched as the maid came out of 1201, gave the cart a shove with her hip, then guided it another ten feet until it came to rest in front of 1203. She rapped on the door, waited long enough to determine there was no one in the room, then inserted a white plastic card into the electronic lock. With a click, the door opened. Leaving her cart on the threshold, she scooped up a stack of fresh towels and disappeared inside.

The man adjusted his tie in the mirror at the far end of the hallway. It was his favorite suit and tie, and he prided himself on his appearance. His fastidiousness was cause for some ridicule from his associates, who liked to remind him that there was no dress code for his line of work. Nobody used his real name, Spieveck, which had been inevitably (and logically) shortened to Spiff. The nickname didn't displease him. Why wear a Knicks sweatshirt and old jeans, he reasoned, when you could get your clothes at Armani Exchange? If others wanted to look like slobs, that was their affair. He liked being taken for a lawyer or a businessman. People did all the time.

Only minutes ago, as he'd walked across the lobby, the concierge had nodded deferentially and said he hoped that everything was satisfactory. "Most satisfactory," he'd replied, before stepping into the elevator. And he wasn't even staying at the hotel!

Reassured that the knot of his tie listed neither to the left nor to the right, Spiff strode down the corridor, edged by the cart, and entered the room. It was almost antiseptically neat, he noted with approval. As he automatically checked out the premises, he heard the maid singing along with her Walkman. He was about to make a noise to alert her of his presence, when she shuffled out of the bathroom and caught sight of him.

"Ah, *madre mia!*" She shrieked and jumped back.

"Terribly sorry. I didn't mean to scare you like that. As you can see, I never made it home last night." He flashed a sly smile. "I guess I won't need maid service today."

Before she had time to turn down the volume of the Julio Iglesias tape on her Walkman, he ushered her to the door and pushed her cart into the hallway.

"*Gracias. Muchas gracias,*" he said, smiling and waiting for her to move on.

"*De nada, señor.*" How ridiculous to pay for an expensive room and not use it, she thought. But one look at the attractive stranger was all it took to know that he'd probably been out all night cheating on his wife. She recognized the type—salesmen, eager to have a good time in the big city. If it meant one less room to clean this morning, far be it from her to voice an objection.

Once she had rounded the corner of the hall, Spiff hung the DO NOT DISTURB sign on the outside doorknob and double-locked the door. Then, he put on a pair of latex gloves, snapping them the way medics did on TV. He knew that no one had spent the night here, as the plump pillows and unruffled bedspread testified. He crossed to the open suitcase on the luggage stand by the window, carefully examining the contents—underwear, socks, T-shirts, cotton sweaters—then depositing them systematically in neat piles on the floor. He saw no reason to toss things around; it paid to be orderly. If you made a mess, you could inadvertently cover up what you were looking for. In the side pockets of the suitcase, he came on a pack of stale gum, a half-filled bottle of aspirin, and a dirty comb.

He ran his hands over the lining of the empty suitcase, searching for hidden compartments.

"Fucking nothing!" he said.

He didn't like talking to himself. It implied a lack of control. But sometimes, like right now, the words just popped out of his mouth by themselves.

Fucking nothing was secreted in the publications on the coffee table, either, save an airplane ticket, which was tucked between the pages of an in-flight magazine called *Destinations*. The drawers in the nightstand by the bed yielded only the standard items supplied by a gracious management: stationery, a pen, a Gideon Bible (he flipped through it just in case), plastic laundry bags, and a menu for room service pushing the continental breakfast at $15 a head. The NO SMOKING plaque on the wall explained the absence of matchbooks and ashtrays. What, he wondered fleetingly, did tourists steal for souvenirs these days?

In the closet, a plaid work shirt, a pair of jeans, and a suit had been hung up on wooden hangers—the theft-proof variety that hook onto metal rings permanently attached to the bar, thereby further frustrating the ashtray collectors. The left shoulder of the suit jacket felt suspiciously stiff to him, so he took the Kershaw Talon out of his pocket and flipped it open. The blade, three inches of stainless steel shaped like an eagle's claw, sliced cleanly through the fabric. The stiffness was only padding meant to give the jacket body and its owner the reassurance of a broad physique.

Spiff regretted spoiling such a nice piece of goods. From the touch, he could tell that it wasn't run-of-the-mill Sears. He made a mental note of the label, Hugo Boss. Just to be on the safe side, he sliced open the other shoulder.

The shaving kit on the marble counter in the bathroom contained the usual toiletries, a package of condoms, and a prescription medicine in an amber plastic container. The bathroom, as spotless as the bedroom, hadn't been used, either. Or else he was dealing with the original Mr. Clean. He checked his watch. Six minutes so far. Another few minutes and he'd be out of there.

He stripped the double bed of its linens, as the maid would have done, pulled the pillows from their cases and patted them down. Then he stood the mattress against the wall and lifted up the box spring, exposing a few hairpins and some dust balls. His nose wrinkled instinctively in disgust, and he let the box spring fall back on its frame with a thud. He was drawing blanks everywhere.

The cushions of the sofa hid no surprises, not even loose change. That left the service bar, an unlikely spot, but one to be checked nonetheless. The shelves were stocked with fruit juices, snacks, and liquor miniatures, which he swept into a wastebasket with a couple of brisk gestures. He strongly disapproved of drinking. Peanuts were another matter. He pocketed a package for later, taking care to enter a check mark in the corresponding square on the "Service Bar Consumption Form" on the Formica counter. What was the point of an honor system, if everybody didn't obey it?

Convinced that he had explored every corner of the room, he took out his cellular phone and dialed a number. He was still waiting for someone to answer when he heard people coming down the hall.

"Shit!"

In another minute, he would have been gone. He tapped his foot impatiently. "Come on. I haven't got all day. Pick up the damn phone."

"Yes?"

Spiff held his breath. In the hall, the sound of raucous laughter grew louder, followed by a door slamming sharply. Whoever it was—revelers returning after a drunken binge on the town, no doubt—had entered the room across the way. Didn't anybody keep normal hours around here?

"Yes? Who is this?" God how that voice irritated Spiff. "Is anyone on the line?"

"Yeah, it's me, Spiff. Nothing here."

"What do you mean? Are you sure?"

It was too early for peevishness. Of course I'm sure, you twit. I'm a pro. I do my job, Spiff wanted to reply. But all he answered was, "Yes, zip."

"First you said there was nothing on him. Now you're telling me there is nothing in his room?"

"You got it. Clean as a whistle."

"Where is it then?"

"Damned if I know."

"But you're being paid to find out. Well, aren't you? I wouldn't call this doing your job very well. In fact, I'd say you were doing it rather poorly."

Spiff resisted the urge to talk back. When clients were upset like this, it was best to let them run their mouths, blow off steam. Eventually, they shut up.

"He has been far more clever than I would have anticipated," the voice concluded at long last. "I'll be in touch."

Spiff heard a click, and the line went dead. He folded up the cellular phone and slid it back into his pocket. His clients didn't always like the way things turned out, but he tried not to let that bother him. All he cared about was holding up his end of the deal. He didn't like a shoddy performance any more than he liked shoddy dress. Standards were going to hell everywhere, and he, for one, wasn't about to contribute to the deterioration.

There was certainly no need to yell, as the client had just done. No need at all. Yelling accomplished nothing and was bad for the blood pressure . . . *everybody's* blood pressure. What it showed was . . . a complete *absence* of respect . . . of . . . of . . . *professionalism.* Yes, that was it! As if he, Spiff, were a pissant just starting out . . . some kind of . . . *rank amateur!*

To calm himself, he flicked open the Kershaw Talon again and walked over to the bed. Then, taking a deep breath and exhaling it slowly, he ran the blade down the center of the mattress from top to bottom. A thin layer of white padding oozed out.

"There! Much better."

The anger was all gone. He felt good again.

He put his ear to the door and, satisfied that no one

else was approaching, ducked out into the hall. Instinctively, he readjusted his tie and slicked back his hair. Halfway to the elevator, he remembered that he had forgotten something.

Hastily retracing his steps, he removed the plastic DO NOT DISTURB from the door handle, flipped it over, then put it back, so that it read PLEASE MAKE UP ROOM.

4

As he lay there, facedown on the stone, his body slowly began to register the morning chill. It crept into his legs and arms and settled into his joints with a persistent ache that pulled him out of his dream and brought him closer to consciousness. It wasn't much of a dream, anyway. Just bizarre, fragmented images. Woods in the spring. A car speeding along a highway. And hands, reaching out from the trees and rising up from the pavement, clutching at the speeding car as it passed, trying to stop it.

Whatever it meant, it wasn't the sort of dream you tried to prolong. There was nothing pleasant about it, nothing to postpone waking for. The images grew progressively fainter while the sensation of cold grew stronger. Then, the man opened his eyes.

He seemed to be lying on a stone mosaic, made up of small black and white tiles. He pushed himself up with his forearms. There beside his left hand was a capital *I*. He looked at it with momentary fascination until the ache coming from every part of his body sapped his concentration. He rolled onto one side and maneuvered himself into a sitting position. He was surprised to see that he was wearing a suit. The knee was torn. He must have fallen

and ripped it. Otherwise, it was a nice suit. Dark green. New. Soft to the touch.

He breathed in the crisp morning air, waiting for his surroundings to come into focus. It seemed to be a circular mosaic of some sort that he was sitting on. The black and white tiles formed letters and patterns. The *I* was part of an inscription. He didn't remember that several hours earlier it had set him off on a flight of metaphysical speculation. He'd forgotten that and a lot more, too.

He studied the other letters—*M-A-G-I-N-E*—and realized he'd been lying on a word. Like a child learning to read, he sounded it out.

"I-ma-gin-e," he whispered to himself. "Imagine!"

He looked around and saw wooden benches and, overhead, a canopy of trees. Beyond them, he could make out streetlights and a row of tall buildings. He concluded that he was in a park in a big city. But what city?

The muffled sound of automobile traffic confirmed his conclusion. He tried to stand. As he did, a shooting pain raced up the back of his neck, causing him to gasp. He automatically reached up with both hands to steady his head. When he brought his hands back down, his fingertips were covered with blood. All he could think was that something was wrong. Not what or how or why. Just something. Questions were beyond him for the time being.

Panic rose in him, along with the sense that his life was in danger. He had to go where the cars were, stop one of them maybe. Struggling to his feet, he managed only a few steps before the ground began spinning. He reeled backward and collapsed on a bench. He gripped the metal armrest and closed his eyes, putting all his concentration into breathing deeply—in and out, in and out—until the dizziness lifted and the ground spun to a stop, like a carnival ride winding down.

The trees came back into focus, their leaves forming lacy patterns against the sky. The sun was striking the topmost floors of the taller buildings, so that the windows appeared to be made of gold foil, not glass. He blinked in wonderment. Then his eyes went to an older, heavier structure to the right. It looked like a nineteenth-century fortress, or perhaps a castle, with its gables and turrets and a roof that came to several sharp peaks in a row. The copper flashing that outlined the building's fantastically shaped roof had oxidized bluish green. From a pole planted on top of the middle peak, an American flag flapped silently.

He stood up and started toward it, oblivious that he was walking over the tile mosaic with the curious word at its center. On the gently curving path that led to the street, he nearly collided with a jogger.

"Watch it, buddy," the jogger snapped.

"Sorry, I didn't see you."

"Well, maybe if you looked where you were going . . . Hey, are you all right?"

No, the man thought. I'm not all right. I need help. But before he could articulate the words, the jogger had resumed his pace and moved on down the path.

At the street corner, he had a better view of the massive building. It was constructed out of yellow brick and brownstone, and from the deep inset of the windows, he judged the walls to be several feet thick. Dark wooden shutters and curtains had been drawn across most of the windows on the lower floors. If there was life stirring within, it was not discernible from the sidewalk.

As he examined the imposing facade, he thought he caught sight of something moving in one of the corner windows, three stories up. A person was hovering in the window, staring down at him, unless his eyes were fooling him and he'd been taken in by an apparition. His senses weren't all that reliable this morning. The form moved ever so slightly, and a pale face flashed briefly in the dark pane. It *was* a person. With silver hair.

Don't go away, thought the man in the green suit. Help me. He lifted his arm and waved at the figure in the window, even though the movement sent splinters of pain through his head. The pain no longer mattered. He had to make contact. "I can see you," he cried out. "You must be able to see me. Please wave back."

The person in the window pulled back into the shadows.

"Don't go away," shouted the man in the street. Desperation took hold of him, and he swung both his arms over his head, crisscrossing them furiously, like a sailor who has lost his semaphores but still continues to spell out a message of distress.

"I see you. I know you're there."

But the figure had disappeared altogether. The third-story window, like those around it, was dark.

The man let his arms fall to his side. He saw some lights blink on in the dormer windows under the gabled roof, then realized it was another optical illusion created by the morning sun. He told himself it didn't matter. The windows were too high up for anyone to take notice of him anyway.

"He's waving at me . . . No, I'm not kidding . . . He's standing right there on the far corner, waving his hands over his head like some demented person. I don't believe it."

Without taking his eyes away from the sight that had so startled him, the silver-haired man stepped back and fumbled in the pocket of his paisley dressing gown for a pack of Benson & Hedges. Trapping the telephone receiver against his right ear in order to free his hands, he lit the cigarette and then shot a stream of smoke at the ceiling. Although it was still early, he was on his fifth cigarette already, which meant that it was going to be another two-pack day.

"I don't know what he's up to," he said, resuming his conversation. "I rather thought you might have an explanation for it." He spoke with a clipped British accent, even though he'd lived in the United States for more than twenty years and could easily have modified his speech, if he so chose. He chose not to, feeling that good diction and adenoidal vowels gave him an edge in his dealings with Americans, who tended to be intimidated by singular pronunciations.

"Oh, I know what you *wanted* to do. But for the moment, one must show a bit of restraint. Once this is settled, you can pitch him in the Hudson River for all that I care. Not yet, though . . ."

He pulled back the damask curtain and checked on the activity in the street. "He seems to be waiting for the light to change . . . A bit unsteady on his feet, which should come as no surprise to you."

To keep his voice from rising, he took a deep puff on the cigarette. Stupid people irritated him, and the irritation showed up first in his voice, which lost all its urbanity as it rose in pitch. When he screamed, he could be as shrill as any fishwife, which is why he tried never to lose his temper. Aesthetically, it was simply unacceptable. Staying calm was requiring an increasing effort of him, though.

"*No*, he's not waving any longer . . . He seems to have stopped looking up here . . . Wait, he's crossing the street . . . He's coming toward the building. My God! What's possessed him! . . . The bloody fool is headed straight for the entrance."

5

Once the man in the forest green suit had successfully navigated the street, he noticed that a moat surrounded the turreted building. He approached it with curiosity, until a startling sight stopped him dead. Black sea monsters were writhing up out of the depths, their gaping jaws ready to devour the unwary.

The monsters were accompanied by a king, whose blazing eyes and tangled hair served as further warning to back off. The man in the green suit sensed he must be hallucinating. Sea monsters in the city didn't make sense. As he stared at them dumbly, their undulations slowly ceased and the ferocious king reverted to what he was—cold metal.

He had been transfixed by the sculpted figures on a wrought iron railing. The king was that god of the sea— the one whose name began with an *N*. Newton! No, not Newton. Not Nestlé, either. Why was he having such trouble coming up with words? His mind was functioning so oddly this morning.

Neptune! That's the one he was trying to think of.

His eyes followed the railing to the middle of the building, where a vaulted passageway led to an inner courtyard. Off to one side was a brass sentry booth. As the man started to turn into the passageway, the door of the booth swung open and a figure in a burgundy uniform stepped out onto the pavement.

"Excuse me, sir," he said. "May I help you?"

The uniform puzzled the man, because it seemed to belong to another time. Palace guards dressed like this in movies and in children's books. He waited patiently for this storybook character to reveal his true identity, as the sea monsters had done. When no transformation came, he pushed on in the direction of the courtyard.

The doorman's arm caught him at chest height and blocked the way. "Hey, wait a second. Where are you going?"

It took all the man's concentration to get the one word out. "Inside."

"Yeah, and who exactly do you want to see?"

He was unable to answer. The whirling sensation had come back.

"Hey, buddy, you doing all right? You look like you had a rough time last night. I think you'd better move on now, okay?" The doorman had seen his share of bums and crazies, not to mention the tourists, who fell somewhere in between. The wisest tactic, he had learned, was to keep up a running patter while ushering them back out onto the sidewalk and pointing them toward the subway. Firmly, he slipped his arm around the man's shoulders.

"Sure must have been one helluva party. Well, happens to the best of us. A few hours sleep ought to fix you up fine. Come on, now. Let's keep going."

Just as he was about to release his grip on the man—and give him a last helpful push—a voice called out, "Is that your new boyfriend, Joey? I always suspected you were cheating on me." Tina stood in the passageway, a pale cherry windbreaker tied around her hips. Watching her go in and out of the building in her skintight exercise gear, a dance bag slung over her shoulder, was the chief advantage of Joey's shift. Her body, although aerobically trained and maintained, had lost none of the natural voluptuousness he had always admired in women, while her face with its dark eyes and full cheeks, reminded him pleasantly of his Mediterranean relatives. He liked her frankness, too, which contrasted with the snootiness of the residents.

"Very funny. This guy had some night last night. Doesn't know where the hell he is. He was trying to get inside."

"He seems awfully attached to you right now!" As she came toward them, her expression changed. "Joey, what's that on your hand?"

The doorman glanced down. The fingers of his right hand were reddish purple. He looked over at the stranger, who was weaving back and forth on the sidewalk, then at his hand again. "Holy shit! It's blood."

"Jeez, Joey. Maybe you should call the police. This guy's not some derelict. Look at his clothes."

"Are you all right?" she asked, reaching out a hand to steady the wavering man. "Would you like us to call somebody for you?"

"Who?"

"I dunno. You tell me."

"Nobody. I can manage by myself."

"You sure of that?"

An incongruous smile broke across his face. "You are very pretty."

"Looks like you're the one got a new boyfriend now," said Joey.

"Well, he wouldn't be half-bad cleaned up." Tina was only partly jesting. The man had sandy blond hair and eyes that, even in their glassy state, were penetratingly blue. He seemed to be about thirty-five, and his build, from what her quick, professional evaluation told her, was that of someone who had been an athlete in his youth, probably a runner or a swimmer, and had never let himself get out of shape. "But I haven't started picking up men off the street yet. Excepting you, Joey. I'd pick you up anywhere."

"Ready whenever you are," replied the doorman, who enjoyed his running flirtation with Tina, not that it would lead anywhere. "Say the word, Tina, and I'm yours."

The man in the green suit spoke up. "Tina?"

"Okay, boys, let's not both of you fight over me."

"Tina?"

"You got it. That's my name. Don't wear it out. So why don't you tell us yours?"

Without warning, the man's knees buckled, and he crumpled to the sidewalk, pulling Tina with him.

"Shit! Joey, call 911."

"Leave him alone, Tina."

"I said call 911!"

As Joey retreated into the sentry booth, Tina loosened the man's tie and checked his breathing. His hands gripped her windbreaker so tightly she had to pry his fingers open one by one. Finally she gave up and let him hold on.

"They're on their way," Joey said on his return. Several commuters, heading for the subway stop on the corner, checked out the odd scene on the sidewalk—curious, but not curious enough to break their stride. The wail of a siren grew louder. The man on the ground opened his eyes.

"How ya doin'?" Tina gave him a look of encouragement.

"Not so good."

"Just hang in there for a few more minutes."

"Am I dying?"

"If you are, that makes me the Virgin Mary."

The crack brought a smile to the man's lips, and he relaxed his grip on her windbreaker.

"There you go. Improving already. You'll be good as new in no time. Just in case, we called for an ambulance."

"Thank you, Tanya."

"The name's Tina, but you're welcome anyway . . . You sure we can't get in touch with somebody? You got a wife? A girlfriend?"

"If that ain't typical," piped up Joey. "You can be out like a light and the first thing they want to know, when you come to, is if you're taken. Better watch out, guy."

"Don't mind this one, mister. He's just jealous because he hasn't been laid since the Bicentennial."

Within minutes, a squad car and an ambulance had pulled up in front of the building. The police car disgorged two cops. The burlier of the two—a Sergeant Edward Callahan, according to his name tag—had the lumbering and unexcitable manner of one who has seen it all. He did the talking. His wiry partner scanned the street nervously, as if half-expecting an insurrection to break out.

"Okay, what do we have here?"

It didn't take Joey long to reveal what he knew. Even with his proclivity for embroidering a story, the details were scant. Callahan made a few notations in his notepad.

Tina had even less to offer.

"Did someone do this to you or did you fall by yourself or what?" Callahan asked, leaning over the man. When no answer was forthcoming, the officer pulled himself back up and shrugged. "A mystery man, eh? I guess you guys better take him to Roosevelt."

The paramedics had already flung open the back doors of the ambulance and rolled a stretcher onto the sidewalk. At Callahan's signal, they eased the man onto the stretcher and belted him into place. Tina could see that the restraints frightened him.

"Hey, it's nothing to worry about," she reassured him. "They don't want you to fall off, that's all." He didn't seem to believe her. In his eyes, she could read the same unfocused terror that seized her daughter in the middle of the night. The kid got so scared sometimes that she wouldn't stay in her own bed, and Tina never had the heart to force her. The stranger seemed every bit as lost and alone right now.

"Lady," one of the paramedics asked. "You prefer to ride in the front or the back?"

"Oh, no. I wasn't planning to come with—"

"Please, Tina," the man cried out. It wasn't until he squeezed her hand that she realized he had been holding it. "Don't leave me."

"Oh, shit!" she muttered to no one in particular. "Why me?" His eyes were locked on her, beseeching and scared.

"Let him go. They'll take care of him," advised Joey.

She made up her mind in a flash.

"I don't know about that, Joey. Hospitals are pretty scary places these days. You can never tell what's going to happen. They're always giving people the wrong medicine. Hell, they can cut off your leg by mistake." She turned to the paramedic. "The back, I guess."

"Saint Tina! Our lady of the StairMaster."

"Can it, Joey. All I'm doing is making sure he gets to the hospital in one piece."

"Don't you have any more clients to work out this morning?"

"No, I had a coupla cancellations at the last minute. And they all want to know why they're not getting any thinner!" She climbed into the back of the ambulance, and Joey handed her the oversize dance bag in which she carried her exercise gear. "Mrs. Shriver in 4-D was my only bubblebutt of the day."

6

To refresh her memory, Deborah Myers quickly riffled through the three-by-five cards in her lap. On them, she had noted dates, quotes, movie titles, and the occasional odd phrase—such as "tabloid vendetta?" and "Crawford/ Ford"—that indicated possible areas of fruitful questioning.

The latter was a reference to the steamy scene in *The Forgotten Summer*, in which Cynthia Crawford, playing a lonely widow, had put the make on the young Christopher Knight in a Thunderbird convertible. The film had been intended as a comeback for the aging actress, whose star was waning. But the scene, in which she had slowly unbuttoned his shirt, exposing his torso to moviegoers for the first time, had capitulated the young actor to fame instead. His boyish ingenuousness, combined with the sleekness of that torso, had driven a fair number of young women wild. Ironically, Cynthia Crawford had come across as slightly predatory, thus hastening the end of her career even as Christopher's was taking off. A year later, she had swallowed more sleeping pills than were healthy for a living person.

That could be one of the "soft spots," Deborah thought to herself. That's how she referred to those areas of a celebrity's past that might, with the proper probing, give way to reveal something underneath. The interview, she liked to tell her staff, was not an efficient truth-gathering mechanism, merely a prenegotiated conversation. The challenge was to get her subjects, wary to begin with, to lower their defenses, if not bare their souls. If a few tears were spilled in the process, so much the better, although she knew that most actresses could turn on the waterworks at will, and she hardly expected tears today from Christopher Knight. Anything that got away from the prepackaged, self-promoting blah-blah would be welcome.

Everyone, she realized, had a reason for doing her program. Politicians sought her out, usually because they were trying to present a more human side of themselves to the electorate. Then there were the sinners—the actor caught in flagrante delicto with a hooker or the actress who'd been picked up for shoplifting pantyhose. They were trying to control the damage and came offering her their repentance in an effort to win the public's forgiveness.

Most performers, though, were simply selling something—a new movie, a tell-all book, or in the case of the supermodels, a glossy 1990s version of what was called a "pinup calendar" in simpler days. They were "the peddlers," hoping to pump up their weekend grosses or wangle a toehold on the best-seller list.

To be interviewed by Deborah Myers was said to be worth a half dozen magazine covers, although the publicists generally went after the covers, too. Lower in the pecking order were the talk shows—late night and early morning. Lower still was the press junket, which required the star to sit in a hotel suite in L.A. or New York for the better part of a weekend. At fifteen-minute intervals, lesser journalists and TV reporters were ushered into the room for their "exclusive" interview. Few celebrities enjoyed this, but some recycled the same tired anecdotes with convincing spontaneity, and the performance played big in Providence or Richmond.

So what, Deborah Myers wondered fleetingly, was the reason Christopher Knight and Jennifer Osborne were granting an interview? It wasn't just to push *In the Beginning*, their new movie, whatever the studio brass claimed. A Christopher Knight movie didn't usually need that kind of send-off. In fact, he was one of the few stars who got more publicity the less he said. At the Oscars, you'd see him and Jennifer walking into the Dorothy Chandler Pavilion, smiling and waving to the crowd, with hardly a word for the reporters, who pressed up against the velvet ropes and thrust their microphones at him, like street people clamoring for spare change.

Today Christopher Knight would say only what he—and his people—wanted him to say. They were probably on a conference call this very minute discussing how best to handle her. No matter. Personally, she had heard enough hype to last a lifetime. She recognized that millions of viewers felt otherwise, though, and she did the show for them.

Oh, who was she kidding? She did it because it was her job. And as jobs went, it paid damn well.

As she tapped her note cards into a neat stack, Christopher and Jennifer came back into the living room together. Deborah seemed to remember that they had gone off in different directions and now they were holding hands, as if to emphasize that there were two of them, and only one of her. Not a good sign, Deborah thought, but what she said to them was, "This will be great fun, you'll see."

"So how do you want to do it?" Christopher asked.

"I thought I'd start with you first, Christopher. Then, Jennifer. Then the two of you together. That was the format we discussed the other day. If it's still all right—"

"I've been thinking I'd really prefer that we do the whole program together," Christopher said.

"Well, you will. Most of it, anyway. The opening segments will be one-on-one, that's all. If you'd rather, I can start with Jennifer—"

"Oh, no, honey," Jennifer said to her husband. "You go first. You'll be just fine."

Thank you, dear, thought Deborah. The old adage—divide and conquer—applied as much to celebrity journalism as it did to war. If there was any chance of getting Christopher Knight to talk confidentially, it would be in a head-to-head encounter. With three, you got conversation. Or argument. Or confusion.

Jennifer was the more known commodity anyway, less publicity shy than Christopher. She had even been Miss July in one of those men's magazines way back when. (The date was somewhere in the note cards.) He was the nut to crack, assuming, of course, he wasn't just a hollow shell, like so many actors.

"This isn't like one of those game shows, where she has to wait offstage in a soundproof booth, is it?" Christopher remarked, with an edge in his voice.

"That awful *Dream Date*, you mean?" Deborah groaned. "I think I'd die a virgin rather than go on that program. If the choice were still available to me, I mean." The quip defused some of the gathering tension.

"If she'd like, Miss Osborne can sit right here," Pete intervened, indicating his folding canvas chair next to the camera. He would be too nervous to use it, anyway.

"Look, dear, I'll be close enough to jump in, the minute Deborah starts getting rough with you," Jennifer said, a little too brightly for Deborah, who sensed the remark was meant as a warning. The two stars intended to put up a united front today. Beware the interviewer who tried to come between them.

An assistant pinned a microphone to the lapel of the actor, who took his place on the white divan. With the hibiscus trees behind him, and the glinting blue ocean beyond them, he looked like a model in an ad for a pricey men's cologne. The audio man announced that tape was rolling, and Pete promptly began his pacing.

"Christopher Knight, did you ever think, growing up, that your life would turn out like it has?" Deborah asked.

"Like what?"

"Well, that you would be rich, famous, successful, married to one of the most beautiful women in the world."

"How about happy?"

"That, too. Did you expect any of it?"

Christopher ran his index finger along the edge of the sofa arm. "I suppose I did."

"Really?" Deborah's eyes opened wide with amazement.

"No, not *expect* it. I thought it could happen. I must have. You don't go into this business unless you believe you've got a chance of succeeding. That's all that keeps you going sometimes."

"I spoke to a lot of your colleagues before this interview. People who have worked with you. For you. Everyone praised your professionalism, your talent. Nobody had a bad word to say in that respect."

"I would hope not."

"Finally, I said, 'But what kind of a guy is he? Is he any fun, when he's off the set?' Nobody could tell me. You seem to keep your distance from people."

"I value my privacy, yes."

"The consensus appears to be that you don't have many close friends."

"I have a few. Obviously you didn't speak to them."

Sensing a mild rebuke, Deborah shifted gears. "You've always shied away from the media. Unlike most actors, who are constantly out there promoting their films, you've taken a different tact. Why is that?"

Christopher Knight wrinkled his brow and gave himself over to a moment of reflection.

"After the success of *The Forgotten Summer*, Cynthia Crawford offered me a piece of advice that I took very much to heart. She told me that the only way to keep your sanity in this business is to make sure your work is bigger than your celebrity."

"I'm not sure I understand."

"The actors I have always admired the most, the ones who made me want to be an actor, are those who have kept the focus on their work. De Niro, Pacino. Elizabeth Taylor or Madonna, people like that, will always overshadow any role they play. They're so famous their fame ends up coloring their performances. They're controlled by their own image."

"Interesting advice. Cynthia Crawford didn't live by it."

"No, she learned the lesson too late."

"Would she be alive today, if she had managed her career differently?"

"None of us will ever know that."

Deborah Myers decided to risk her first probe. "There were rumors of a romantic involvement between you two."

"Rumors! What would you do without them?"

"The rumor was that you had a stormy relationship and the breakup contributed to her decline. Any truth to that?"

Christopher's sigh was barely perceptible. "No. I would have been honored. She was a wonderful woman. Misunderstood."

Deborah nodded, her eyes moist with understanding, then pulled a card from the deck in her lap.

"Are *you* misunderstood? Here's what one of those colleagues told me. 'Christopher Knight lives his life as if he knew exactly when his final day would be and he's in a hurry to get everything done in time.' How do you react to that?"

"I had never thought of it quite that way . . ."

"All I hear is how hard you work. Night and day. One picture to the next. Acting, now producing. 'He doesn't stop.' "

"You never know when it all might end, I guess."

Deborah Myers leaned forward and reached out a hand, a gesture (she knew) that showed her sympathy and concern. "But you're at the very height of your career. Are you really afraid that it is going to end?"

"It ends for everyone, doesn't it? I have no illusions about that. Eventually, it will end for you, too, Deborah."

Deborah Myers chose not to pursue the point.

7

*S*teve Carroll wanted to be famous. He couldn't have said when the desire first came upon him any more than he could have pinpointed the moment he realized that he was good-looking, but the two were connected in his mind. He knew that he was as good-looking as Redford or Newman or any of those other relics his mother mooned over. And he knew, too, that there was something to be gained from that, something more than the charged stares that had come his way for as long as he could remember. His looks gave him an advantage over people, and that advantage multiplied a thousand—no, a hundred thousand times—was what he thought fame must be like.

His height and broad shoulders made him appear older than he was. If he was wearing his one sport coat, he could drive over to Poughkeepsie and pick up any Vassar coed he wanted. And here he was, not yet out of high school. He'd tell the girl that he was home from Yale for the weekend, visiting family, and that they'd get together again in another couple of weeks. But, of course, they didn't. Once he'd gone to bed with a girl, he lost interest. The excitement wasn't in the conquest, really. It was in the pretending that made the conquest possible.

He could feel himself getting carried away each time. It was as if great weights were slipping from his body, and he was free of the past and his mother and all her dreary expectations for him. Free to remake himself, as whim or circumstances demanded. And how women fell for it.

It hadn't occurred to him that his propensity for role-playing might lead anywhere until he'd been coaxed into going out for the senior play and, never having acted on a stage before, landed the lead. It was a stupid play about a football player who gets in a jam after he makes two dates for the prom. The role required no great exercise of his imagination or anybody else's, for that matter. Any girl at the high school would have leapt at the chance to go out with Steve Carroll, so the prospect of him with one girl too many on his hands was wholly believable. Still, he had pulled the part off with some flair.

Linda had sat in the front row both nights, applauding as loudly as everybody else. She had actually enjoyed seeing him strut around. When one of her girlfriends asked her if she wasn't jealous, she answered tartly, "Why should I be?" She and Steve had been going steady for three years. "Besides, he's just performing," she said.

Neither Linda nor her girlfriends were aware of the excursions to Poughkeepsie or the string of disappointed coeds. Steve's closest pals didn't know, either. He was good at secrets. Keeping them required little effort on his part. Secrets fortified him and made him feel less vulnerable, so why would he spoil that feeling just for the momentary pleasure of boasting about his latest sexual escapade? The satisfaction of not telling was so much greater.

Lately, Steve had begun to nurse another secret: He was thinking about becoming an actor. The experience of the senior play had done something to him. Several of his teachers had come up to him afterward and told him he was a natural, bound to go far. Maybe that's when the seed was planted. The prospect that there could be money in acting, an actual career, was one he had never considered before.

"So when are you off to Hollywood?" said a pal later as he passed the other way in the school corridor. It was just a wisecrack, but Steve asked himself if the guy hadn't read his mind.

The thought of a career was still with him as he drove his prized Impala down Linda's street that Friday night. She was out on the porch already, hugging herself nervously and keeping a sharp lookout for the car. As soon as it came into view, she scrambled down the steps and cut across the lawn. Steve had barely pulled up to the curb before she had flung open the door and slid onto the seat.

He thought he glimpsed her parents behind the lace curtains, peering out the front window. Usually, he went in and chatted with them for a few minutes. Linda's father was a sports fan and liked to run on about the Yankees. Her mother never failed to ask, "Where are you lovebirds going tonight?" With a gentle smile, though, to show she wasn't prying.

"What's the trouble?" Steve reached over and caressed Linda's cheek.

She jerked away. "Drive somewhere."

He could tell that she had been crying. Her dark eyes were red and watery, and her cheeks were splotchy. She hadn't bothered to comb her hair, which fell in flat, unattractive swaths about her long face. There were few hints of the prettiness he usually found in her.

"Where?"

"Anywhere. Just get out of here! Please!"

41

He shifted the Impala into drive, swung the car out onto Chestnut Street, then at the intersection, took a left on Belmont Avenue. At regular intervals, the streetlamps cast down pools of light that shone through the windshield and briefly illuminated the couple, like a series of slow-motion flash bulbs. He stole a quick glance at her.

"Did something happen? Is Grandma Wilde all right?"

"She's fine."

"What then?"

She turned away and pressed her forehead up against the car window.

"Come on, Linda! Stop playing games. Why have you been crying?"

From experience, he knew that the silence would last only so long. Unlike him, Linda Anderson couldn't keep secrets. But she gave no sign of unbending tonight. He used a more insistent tone.

"Is everything all right?"

She shifted uncomfortably, then pushed her hair away from her face as she looked at him.

"I'm pregnant."

The confession hit him like a blast of cold air and took his breath away. She could have been saying "I'm tired" or "I'm bored" or "Let's not go to the movies." It was so matter-of-fact.

"What?"

"Pregnant. Expecting! You know, a baby!"

He wondered who else knew. Her parents? Was that why she hadn't invited him in tonight? He was going to have to say something soon, but what? He couldn't think of anything appropriate. His mind had emptied out. He wasn't even conscious of driving.

"Didn't you hear me, Steve?"

"I heard, Linda."

It wasn't an answer, just three words signaling that he was in the car, next to her, nothing more. Her hands flew up to her face, and the sobbing started again.

He pulled the Impala over onto a patch of gravel bordering an empty lot, turned off the ignition and sat there, aware of the blare of a television coming from one of the nearby houses. This wasn't meant to happen. They'd always taken the necessary precautions. That's what she said anyway. He'd certainly done everything he was supposed to. He'd given her a charm for her charm bracelet to mark each of their three years together. Next week, he was taking her to the prom. He'd already ordered the corsage at Rose 'n' Blooms, old Mr. Rosenbloom's florist shop. Now she was . . . she was springing this . . . this surprise on him.

He reached over and pulled her hands away from her face. "Are you telling the truth?"

"Do you think I'd make up something like this? I'm sorry, Steve. I saw the doctor two days ago."

In the white light of the streetlamp, her face had an ashen pall, relieved only by the moistness of her tears. He had never seen her so lost. "Tell me everything's going to be all right."

"Yeah . . . sure, it is . . . Of course, it is . . . ," he replied. But as he fumbled for the reassuring words—and the conviction that they demanded—he knew that he was acting. He no longer loved her. He asked himself if he ever had.

8

Munching peanuts, Spiff passed through the hotel lobby and out the glass door, then paused on the sidewalk to consider his options. A brisk stroll in Central Park was a possibility, but he was wearing his good shoes, the Guccis, and didn't want to risk scuffing them.

He contemplated grabbing a cup of coffee and a bagel and taking in a movie later. A new Sony cineplex—fourteen theaters under the same roof—was just a couple of blocks over. The idea of playing hooky appealed to him. Then he remembered that the movie he was really looking forward to, *In the Beginning*, didn't open until the end of the week. Jennifer Osborne in the buff—that was all anyone was talking about on TV. The posters that had recently bloomed in the subway showed her discreetly covered by foliage, but the R rating meant there wouldn't be much foliage in the movie.

He wouldn't let his sisters carry on like that. Of course, his sisters had better sense than to think of even trying. They respected themselves. Someone like Jennifer Osborne was little more than a highly paid stripper, when you came right down to it.

He wondered how he would feel if he were Christopher Knight, knowing that the whole world was salivating over his wife's breasts and who could say what else. Did he get off on that? The film took place in the Garden of Eden, so they both probably pranced around in the raw. That was Hollywood for you today. The actors were all exhibitionists. Even the big, expensive movies were nothing but jack-off films in disguise. They sure didn't make them like they used to.

He'd read in one of the tabloids that between them Jennifer Osborne and Christopher Knight were paid twenty-five million bucks for the film. While he didn't like to think that that put a different slant on things, he recognized that for most people it did. A $50 hooker was a whore, but a $2,000 call girl was an escort. Hell, who was he fooling? His sisters would show their tits in Times Square in an instant, if they thought they'd get a fur coat out of it. People did anything for the almighty dollar!

Fortunately, the plainness of his sisters made the issue purely theoretical, so he told himself that there wasn't much point in getting too worked up about it. The cellular phone in his pocket beeped. Any further musings about *In the Beginning* were going to have to wait. He'd think about Jennifer Osborne's breasts later, when he was alone and could give the whole pornography problem his undivided attention.

"Spiff?"

He recognized the voice immediately and stepped out of the flow of pedestrian traffic. "Yeah?"

"Our friend has been taken to hospital."

"No shit! By who?"

"By the police, that's who. They just put him in a bloody ambulance."

"Which hospital?"

"Roosevelt, I would imagine. It's the nearest. What do you think he's telling them?"

"I don't have a clue."

"Well, maybe you should get over there and find out. See if he's come to his senses and is willing to cooperate now. I want this problem solved."

"If I'd finished him off in the first place, you wouldn't have this problem."

"But I still wouldn't have the goods, as you say, now would I?"

"If you'd like my opinion—" Spiff didn't get the opportunity to say any more. The caller had hung up on him again. It was getting to be a habit with the man.

He stood there with the dead phone in his hand and contemplated calling the man back to say that this arrangement wasn't working out. He wasn't a lowly servant, for Chrissakes. He'd been hired for his *expertise*.

Instead, he bent over, picked up a rock and, flinging it with pinpoint accuracy, caught the backside of a pigeon perched on the edge of a trash can. The bird flapped its wings and fell to the ground, unable to fly. Spiff watched it flutter pathetically in circles for a while.

When he headed west to Roosevelt Hospital, there was a spring in his step.

A siren wailed and somebody said, "We have a white male, midthirties, with head injuries, coming in."

Opening his eyes required too great an effort, so he kept them shut and tried to visualize what had happened. It seemed like such a long time ago that . . . what? He remembered cold concrete and people hovering over him solicitously. And uniforms. But the random images bobbed on the surface of his consciousness, without pattern or purpose, like flotsam on the ocean.

From out of the blackness came another voice: "Hey, stay with us, buddy. You hear me?"

He did. He was, in fact, aware of a buzz of activity around him, and a hand gripping his hand tightly. His eyelids flickered and the darkness in his head was replaced by fuzzy shapes, heads of people surrounded by halos of white light.

A woman was sitting next to him. She had black hair and a pretty mouth. Her name escaped him, but he recalled that she was friendly, and he was comforted by her presence.

"Jesus H. Christ," she was saying. "Are you trying to give me a heart attack? I thought we'd lost you. I scare pretty easily, just so you're aware."

"Looks like he's back with us, lady," one of the paramedics said. "How you doing, guy? You can relax now. We're here."

The ambulance backed into a wide bay that could have been a loading area, except for the illuminated red cross that identified its real purpose. Beyond the electronic sliding glass doors, several people were clustered at the end of an oblong workstation.

Tina recognized the two policemen, who had showed up earlier at West Seventy-second Street. The one named Callahan was conferring with a middle-aged woman who had the pinched air of an overworked administrator and clutched a clipboard to her ample bosom. The younger woman next to her, with a stethoscope around her neck, seemed to be a doctor. They all looked over as the gurney was wheeled in.

It had been a busy night, and the linoleum floor, overdue for a good scrubbing, testified to the activity. The harried staff had attended to everything from a vicious stabbing to a serious case of the DTs, not to mention the twisted ankle of an East Side dowager who had been in too much of a hurry to reach her limousine after a concert at Avery Fisher Hall. The neon tubing in the ceiling cast a bright, white light that made even the healthy appear slightly moribund.

Tina's instinct was to find the waiting room and park herself there until the preliminary procedures were over. But just then, the doctor glanced up and gestured for her to come over. "Can you tell us what happened, miss?"

She had hardly anything to tell and thought they must take her for a kook—some dizzy, self-appointed Florence H. Nightingale on a mission of mercy. The cardinal rule of the city held that to get involved in a stranger's affairs was to invite trouble. Everyone knew it and obeyed it. Everyone sane.

"Are you a relative?"

"Uh, no. I was just helping. I mean, he asked me to come. It didn't seem right to abandon him. The blood and all. Somebody's gotta . . . you know . . ." Her explanation trailed off into an airy, half-sketched gesture.

"Let me take a look." The doctor gently turned the man's head to one side, exposing a gash of matted hair and coagulated blood at the base of his skull. Tina directed her gaze elsewhere.

"Not pretty," the doctor said, "but it may look worse than it is. His pulse is steady. We should probably do a CAT scan, just to be safe."

"Hello, sir . . . sir?" The woman with the clipboard bent down so that her face was level with the man on the gurney. "Can you tell us your name? Don't close your eyes . . . I need a name, an address, and a social security number."

"Hey, buddy, can't you hear the lady?" Callahan said. "Not speaking, huh? Check his pockets, Carl." The second policeman stepped forward and perfunctorily frisked the man on the gurney.

"Zero," Carl said. "Whoever mugged him done a good job. There's no wallet. No wristwatch. Some loose change is all. A set of house keys, I guess. Wait a second." From the man's right-hand jacket pocket he extracted what appeared to be a credit card, except there were no markings on it. "What's this?"

Callahan examined the card. "It's a hotel key. Ain't you never stayed in a hotel?"

"Yeah. Every summer. Howard Johnson's. But they give you a real key with the room number on it. Not one of these *Star Trek* gizmos. So where's the name of the hotel?"

"That's the point. You lose it, no one knows."

"Knows what?"

"Where the hell you're staying. Put it back for now. The guy must be a tourist or a businessman. Probably wandered off where he shouldn't have. They forget they're not in Cleveland. With luck, someone will call the station to report him missing. All we can do right now is file a John Doe report." He made some scribblings in his notebook. "Let's go Carl."

"Excuse me," Tina said, tapping Callahan on the shoulder. "Are you going to leave him just like that?"

"You got any other suggestions, lady?"

"Not right off the top of my head, no. But what if he's

not from around here. I mean, suppose he doesn't know anybody?"

"If he's not from around here, then he's got a nice place to sleep for the night and someone to watch over him. That's more than a lot of people in this city can say."

"But—"

"Look, when he comes around, tell him to get in touch with the detective squad on West Fifty-fourth. They'll do the necessary follow-up." He handed Tina a business card. "Come on, Carl. We're outta here."

At the sign from the doctor, an orderly wheeled the gurney toward the far end of the emergency room. Cubicles with flimsy white curtains for doors lined the walls. The curtains hung from runners in the ceiling so the staff could open or close them with a flick of the wrist. Most were closed, affording their occupants at least the illusion of privacy.

"It'll be a while before we can get him upstairs for tests," the doctor said to Tina. "Give us a few minutes to clean him up, and then you can keep him company."

Expecting no response, she immediately sailed off in the gurney's wake, leaving Tina to ponder why they called the place an emergency room, if all you did was wait. The noise level surprised her. She thought of hospitals as quiet places of healing, where doctors communicated with one another in tones of hushed urgency. Here, orders were barked at top volume, carts clattered up and down the aisles, and occasional moans pierced the curtains. It was like the supermarket in her Queens neighborhood on Saturday morning.

She gave herself another half hour, max. Then she could head home with a clear conscience, good deed done for the day. She knew her brother would rag her for acting impulsively, but she liked to help people. Sometimes it led to complications; most of the time, people really needed the help. Anyway, if you didn't give them the benefit of the doubt, what the hell kind of planet would this be? A couple of hours of her life are all she'd have wasted.

And not wasted, really. If this guy was from out of town, she'd have shown him that all New Yorkers weren't assholes. He had looked so damn vulnerable, his eyes swimming in confusion. She'd always been a pushover for guys with innocent faces and puppy dog eyes—even those who turned out to be real bastards. For some reason, although she couldn't say why, this guy struck her as different.

"Knock, knock." Tina parted the white curtain. "How we doing?"

The wound on the back of the man's head had been dressed and bandaged, and his forest green suit was hung up on a hook.

"Where am I?"

"So, we've decided to talk, have we? You're at Roosevelt Hospital."

"Where's that?"

"New York. The Big Apple. Ever heard of it?"

"What happened?"

"That's the sixty-four-thousand-dollar question." He was trying to sit up. "Easy now." She helped him swing his legs over the side of the bed. A little color had come back into his face.

"Tell me a secret."

"What?"

"Your name."

His features stayed blank.

"Have it your way. Where you from?" Still no answer. "Well, you remember me, don't you? Tina. Tina Ruffo."

"Ruffo?"

"Yeah. Italian. Can't you tell? . . . Sicilian, actually . . . My grandparents came from Messina . . . My grandfather had a fruit stand. No kidding! . . . Apples, oranges, pears. That sort of thing . . . Yeah, he used to bring all the best stuff home for us . . . What's wrong? Am I babbling?"

He smiled broadly, then raised his hand to the back of his head and the smile vanished.

"What's that?"

"Oh, your bandage. You got roughed up pretty bad and collapsed a few hours ago by the Dakota."

"North Dakota?"

"No. It's a big-deal apartment building. Where John Lennon was shot. You know somebody there, perhaps?"

He slowly shook his head in puzzlement.

At least, she thought, he was sitting up and speaking. "I wonder where the doctor is. If they keep us waiting much longer, we'll both qualify for Medicare."

She stepped outside the curtain, just as an Indian orderly, steering a laundry cart full of dirty sheets, padded by. "Excuse me . . . sir . . . mister . . . hey you!" Another American who didn't speak English, she thought. Hardly anybody did in the city anymore. Across the room, a woman on crutches was cursing loudly in Spanish.

"John Lennon was shot?" The surprise in the man's voice drew Tina back into the cubicle. "When?"

"Only about a hundred years ago. Where have you been all this time?"

"I don't know."

"What do you mean you don't know?"

His brow furrowed.

"Okay, forget about John Lennon for a sec. Let's begin at the beginning. Who the hell are you?"

He stared at a dark crack in the linoleum floor, as if it were some sort of magic code that contained the answer to the riddle. Right now, he couldn't imagine anyone asking him a more perplexing question.

9

Deborah Myers knew that it was unwise to ask herself how an interview was going while she was in the midst of it. It didn't matter that over a long career the only completely worthless interview she could remember, one that had resulted in virtually no coherent footage, had been with a rock star so high on drugs that he had fallen asleep on her. Deborah usually felt as she did right now: vaguely stymied.

The half-hour taping with Christopher Knight had produced no "special moments," just glimmers of a human being, and someone guarded and defensive at that, not exactly overjoyed to answer questions. He had opinions, but most of them had to do with the need for maintaining privacy at home and on the job, which didn't make Deborah's task any easier. Unless she got more fire out of Jennifer Osborne, viewers would abandon her by the hundreds of thousands for that fool *Emergency Squad*.

Perhaps she would exchange some womanly confidences with the actress, on the theory that candor usually begets candor. Her own confidences could always be conveniently edited out later. Jennifer certainly had a controversial past, if an eight-page photo layout in

Playboy could still be considered controversial. Jennifer's explanation for baring it all—"I didn't have the stuff to be an Avon lady"—was widely circulated at the time. The photo spread had led to her first bit parts in the movies and contributed to her early notoriety as some kind of sex goddess.

There had been the inevitable stories (unverified) of affairs with her leading men, but she had taken care not to appear in public with any of them. Then she'd married Christopher. Although her voluptuousness didn't change, the press on her did: she became half of a golden couple, her dubious past paling in comparison with the glittery present. One of the tabloids bribed a waiter at the wedding reception to take shots of the couple, who were caught in the not-very-compromising act of cutting a three-tiered cake. Two of Jennifer's assistants had been summarily dismissed last summer and had threatened to sue. But several months later the suit was quietly dropped and the tabloids had been frustrated ever since in their quest for dirt.

Surely, Deborah told herself, there was more to the star than a feathery voice, blonde hair and perfect breasts, rumored to be her own. The premise that what you see is sometimes all you get, even with movie stars, was unacceptable, however true. Thinking like that, Deborah knew, would have invalidated most careers in popular journalism. The public perceived her as a kind of celebrity detective, tracking down the elusive, cornering the mysterious, and wrangling confessions from those whose biggest crime was their fame.

"Tape is rolling."

Deborah assumed her most probing expression, and

the resulting v-shaped furrow between her eyes momentarily undid the costly work, not yet a year old, of Manhattan's finest cosmetic surgeon. She generally tried to avoid squinting of any sort, fearing the long-term consequences, but this was an exceptional occasion. "How do you think people see you, Jennifer?"

"The way they see most actors. By lining up and buying a ticket."

"Come now. You know what I mean."

"Do I?"

"Let me rephrase the question. You have an image—sexy and alluring. Is that something you're conscious of?"

"I'm an actress. I play different roles. Some of them have been sexy, alluring women. But the time will come when I won't play them anymore. I'll play mothers, then mothers-in-law, then crones, if I'm lucky. That's usually how it progresses. Then, I bet you'll ask me what it is like *not* to be young and sexy anymore."

"That day is a long time away and by then I'll be much too old myself to ask any questions at all. Anyway, it's hard right now to imagine you being anything but beautiful, Jennifer."

Deborah hoped the compliment didn't sound too calculating, but it was true that Jennifer Osborne would age gracefully. The high cheekbones augured well. And the compliment might melt some of the chilliness that had permeated the room. The actress smiled modestly, but Deborah couldn't determine how real the smile was. She concluded it was probably a reflex reaction, like a leg jerking when tapped by the doctor's rubber hammer.

"Does it bother you what people think?"

"Heavens, no. I can't control that. None of us can, so it

would be a pretty foolish thing to worry about it. I worry about what I *can* control—what I eat, how I live my life, how I play my parts. I'd like to contribute something positive, not just add more trash to the heap."

Okay, Deborah said to herself, here we go. "Some would say a layout in *Playboy* is more trash on the heap." Again, that perfectly shaped smile. "You can't deny, Jennifer, that there has been nudity in a lot of your pictures."

"I don't see what's wrong with that."

"Not everybody would agree with you."

"Everybody wouldn't, true. People get themselves terribly worked up over issues of no consequence these days."

"Can you understand why in this case?"

"Frankly? No."

Deborah withdrew a card from the deck in her lap. "In a recent column in the *Boston Globe*, the Reverend Paul Greenway accuses you and your husband of using the gospel for titillation. He says he doesn't like what you're doing to his Bible. 'Let's keep the genitals out of Genesis' are his exact words."

"*His* Bible? How possessive of him! Why are certain people so quick to criticize a film they haven't seen? Anyway, to my knowledge, Adam and Eve didn't have designer wardrobes. Perhaps Reverend Greenway knows better."

"Then his criticism is meaningless to you?"

"I worry for Mrs. Greenway. Her husband is spending too much time thinking about my genitals. Unless he's thinking about Christoper's genitals, which would be even more troublesome for her."

Several of the crew members guffawed, and Pete forgot his nervousness and stopped pacing. Jennifer Osborne, it was apparent, had more than beauty; she spoke her mind. The melting softness of her looks was deceptive.

"You should get the reverend to come on your show and explain himself, Deborah. 'Sex and the Pulpit'—that would be an awfully interesting topic for discussion, don't you think?"

Deborah did. More importantly, she had begun to think that this interview might be salvaged, after all.

"So you're not worried about pleasing everybody?"

"Heavens, no. The only person I have to please is myself. And Christopher, naturally." Jennifer looked past the camera to her husband, who had been listening attentively to her answers. Their eyes connected briefly. Deborah could see that something was exchanged in the glance but was unable to interpret the silent message, which had been transmitted too fast. Did Christopher approve of his wife's outspokenness or was he counseling her to pull back?

"We made a pact a long time ago," the actress continued. "All that counts is what we think of each other."

"A pact! Sounds like a secret club!"

"No, just a marriage."

"What about 'for richer or poorer? In sickness and in health?' However it goes . . ."

"Oh, absolutely. Every last bit of it," the actress responded brightly. "Till death do us part."

10

"Transient global amnesia can last from a matter of minutes to months. There's no telling in advance, and we'll want to do some tests, of course. But my guess would be that in a few hours everything will start to come into focus. At most, a day or two. What's happening to you is not all that unusual for someone who's suffered a head injury."

The doctor, a slight woman in her midthirties, was probably attractive, Tina judged, when she got herself dressed up. But the long night shift had left dark circles under her eyes, and the institutional lighting made her skin appear gray. If she wore makeup, it had worn off hours ago.

The man on the hospital bed was listening raptly, but Tina wasn't certain how much he was actually understanding.

"You've had a concussion and some bleeding from the left ear, so the disorientation you're feeling is, well, I don't want to say normal. But it's understandable. Do you remember getting in the ambulance with this woman?"

The man looked over at Tina and his face lit up. "Yes, she helped me."

"Well, that's encouraging," the doctor said, directing

her explanation to Tina. "Most people think amnesia is just forgetting what you once knew—who you are, where you live, that sort of thing. The past is erased, so to speak. But once the condition sets in, it can also mean you don't acquire any new memories. The brain no longer files experience away, so the present can be destroyed, too."

She turned back to the man. "We have to consider it a very positive sign that you remember your friend here. You've been through a traumatic experience. You were attacked. There are bound to be mental as well as physical ramifications."

"You think I was attacked?"

The doctor fought a weary sigh. In another few minutes, she would go off duty and could forget the pains and anxieties—and the questions, always the frightened questions—of the last twelve hours. A little amnesia, she reflected wryly to herself, wouldn't be such a bad thing right now. She marshaled her concentration.

"We're assuming that's what's happened, since you don't have a wallet on you or a watch or anything of value. But don't worry about that. If anything starts to come back, tell your friend here, or have someone write it down. Or write it down yourself. You never know what will trigger a memory."

"Do I still know how to write?"

"Yes, you do. And drive a car and ride a bike and add and subtract, too. The funny thing about memory loss, whether temporary or permanent, is that you don't lose certain acquired skills. That information is stored in a different part of your brain. We'll be admitting you shortly, and one of the resident doctors will explain all this in greater detail. Meanwhile—"

The man rose off the bed at the mention of having to stay in the hospital. He was supposed to be somewhere else. He had important business to conduct, people he needed to see. He was pretty sure it was today. Unless it was yesterday. Which?

His confusion was immediately apparent to the doctor. "I know nothing makes sense to you right now, but it will," she said. "Things will start to come together like a giant jigsaw puzzle. Just take it easy and get some rest." She turned to Tina. "I'll be sending someone down to get him. It shouldn't be too much longer now."

Brushing a strand of hair out of her face, the doctor managed a reassuring smile—the last one of her shift—pushed the white curtain aside and left. Tina felt the man on the bed looking at her with that mixture of expectation and helplessness that churned up her gut, whenever she saw it in the face of her daughter, Angelina. No words were necessary: the imploring look was always enough, calling on her to heal a bruise or soothe hurt feelings.

Tina wished she were better able to resist it.

Her intention had been to assure that the man got the right medical attention, maybe telephone his family and then be off. But who knew if he had a family? For the moment, she seemed to be the only person in the entire world he recognized, and her nagging conscience was telling her it would be rotten to abandon him.

That was what came of having spent so much of her own life trying to rescue people—her mother, who had wasted away to cancer by fifty, and the younger brother she had ended up raising. Then there was "Angelina's father," as she now referred to the musician who had been her husband for two rocky years, before he'd deserted them both for a gig on the West Coast and a blonde rock singer with a nose ring.

When one of Tina's clients, a psychotherapist named Meryl, told her she was turning into the classic codependent, Tina retorted that Meryl was becoming a classic pain in the ass. But more and more she recognized the truth of what Meryl had said.

"You wouldn't be wanted by the law by any chance? I mean, you're not some crazy person, right?"

The man moved his head from side to side. "Not that I know of."

"Not that I would tell anyone. Half my family has been wanted at some point. And the other half are psychos, when I think about it. You think I'm joking! I told you I was Sicilian. So how about Andy?"

"What?"

"Andy—does that sound familiar? You look like you could be an Andy."

"No."

"Arthur, then? . . . Bob . . . Bruce . . . Clarence . . . Daniel . . . Ernie . . . Frank . . . Tell me if I'm getting warm, at least? . . . Gary . . . Harry . . . John . . . *K?* What's a name for *K?*"

The man spoke up confidently. "Kevin!"

"There you are! See how easy that was! So your name's Kevin?"

"No . . . not Kevin . . . Kevin is my . . . is a . . ." His mind was like quicksand, swallowing up faces before he could put a name to them. "The doctor said it would come together, like a puzzle. But it's all . . . pieces."

Tina realized she had better distract him somehow, make a game of the situation, before the desperation returned in force. It worked whenever one of Angelina's moods threatened to escalate into a tantrum. And the man was behaving no differently from a child right now.

"Hey, hey, you're not going to give up before you've started, are you? We can figure this out, the two of us. You'll see. We already know a lot."

"We don't know anything."

"We do, too. You have a hotel key in your pocket." Tina reached into his coat jacket and pulled out the oblong of plastic. "Do you remember checking into a hotel?"

"No."

"Well, you must have. And this is not a cheap suit, I might add. Hugo Boss. So you're not poor. That's good news. You're not some bum who can disappear off the street without somebody noticing you're gone. Why they're probably looking for you right now. It's just a matter of time before they find you. The least you can do is give them a little help."

The pep talk had the desired effect of stemming the man's panic. He stood up, waited while a wave of vertigo washed over him, then emptied his pants pockets. There wasn't much to empty. The left pocket contained exactly eighteen cents. The right yielded a folded piece of stationery with *Hotel Mayflower* in flowery script across the top and, just below it, the hotel logo, a drawing of a horse and buggy in Central Park. A phone number was scrawled on the paper.

"See there!" said Tina, excitedly. "You *are* staying at a hotel. The Mayflower is just a few blocks from here. Not far from where we found you. That plastic card must be the key to your room. Now we're getting somewhere. Did you write these numbers?"

"I don't know."

"You don't know jack-shit today, do you?" His face collapsed. "Oh, come on. Don't get moody on me again. That was just a little joke. If we don't keep our sense of humor, we'll get nowhere." She fumbled around in her dance bag for a ballpoint pen and tore a blank deposit slip out of her check book. "Okay," she said, handing him the pen and paper, "Write this down: eight . . . seven . . . three . . . four . . . zero . . . one . . . six."

As soon as he had finished, she put the deposit slip up against the hotel stationery. "No question, it's your writing all right. We'll have to give this number a call. Maybe it's a friend. How about going through your back pockets? I'll see if there's anything else in your jacket."

A cry of triumph went up. "Well, if I ain't Agatha H. Christie herself! Guess where you were last night."

"Where?"

"You went to a show."

"I did?"

"Well, you have a ticket stub dated May seventeenth. That was yesterday. For the Vivian Beaumont Theater at Lincoln Center. The show was *Crime and Punishment*. Oh, my! I heard it was rotten. Why did you go see that?"

Seeing the panic in his face, she promptly answered her own question. "Oh, you probably knew someone in it. That's the only reason anyone goes to anything these days. A lot of my friends are actors and dancers, and I'm always having to haul myself off to see some piece of crap and then tell them afterward how sensational it was. Half the time I don't know what's going on. So maybe you're friends with someone in the cast."

"I saw a movie?"

"No, doll. You went to the theater."

Just then an orderly, carrying a white hospital gown, stuck his head through the curtain. "The doctor wants you to put on this. We'll be moving you upstairs in a little while." When he spotted Tina, he did a double-take and allowed his eyes to travel the length of her body. "I guess you don't need me to help get his pants off, do you?"

She caught the smirk in his voice.

"Thanks, pal. We'll manage without you."

"I bet you will," he snickered and left.

"Wise guy!" she muttered at his departing form. Turning back, she noticed that the man was fumbling with his shoelaces. "Oh, here, let me help you."

Wearily, he extended a leg, and she tugged off the right shoe, then the left shoe. A small key fell to the floor. It had an orange plastic tip, imprinted with the number 102.

"What's that?" the man asked.

"Looks like the key to a locker or something. The kind they have at a bus station or airport."

"What's it doing in my shoe?"

"My best guess would be that you put it there for safe-keeping. Not a bad idea in New York."

She peeled off his socks, feeling mildly embarrassed that she, a grown woman, was undressing a grown man and a fairly attractive one at that. When was the last time that had happened? "Look, I'll slip outside for a second, while you get into the hospital robe, okay?" She put the orange key in the pocket of her windbreaker, along with the flat plastic hotel key and the ticket stub.

"You're not going, are you?" cried the man.

"I'm just giving you a little privacy while you change your clothes."

"But you're not leaving . . ."

I guess not yet, she thought to herself, glancing at her wristwatch and noticing with surprise that it was almost noon. Angelina's school let out at two-thirty. The day was flying. At this point, though, a few more minutes weren't going to make much difference.

"No, of course I'm not leaving. How could I? My new career as host of *Unsolved Mysteries* has just begun."

Several people puffing on cigarettes hovered just outside the emergency room entrance—exiles banished to the street until their craving for nicotine was appeased. Spiff paid them no mind as he strode up. But his attention was immediately drawn to the woman in a tight tank top that left little to the imagination.

He paused at the double glass door and gave a nod in her direction. "Well, well, Who do we have here? How is the lovely lady this morning?"

"Fuck off, buddy." Tina turned her back to him, thinking that the pigs were out in force this morning.

Spiff let the rebuff roll off and wondered why nobody had any manners these days. All he'd done was ask how she was and tip his hat—figuratively, of course. He'd stopped wearing a felt hat about a decade ago, after someone had told him it didn't make him look distinguished, just shady. But he liked to think he conducted himself in public, *as if* he were wearing a hat.

His error was assuming that the young woman in the tank top was a lady. Going around and flaunting every curve in her body like that! What did she expect? When he was growing up, they had a name for her kind.

"Ball-busters," he snarled, before catching himself.

Still, it was true. That's what they called them, and their numbers were definitely on the rise. By his calculation, they made up about 90 percent of the female population today. He offered a silent prayer of thanks that his sisters belonged to the other 10 percent.

He crossed the waiting room to the front desk. Behind it, a security guard controlled the traffic into the ward itself, stopping most visitors and redirecting them to the worn, black vinyl sofas and chairs that furnished the room. About half of them were filled right now. The place had a dingy air of resignation to it, Spiff thought. So many docile people, accepting the nasty turns that fate had sprung on them or their loved ones. It was pitiful. He pushed by the guard.

"Excuse me, sir—"

"My brother's in there," he said, barely breaking stride.

The guard started to follow after him. "Sir, you can't go in without a—"

Spiff spun about. "Look. My brother is dying. Time is crucial. I can't be bothered with stupid paperwork now." Admiring the controlled emotion in his own voice and the slightly superior attitude—not rude, so much as firm— Spiff passed into the emergency room itself. The guard registered a second protest, feebler this time, then gave up and returned to his desk.

It didn't take Spiff long to scout the layout. Around a central workstation, cubicles lined three sides of the room. Those with drawn curtains, obviously, were occupied. It was a simple process of elimination.

The attention of the staff was momentarily concentrated on the latest arrival, a middle-aged woman with blood on her face, who was writhing on a stretcher. From what he could overhear of the doctor's conversation, Spiff gathered that she had been in a nasty automobile accident and had been thrown up against the windshield. The driver of the car and a pedestrian, injured by flying glass, were being brought in as well, in a separate ambulance.

"I want my son!" the woman on the stretcher was screaming. "Where's my son?"

Spiff profited from the diversion to begin his circular exploration of the ward. Like the magician's art, so much of his profession depended on timing. The magician got the audience to observe his right hand closely while he pocketed the fifty-cent piece with his left hand. Spiff waited until life itself created the proper distraction, then went about his business, unnoticed. If someone *did* notice him, his respectable appearance rarely aroused suspicion.

He recognized the green suit jacket first, hanging from a hook on the wall of the cubicle. The man was by himself, seated on the edge of the bed and gazing despondently at the folded hospital gown in his lap. Without parting the curtain, Spiff studied him closely. No question that the spirit had been taken out of him.

For how long, though? It was Spiff's belief that you had to keep the pressure on. Without special . . . encouragement, people reneged on their promises and reverted to their old ways. The man sitting on the bed hadn't cooperated last night. He could have, too, and spared himself a lot of unpleasantness in the bargain. This could all have been settled by now. But no . . .

Spiff sighed. Human beings could be so pigheaded. At this point, though, it really came down to a matter of principle. He was a professional, who got the job done. He had a reputation to uphold. So who was this guy to fuck with it? The nerve!

At the far end of the emergency room, the other victims of the car accident had arrived, mobilizing the staff and creating the very diversion Spiff hoped for. No one, he knew, would bother with the man in the cubicle for a while.

Now was the ideal moment to pay him a quick visit and give him a few reminders of last night. He flicked the curtain open, stepped inside, then flicked it shut.

"So have we learned our lesson?"

11

Steve Carroll sat in the living room with his mother, neither of them talking, and waited for Linda and her parents to arrive. Earlier Kate Carroll had put all her energy into cleaning the modest room—making it "presentable for guests," she said—but her efforts couldn't change the essential shabbiness of the decor nor had they relieved her anxiety. Now waiting sapped all her strength.

Given the situation, guests struck Steve as a curious word, although typical of his mother, who had always labored to put the best appearances possible on their diminished circumstances. For the first time since his father's death, five years ago, Steve was glad the old man wasn't around. It meant one less person to regard him as a failure.

He steeled himself for whatever unpleasantness lay ahead. He was sure he would get a severe dressing-down in front of everybody, and he would probably be ordered to help pay for an abortion. What did an abortion cost? $500? $1,000? No doubt the Andersons would demand that he stop seeing Linda altogether, and his mother would agree to all the conditions. Far be it from her to have an opinion of her own.

His anger was concentrated on Linda for causing this mess in the first place. There had been no reason to inform her

70

parents. He and Linda could have dealt with the problem by themselves. It would have been their secret and brought them even closer together, if she hadn't panicked. Now they had a circus on their hands. In a few minutes, he thought, the real fun would begin.

He saw his mother's back stiffen as an automobile pulled into the gravel driveway that ran alongside of the house. Kate Carroll retreated into the kitchen and checked the coffeepot, then came back and stood meekly by the front door. Mr. Anderson entered first, followed by his wife, who had a protective arm around the shoulder of their daughter. "Good mornings" were mumbled, and Mrs. Anderson and Linda perched gently on the edge of the couch, as if they were afraid that any dent they made in the cushions might be permanent. Steve tried to catch Linda's attention, but her eyes were fixed on the faded floral design of the carpet.

The three women remained silent while Mr. Anderson walked about the room, stroking his chin, before coming to a stop in a shaft of sunlight that streamed through the bay window. It looked as if he were standing in a spotlight. "I don't need to say that this has been quite a shock for us," he said. "As you know, Kate, we've always been very fond of Steve. We've trusted him, just as we have trusted our Linda. What I've had to face—what we all have to face—is that we live in a changing world. Kids grow up faster and faster these days. They see things on TV and in the movies . . . It's just that you don't like to believe those things will ever happen in your own family."

Mrs. Anderson put a handkerchief to her mouth to muffle a sob, and Kate Carroll's shoulders drooped perceptibly. Linda still couldn't bring herself to lift her head. They made a pathetic lot, Steve thought, except for Mr. Anderson, who couldn't help savoring the role he was playing in the lives of these helpless women and the authority that his wayward daughter's misfortune conferred upon him.

"I know, Steve, that you've talked of taking some time before college and seeing a bit of the world," he said. "I presume you understand that's no longer possible. The situation is different now. Without promising too much, though, I think I can arrange an entry-level job for you with the company.

"You'll have to prove yourself, naturally, and it wouldn't happen overnight, but if you buckle down and show us that you're serious, I am confident that you can move up the ladder in time."

He cleared his throat. "As for the living quarters, the only alternative for the present seems to be our house. At least, until the baby is born. By then, you will have saved up some cash and we could find a place for the two of you that would be comfortable and not too expensive. Oh, I realize that young people need their privacy. But in the meantime, there's nothing wrong with the two rooms in the attic . . ."

As he droned on about what a cozy apartment they would make, if properly fixed up, Steve stopped listening. His temples throbbed, and the thumping noise drowned out the man's words. Mrs. Anderson's sobbing had ceased, he noticed, and she was gazing at her husband with undisguised admiration. Linda had raised her head at long last and was smiling tentatively. Even his own mother had shed the despondency that usually enfolded her like an old housecoat.

It wasn't possible! They were all shoving him into a box and preparing to clamp down the lid. Why didn't they just take out a pistol and shoot him? His life wasn't going to be over at eighteen. He had plans. He was going to Hollywood and be somebody. That's all he'd been dreaming of lately.

Live in the Anderson house? Were they crazy? He could picture it—constantly having to thank Mr. Anderson for his generosity! Kissing up to Mrs. Anderson every day of the week. Not to mention devoting the next twenty years of his life to Linda and some snot-nosed kid. There wasn't a chance in hell.

For a while, laughter mixed with the throbbing in his temples. Then, he heard a voice, calling him. "Steve . . . Steve . . ." His mother was talking.

"What, Ma?"

"Don't you have something to say to Mr. Anderson?"

The unexpected turn of good fortune had put a rapturous glow on her face. After five years of struggling to raise Steve by herself, she felt a huge relief that someone strong had come into their lives, someone who could provide the discipline and the moral leadership she hadn't, someone who would set an example for her son. The Andersons belonged to a better class of people, one to which this impending alliance now allowed her to aspire, and her eyes were watery with gratitude.

Paul Anderson let himself bathe in the satisfaction of a job well done, before pointing out that he was only doing what any self-respecting father would do. They all had the children's interests at heart, didn't they? To show there were no hard feelings, he clasped Steve's hand firmly and gave it a shake.

Steve surveyed the happy faces, closing in on him, and asked himself what he was supposed to do now. Hug Linda? Kiss his mother? Or stand there and continue to say nothing. The only thought that sprang to his mind was that if everyone in the living room burst into flames at that very instant, he wouldn't bother to piss on the fire.

12

Tina Ruffo blinked in the sunlight. While she'd been in the emergency room, a breeze had blown away the clouds and the full glory of spring had settled over the city, lending a touch of enchantment even to the treeless stretch of sidewalk in front of Roosevelt Hospital. After the odor of disinfectant, the air was fresh to her nostrils, and the UPS truck rattling down the street reminded her that, whatever the misery behind the sliding glass doors she had just passed through, the real world continued to go about its business and she should, too.

She definitely got carried away with people and their problems. She couldn't help it. Sometimes it just meant giving a homeless person a dollar or helping an elderly person on or off the bus. But once she'd ridden all the way to Brighton Beach on the subway while a Russian immigrant told her his travails in terrible English, because she didn't have the heart to interrupt him and get off at her stop.

Angelina's father was the best example. She'd rescued him, too, or tried to. He was an artist, and holding down a regular job, he had said, would kill his creative spirit. Not only had she swallowed the line, she'd supported him for four long years, put up with moods, rallied his spirits when they were down, which was often, and listened to his rock songs, which were pretty bad. Then to show his appreciation, he'd run off with the first blonde bimbo, who happened along. Maybe it was the second.

Now here she was, holding the hand of a man who didn't know his name, where he came from, or how he'd gotten a nasty wound on his head. She would go back inside the hospital presently and make sure everything was under control, but then it was definitely good-bye and back to Queens. Hadn't she earned her good conduct medal for today?

The attempt at self-mockery gave way to the sensation of physical well-being. The warmth of the sun felt good on her face, and the noises of the city seemed to come from far away, as if muffled by a blanket. She walked away from the entrance bay and leaned up against the wall, relishing the moment's peace.

She had succeeded in putting all thoughts from her mind when a metal door next to her suddenly clanged open and jolted her out of her reverie. A figure darted by, heading east on Fifty-ninth Street. He had managed to slip his left arm into his jacket, but the other sleeve flapped behind him, and as his body stumbled forward, his right arm kept reaching back comically for it. Tina recognized the color, forest green. It was the man, *her* man. What the devil was happening now?

"Hey," she called out. "Where are you going? Wait a sec." The sound of her voice made him pick up his speed, although even with the added effort, his pace amounted to no more than a brisk walk. It took her only a few moments to catch up and place a hand on his shoulder. Terrified, the man spun around, nearly losing his balance.

"Hey, it's me. Tina."

He was breathing heavily. Tina instinctively reached out to steady him and for the second time that morning, found herself holding the stranger in her arms.

"What's the matter? What are you doing? Did they send you home already?"

The man gestured back toward the bay, where the ambulance had deposited him several hours earlier. "They're going to kill me."

"What?! . . . Oh, everybody feels that way about hospitals," she said. "You're not alone in that department. The doctors and nurses may not be the friendliest people on the planet, but they're trying to help. Believe me, they want you better."

"He asked me if I'd learned my lesson."

"Who did?"

"A man in a dark suit."

"The doctor, you mean?"

"He wasn't a doctor. I thought he was at first because he asked me if I was going to cooperate now. I said yes, I wanted to get better. He said that was good. If I would just hand over everything, nice and easy, there would be no more trouble."

"Trouble? Hand over what?"

"That's what I asked. I don't know what he was talking about. Then he got mad and said he didn't want to have to teach me another lesson. 'Last night was just a warning,' he said. 'Next time will be worse.' "

"Next time?"

"Next time, I won't just have a headache. I won't be so lucky. They won't be so nice to me next time."

"Who? These are friends of yours?"

" 'No more games,' he kept repeating. Then an orderly

came in, and I asked to go to the bathroom. As I was going down the hall, he said, 'I'll be waiting here when you get back.' "

The man scanned the street, which was empty, except for the coffee vendor who had serviced the last of the morning trade and was now closing up his stand. The smokers, who had been huddling by the emergency room entrance earlier, had stubbed out their cigarettes and returned inside.

Great, Tina thought to herself. In addition to all his other problems, the man was a raging paranoiac. Why hadn't she just minded her own business today and stepped over his collapsed body, like any sane New Yorker would have done?

"I've got to hide," he said.

"You're in no condition to go anyplace. What we're going to do, you and me, is go back in there. I'll make sure nothing happens to you. Trust me."

She was talking to him again as she would to a child, her tone both coaxing and placating. Reluctantly, the man took the hand she extended to him. Tina started to lead him back, when he dug in his heels and gave her arm a jerk.

"There he is!"

"Who?"

"The person I just told you about."

Spiff had come outside and was talking on his cellular phone. Tina recognized him instantly as the businessman who had tried to pick her up earlier. She hadn't given him a moment's thought then and, honestly, saw no reason to now, except that the man at her side seemed legitimately terrified. He pulled her into an alcove, where they were hidden from Spiff's view.

"You've got to take me to the hotel," he insisted.

"What hotel?"

"The one like a ship. You said I had the key to a hotel room. Can you show me where it is? Quick, before he finds I'm gone."

She realized that he was talking about the Hotel Mayflower, which was only a few blocks away. The room key was still in the pocket of her windbreaker. She peered around the corner of the alcove. The businessman had finished his conversation on the cellular phone and was running a comb through his hair, preparing to go back into the hospital.

"He doesn't know I'm gone. Please, we've got to hurry."

Hugging the side of the building, he scuttled toward the end of the block. Tina heaved an impatient sigh as she watched his arms flap. He was nuts! A real fruitcake! She considered going back to the ward and enlisting the help of an orderly. But if the guy was mad, there was probably no keeping him at the hospital against his will. She really could have used the services of a friendly police officer about now. Not those two cops who had accompanied them to the emergency ward. They'd barely gone through the motions. Hell, it wouldn't have surprised her if the one called Callahan had taken off the rest of the day.

The intersection was dominated by an imitation Gothic cathedral, its cumbersome spires sooty from years of automobile exhaust. The man hesitated at the curb, jerked his head back and forth, then lurched to the right. Tina took after him, shouting as she went, "Mister, mister, you're going the wrong way. The hotel is the other direction."

The confused expression in his eyes lifted as soon as she came abreast of him. He was like some lost kid at a county fair, she thought, who suddenly lights up with joy when he spots his parents.

"Listen to me now," she said firmly. "I'll accompany you to the hotel. But that's it. The end. *Finito.* Then I am definitely going home and you will have to manage on your own. *Capiche?* So whatever it is you do with those blue eyes of yours, you can stop doing it right now."

By the time they reached the hotel, the man's panic had subsided and he no longer was quite so crazed. They paused under the portico while she straightened his coat collar and attempted to smooth down his hair. Perhaps no one would notice the tear in the knee of his pants. She fished in her pocket for the blank plastic card, hoping it was what the cops had said—a new-fangled room key. If not, she didn't know what she'd do.

"I think you better leave this up to me."

The reception desk was staffed by a buxom woman with her hair in a tight bun and a young man of college age. Tina hung back until the woman retreated into an inner office, then approached the young clerk. The badge on his vest pocket identified him as a TRAINEE.

"I'm sorry to be so stupid," she said as she slid the plastic card across the counter. "I've forgotten our room number. Could you help me?"

The clerk swiped the card through an electromagnetic trough, attached to a computer, and waited for the information to pop on the screen. "Here it is. Name, please?"

Tine pretended she hadn't heard. "People must do this all the time. The old-fashioned keys were so much easier. But that's progress for you! No stopping it, is there?"

"No, ma'am. May I ask—"

"Of course, no one's trying. To stop progress, I mean. That's just one of those expressions. Look, I don't mean to rush you, but my husband isn't feeling well."

The clerk looked at the man beside her for the first time and noticed the bandage. "Oh, I'm sorry—"

"Not your fault. He took a spill in the street. Missed the curb and down he went! Anyway, I'd like to get him back to the room right away, so if you could hurry."

"Yes. That would be 1203, ma'am."

"I thought so," she said triumphantly. "He kept saying it was 1208. I knew it was 1203. You're a doll."

The corridor on the twelfth floor was deserted. The previous evening's guests had already checked out while the new ones wouldn't check in for another hour or so. The woodwork and doors were painted a violent raspberry color to match the worn carpeting, which was nearing the end of its usefulness. The only decoration on the walls was an arty photograph of a wineglass, which served as an advertisement for the Conservatory Restaurant on the ground floor.

"Does this look at all familiar to you?" Tina asked, wrinkling up her nose.

"No."

"Jeez, how could anyone forget? Well, all I can say is I hope we're not walking in on your wife or your girlfriend or someone else. I'm in no mood for a scene. Another one, that is." Hooked over the doorknob to 1203 was the notice PLEASE MAKE UP ROOM. "Well, *somebody* stayed here last night."

She inserted the card in the slot in the door and jiggled the handle, which failed to budge.

"Pull it out," he said.

"What?"

"Pull the card out or the door won't unlock."

"The things you *do* know!" she marveled. As the door clicked open, her jaw fell. "Holy shit!"

A bizarre sight greeted them: clothes piled up on the floor in neat pyramids, sofa cushions standing on their side, bed linens draped over the headboard. From a deep slash in the mattress, foam rubber stuffing oozed like pus from a wound.

"What happened?" he asked.

"It must've been a helluva party or else you have some strange nesting habits."

They stepped into the room carefully, not touching anything, as if they had stumbled upon the site of an archaeological dig and were fearful of destroying an important artifact. Tina plucked a pair of Calvin Klein briefs from a pile at the foot of the bed.

"Do you normally leave your clothes in little piles on the floor like this?"

The man studied the empty suitcase intently and tried to recall whether or not he had unpacked it. He didn't think so. Who had, then? As he ran his fingers over the lining, a memory stirred in his head, a memory of traveling someplace warm and sunny, where people went to relax. He could see them, as if through a lens, laughing and carrying on for the camera, having a swell time. But it wasn't here. The memory came from somewhere else. The harder he tried to pin the image down to a time and a place, the blurrier it became until it vanished.

He went to the window, pulled back the curtain, and gazed down onto the treetops and a sea of green leaves. A massive marble pillar, topped with gilded statuary, marked the entrance to the park. Joggers and roller-bladers were out in numbers, and a horse-drawn open carriage silently transported its passengers east toward Fifth Avenue.

"I hope these aren't your favorite threads." Tina held up a sports jacket she'd taken out of the closet. "Can you believe this? It's been all cut up. Like with a knife or something. Why would anyone ruin a perfectly good jacket? Or do that to a mattress, for crying out loud? You don't suppose you did it yourself, do you? In some kind of a deranged fit?"

The man's forehead stayed pressed against the window. "He's there!" he cried out.

"What now?"

"The person from the hospital. The one who said last night was just a warning. He's down below. Over there."

Spiff was seated on one of the benches up against the wall of the park. He was back on his cellular phone again, and his eyes went from his wristwatch to the entrance of the hotel to the wristwatch as he talked. His legs were crossed and his right foot jiggled nervously.

"Him again! The jerk I told to fuck off," Tina said. "What in the hell do you think he's doing—"

She cut herself off and swallowed hard. "Holy Mary . . ."

What if the man had been telling the truth when he said he'd been threatened? Much as she didn't want to think so, there was a certain logic to everything that had happened. The attack in the park, the bizarre episode in the hospital, now the ransacked room—perhaps they *were* related.

What kind of a jam had she managed to get herself into? This was no garden variety mugging.

She grabbed him by the shoulders. "What did you do? Answer me. Why are they after you?"

"I wish I knew. Nothing!"

"Well, you better figure it out soon, because from the look of it, they don't appear to be fooling around. Somebody rifled through this room and somebody attacked you last night in the park. And right now somebody is keeping your butt under tight observation. So don't just stand there and tell me you've done nothing!"

"What do you think they want?"

"You're asking me? Maybe you owe some money. You play the horses? That's what it usually is in my neighborhood. If you don't pay your debt on time, they break a bone a week until you do. I'm Sicilian so I know about these things. Not that anyone in my immediate family is involved, thank God. Just a couple of cousins. *Second* cousins . . ."

She stopped herself. The blood was draining out of the man's face and he looked woozy again.

"Sit down. Let me get you some water."

She darted into the bathroom and turned on the tap, letting the water run so it would get cold. While she was waiting, she noticed a small amber plastic prescription bottle on the counter, nestled among the toiletries. She picked it up and read the label. All at once, a glimmer came into her eyes.

She filled the glass, shut off the tap, and hurried back into the bedroom. The man had collapsed in a chair and was absently kneading the curtain with his left hand.

"Brent?" she said to him.

"Yeah?" he replied without looking up.

13

"Brent Stevens."

"What?"

"That's your name—Brent Stevens. If this is your room and these pills belong to you. And since the key was in your pocket, a person doesn't exactly have to be Angela H. Lansbury to put it together. Guess what else."

Tina held up the plastic prescription bottle. "You live at 514 Maywood Avenue in Los Angeles. Lucky you! I always wanted to go to L.A., but I never felt I was pretty enough. Too ethnic."

The man took the prescription bottle and examined the label. He had no idea what it contained, but Tina seemed to think the name and address were his, so perhaps they were. Brent Stevens had a familiar ring to it, although it sounded made up. Maybe he had a nickname people used instead.

He thought he could picture Maywood Avenue—a pleasant street, lined with flowering trees and snug one-story bungalows. Or was he just imagining what a street called Maywood would look like? He waited in vain for a click in his head, a flash of illumination to assure him that, yes, he lived in one of those cozy houses.

"Hey, you're thinking too hard," Tina said, reading his uncertainty. "Relax. When I called your name, you answered, didn't you?"

"Yes."

"There you are! Some part of your brain responded automatically. I'd say that's a pretty big piece of the puzzle . . . And here's another one."

She waved an airplane ticket at him. "It was sticking out of a magazine on the coffee table. American Airlines flight number forty-six to Los Angeles. May nineteenth at eleven A.M. That's tomorrow. And see where it says the name of the passenger? 'B. Stevens.' That's you. It looks like you're going to be back on Maywood Avenue in no time at all."

He studied the ticket intently.

"I've just got one question, Brent."

"What?"

"They weren't looking for drugs in this room, were they? You're not a pusher. Because if it's drugs, I don't care if your name is Walter H. Cronkite. I'm washing my hands."

Brent shook his head. "No drugs. Unless . . ."

"Unless what?"

"These?" He held out the prescription bottle in the flat of his palm.

"Oh, no, doll. That's Claritin. It's on the label. For allergies. I take the stuff myself. The pollen is hell on my sinuses."

"Mine, too?"

"Yeah, yours, too. So we got one thing in common, you and me. Postnasal drip . . . Is that guy still down there?"

She went to the window, and they both looked down into the street. Spiff's place on the park bench had been taken by a grizzled woman with a shopping cart, which overflowed with the booty of the scavenger. A piece of rope was knotted to the handle of the cart. The other end was tied around the neck of a spotted mongrel. The woman's knit cap and thick overcoat indicated that she spent most of her nights outdoors.

"He's gone. Whew! You're positive it was the same guy from the hospital? Because men in suits all look pretty much alike to me. It's not like they dress to stand out in a crowd." Tina was beginning to wonder if she hadn't jumped to a few hasty conclusions earlier. "At any rate, he's no longer there, so maybe we ought to put some order in this place before they kick you out. I hate to think what they're going to charge you for the mattress!"

They tugged the mattress back onto the bed frame, and Tina set about making the bed while Brent straightened the sofa cushions. She slipped the pillows into their cases, fluffling them up in the process. One of the pillowcases had hidden the telephone on the bedside table. The light at the base of the instrument was flashing yellow.

Brent stared at it. "What's that mean?"

"The light? Probably that you've got a message. Pick up the phone. It says to press six."

With trepidation, he raised the receiver to his ear, then angled it so Tina could hear.

"Welcome to Audex," said the automated voice of the operator. "You have four messages. To hear messages, press the pound sign. To repeat messages, press the star sign. For help at any time, press *O* and an operator will come on the line."

He pressed the pound sign.

"Call received Tuesday at 10:43 P.M.," said the automated voice. It was followed by a brief silence, then a woman came on the line. "Hi, Brent. This is Lisa. Just confirming our meeting for tomorrow morning at nine-thirty. Hope you had a good flight and that the room is satisfactory. Look forward to meeting you. See you then."

"Call received Wednesday at 10:19 A.M." The same woman was phoning, only her cheerful tone was more busi-nesslike. "Brent? This is Lisa. Is anything wrong? Where are you? We were expecting you forty-five minutes ago. In case you lost the address, we're at 635 Madison Avenue."

"Call received Wednesday at 11:48 A.M." This time, the voice was hard. "Brent, this is Lisa again. I don't have to tell you how disappointed we all are that you didn't show up. We've been very generous with you up to now and I think you owe us an explanation. I'm in all day."

"Call received Wednesday at 1:05 P.M." "Brent? . . . This is no way to do business, dammit!"

"End of messages."

Baffled, Brent hung up the receiver while Tina scrib-bled a note on the pad by the telephone.

"It seems you had a meeting at 635 Madison Avenue and some broad named Lisa has got her tits in an uproar because you didn't make it. Maybe if she knew you were in the hospital with your head cracked open, she'd be a little more understanding. Then again, maybe not. Sounds to me like she's got an attitude. Well, Miss Bug-Up-Your-Butt, sorry to let you down, but we had more urgent prob-lems to deal with . . . What now?"

Brent was back at the window, his forehead pressed up against the windowpane. "The man's returned."

"Who? You're kidding."

"Over there. Beyond the lamppost. Isn't that him?"

"Shit!"

South of the bench, where the old crone with the mongrel dog still sat, the sidewalk widened to form a rectangular overlook that jutted into the park. Spiff stood at the outermost edge. His head was arched back, and he was scouring the front of the hotel, his eyes moving systematically from floor to floor, window to window, as if he were trying to locate one room in particular.

Brent ducked back, pulling Tina with him. "What's he doing?"

"Put it this way: I don't think he's a building inspector."

"Do you think he'll come up here?"

"Not necessarily. Not yet, anyway. Oh, how the fuck would I know? He could be waiting for reenforcements."

She turned Brent's face toward hers. "Did that guy really threaten you in the hospital?"

"Yes, he did."

"Then we should call that detective right now." From her pocket she withdrew the business card Sergeant Callahan had given her earlier.

"And say what?"

"What you just told me," she answered, dialing the number. As she was about to hand Brent the receiver, a recorded voice invited the caller to leave a name, number, and brief message. "Forget it," she said. "Who's got time to play phone tag with New York's finest? Whatever that guy in the street is up to, I don't think we should stick around and find out. If you plan to get that plane home tomorrow, I'd say it was wise to check out of this hole."

"Where am I going to go?"

"I've got an idea. Just get your toiletries from the bathroom. I'll start packing."

Galvanized by a sense of purpose, Tina scooped the clothes off the floor and tossed them into the suitcase. Then she emptied the closet, clucking again at the damage to the sports coat. She was ready to fasten the latch when Brent shuffled out of the bathroom and handed her a leather shaving kit. He was disoriented all over again.

"Did you get everything?" Without waiting for the answer, she closed the lid. "How are you feeling?"

"I'm all right."

"Because you look like a train wreck. Do you think you can handle the subway all the way to Queens?"

"What's in Queens?"

"My house. But it's just for tonight, and then I'll get you on that plane tomorrow. I couldn't live with myself if I ended up reading about you in the *Post*. So don't get the wrong idea, okay? I live with my younger brother, who'll break your legs if you start acting weird. Although when he sees I'm bringing a stranger home, he'll probably break both of mine."

"He's fucking with us big time."

Spiff shifted the cellular phone from one ear to the other, tapped his foot nervously on the pavement. "He said he would cooperate, but when I asked him to hand the stuff over, he claimed to have no idea what I was talking about. Acted all innocentlike and pretended he'd never seen me before. The guy's slick all right. For a minute, I almost believed him.

"So I told him last night was nothing. Last night was party games, I said, compared to what's in store if he doesn't deliver. He gave me this blank look. I might as well have been talking Greek. Then some orderly came in and took him to the bathroom. He didn't return for about ten minutes. So I went and looked. And the sonavabitch is gone! He'd given me the slip. He sure is one helluva performer is all I'm saying."

"Gave you the slip?" A note of shrillness crept into the voice on the other end of the line. "I must say the fat's in the fire now!"

Spiff suppressed an urge to scoff. Why couldn't the British talk like everybody else? As far as he was concerned, there had been a failure of communication from the start. The client spoke about "tidying up a messy situation" and "putting things to right, if you know what I mean." The trouble was nobody did.

"Fat's in the fire," he echoed. "Yeah, I guess you could put it that way."

"Don't mock me."

"Sorry. Wasn't."

Spiff's patience was fraying. If people would just let him do his job! But no! Clients always insisted that you do it their way, until *their* way proved no good. Then they got haughty and demanded to know what had gone wrong. But they were paying the bills, so you had to humor them.

As the client ranted on, Spiff picked up the pace of his tapping foot, like a bandleader keeping time to a quickening fox-trot. He didn't notice the old crone with the knit cap hoist herself off the bench. Her body was bent and she advanced slowly, laboriously shuffling one tattered house slipper in front of the other, the uneven paving stones impeding her movement.

"Spare change, mister?" she muttered when she got closer. "Quarter, dime, nickel?"

Getting no answer, she gently tugged at Spiff's coat sleeve.

Spiff's reflexes clicked in. He spun around and inadvertently clipped the woman's shoulder. The blow jeopardized her already precarious equilibrium, and she staggered backward, her tiny eyes ablaze.

"Fascist! Dictator!" she screamed.

"Shut your trap, okay, lady?"

"I beg your pardon. What did you just say?" the voice on the line asked indignantly.

"Not *you!* I've got street people attacking me now."

The spotted mongrel, yapping shrilly, strained at its rope. Spiff gave it a kick, setting off another round of insults from the crone.

"Hitler. Mussolini . . . *Nixon!*"

"I'll come down and give you a hand, if you can't manage."

Spiff chose to overlook the client's sarcasm. "Thanks, it's under control . . . Look, you wanted this guy to know we mean business. He knows now. Take my word on it."

"Whole lot of good that does us if he still has no intention of cooperating and we don't even know where he is."

"He's got to go back to the hotel sooner or later."

"Then get over there."

Spiff felt a brief swell of satisfaction. "I'm standing out in front of it."

"Then go inside. Find him!"

"That's what I was—"

"*Now, you idiot!*"

Spiff gritted his teeth. What did the client think he was going to do? Fly off to Cuernavaca? He turned to cross the street and ran smack into the crone's shopping cart. Furious, he shoved it out of his way.

The cart teetered briefly on the curb, then fell over sideways, spilling the woman's sorry possessions into the street with a clatter.

Brent insisted on carrying the suitcase from the elevator to the front desk. Tina hooked her arm around his free arm and stuck close to his side. She was reasonably certain that checking out would present no difficulty. He would have shown the clerk a credit card when he arrived the day before, and the clerk would have taken an imprint. It didn't matter now that the card was gone.

They made, she realized, an unlikely couple—she, still in her exercise gear, her dance bag slung over her shoulder; he with his head bandaged and a dazed look on his face. People would probably take her for a temperamental wife who'd clobbered her nice husband in an argument. No, they wouldn't. This was New York. They'd take her for a dominatrix and her customer.

"Room 1203," Brent said to the desk clerk. The buxom woman with her hair in a bun was back on duty.

"Certainly, sir." Authoritatively, she punched some keys on her computer. "We have you leaving tomorrow, Mr. Stevens. I trust nothing was wrong."

"Nothing at all," Tina replied. "Just a last-minute change of plans."

"I see." The woman produced a credit card voucher. "Do you wish to leave the charges on your American Express?"

"Please."

"This will just take me a moment."

As the clerk busied herself with paperwork, Tina surveyed the lobby. Two businessmen on a sofa were scrutinizing blueprints spread out on the coffee table before them, and a bellhop was wheeling a luggage cart through the glass doors. A yellow cab pulled up to the entrance, blocking her view of the street.

When it drew away, she caught sight of the man, his back turned. He appeared engrossed in a conversation on his cellular phone. The homeless woman with the dog was shuffling toward him. Then, suddenly, the man swung around and whacked her, knocking her backward. The dog was yapping like crazy.

"We better get moving," Tina said. The clerk had withdrawn into the back room. Why was checkout taking so long?

When the clerk came back, she was carrying a large manila envelope, which she slid across the counter. "I believe this is for you, Mr. Stevens. It was left here last night. I'm sorry it wasn't given to you then. And here's your copy of the bill. We hope you'll come back and stay with us again." The thank-you smile, purely business, excluded Tina.

The label on the envelope read simply: BRENT STEVENS, MAYFLOWER HOTEL.

"Should I open it now?" he whispered to Tina.

"Yes, but make it snappy. You know who is still outside."

"You don't think it's a bomb?"

"If it is, this is as good a place as any for it to go off! Did you see that wallpaper? . . . Joking!"

They huddled by the bell captain's stand as he sliced open the flap of the envelope with his index finger. Inside was a plain white business envelope. He tore off the end, blew air into it, and pulled out a handwritten note: "Look forward to tomorrow's meeting. Enjoy yourself tonight on us. Best, Lisa."

"Her again!" remarked Tina.

"Yeah, but look." Amazed, Brent extracted ten brand-new $100 bills from the envelope.

"If I'd known in advance, I'd have ordered us a car service! Too late for that! I hate to point this out, but our man is heading toward the hotel right now."

On the far side of the street, Spiff swiveled his head back and forth, waiting for a break in the traffic.

"What do we do?"

"We don't have a choice. This way."

To the left of the reception desk, a corridor led to the Conservatory Restaurant, which occupied the southeast corner of the building. With any luck, Tina thought, it had its own door onto the street. Coming from the hospital, she had noticed a subway entrance on the nearby corner, one of several that fed into the underground corridors of the Fifty-ninth Street/Columbus Circle station. If they could reach the stairs to the subway without being detected, they could lose themselves in the crowd below. It was their best chance.

Tina grabbed the suitcase and pushed Brent ahead of her and down the corridor. The restaurant was deserted and the maître d's podium stood unattended. A few customers were imbibing at the bar, and off in one corner, a busboy was folding napkins into flowerlike shapes in anticipation of the dinner crowd.

"Can I do anything for you folks?" the bartender called out jovially as Tina and Brent made their way hastily across the room. Distracted by the greeting, Brent accidentally brushed up against a table, pulling the linen cloth partially off and sending silverware clattering to the floor. The noise startled him and he froze.

"Jeez, don't stop now," Tina snapped. She glanced over her shoulder. The man had entered the lobby and was striding briskly toward the bank of elevators. It wouldn't be too long before he discovered that room 1203 was empty and that Brent had checked out.

"Everything okay?" the bartender asked, less jovially this time.

Tina's hunch had been right. The Conservatory Restaurant had an outside entrance. She gave Brent a firm shake and pointed him toward it.

"Couldn't be better!" she called back to the bartender.

A sharp smell of urine floated up out of the subway. Several posters for *In the Beginning* had recently been slapped up on the white-tiled walls, and they had already been defaced. "Rot in hell, sinners!" someone had written with black spray paint, and there were large *X*s over the beatific faces of Jennifer Osborne and Christopher Knight. Tina kicked aside an empty beer can wrapped in a paper bag. Scrambling down the stairs, she could hear the roar of a train arriving in the station.

All at once, she sensed that Brent was no longer following her. He'd come to a stop in front of one of the movie posters and was looking at it raptly.

"Jesus H. Christ, this is no time to dawdle," she called out to him. "Step on it!"

The turnstile was directly ahead. They broke into a run.

14

"Which of you wants to tell me about your first date? Christopher?"

"I don't think there was one. Jennifer knocked at my door and asked if she could spend the night."

"What?" Deborah Myers's stenciled eyebrows shot up.

The actor slipped his arm around his wife. "You'd better explain, Jen."

"I assume this isn't going to be too racy for TV?" Deborah protested, secretly wishing the opposite.

Over the years she had come to the conclusion that most so-called golden couples were really made of decidedly mixed metals; one spouse was always more golden than the other. Elizabeth Taylor exerted a greater fascination than any of her husbands. Lucy had eclipsed Desi. Tom Cruise outshone Nicole Kidman.

Christopher Knight and Jennifer Osborne were different. Appealing as they were individually, Deborah found them more intriguing as a pair. They enhanced each other, and not just physically, either. One plus one made more than two. Seated side by side, as they were right now, they gave the impression that they shared something special, something that was theirs alone, although Deborah would have been hard put to say what it was.

"We were in a small town in Nova Scotia, filming *The Return*. The absolute end of the world," Jennifer recounted. "The film company had taken over the one hotel in the area. And my mother came to visit! I had to share my room with her, naturally, and well, her snoring kept me up half the night."

"One morning, I heard this knocking at my door," Christopher interrupted. "It was Jennifer. Looking . . . not her best."

"Christopher!"

"Well, you weren't, dear. You looked pretty dreadful, in fact. 'I understand you have the only two-bedroom suite in this hotel,' she said. Very straightforward. I replied that I did. 'Do you mind if I use one of the bedrooms?' she said. 'My mother is keeping me up until all hours. In a few days, even makeup won't be able to do anything about the circles under my eyes.' I couldn't very well say no, could I?"

"So I moved in," Jennifer concluded.

"Just like that?" Deborah Myers's eyebrows, always more mobile than the rest of her face, swooped up again.

"The arrangement made sense to me. He was the star of the movie and I had only featured billing. But I had to get some sleep, too. It *was* in everybody's best interests."

"And did you? Get any sleep?" (Deborah rarely passed up the chance to inject a little innuendo into her interviews.)

"Oh, I slept like a baby. We hardly saw each other. We were on different schedules and had only a couple of scenes together. Christopher brought me my morning coffee a few times, which was adorable of him. So I guess our first date was breakfast."

"When did it progress to dinner?"

"Much later. Once the picture was done and we'd gotten back to Los Angeles. Christopher finally asked me out. I think he realized he couldn't live without me."

"I missed our breakfasts."

"Well, I must say, the two of you kept it awfully quiet," Deborah declared with a hint of censure. State secrets were of small interest to her, but in matters of dating and courtship, she subscribed to a policy of full public disclosure. "Nobody knew you were seeing each other. Not a word in the gossip columns. And then, bam! You're married!"

"We just realized we were right for each other."

"But doesn't a Hollywood marriage frighten you? The pressures, the temptations?" Deborah scanned a card in her lap. "I believe it was *Fanfare Magazine* that polled its readers whether or not they thought the marriage would last. Eight out of ten responded no."

"Eight out of ten were wrong," Christopher crowed.

"Anyway, it's not a Hollywood marriage," Jennifer added. "It's our marriage. *Fanfare* is just selling magazines. It's all part of the business. You should understand that better than anyone, Deborah."

Deborah did, much as she was reluctant to admit so on the air. *Fanfare* was lower on the food chain than her specials, which were technically classified as news. (Okay, *soft* news, but that was still news.) But they all trafficked in celebrity, every one of them, from the nightly newscasts to the checkout counter scandal sheets.

Her sponsors happened to be selling upscale things like all-terrain vehicles and family health plans, whereas *Fanfare*'s ad pages trumpeted the merits of mentholated cigarettes and memorial dinner plates from the Franklin Mint. It was all the same hustle. For that matter, what were Christopher Knight and Jennifer Osborne doing this very morning, if not selling an overbudgeted movie epic that had probably tested poorly in sneak previews?

She would have to bring up the film shortly. Time was running out, and *In the Beginning* would be a hot topic, at least until moviegoers got the opportunity to see it. Anyway, she had no choice. The preinterview agreement specified that Deborah would talk about *In the Beginning* and air two minutes of footage of the film on the telecast.

"Before you ask us another question, may I say something?" Jennifer's request caught Deborah off guard.

"Please, be my guest." The hostess leaned back in her chair, wondering what this was about and praying it wasn't a pitch for Save the Whales.

"It's something I haven't told anyone yet. Not even Christopher. I do hope you don't mind my doing it this way, darling."

"Now you've got us all on the edge of our seats," said Deborah, leaning back even more. "Don't make us wait any longer."

"Well, it's just this . . ." The actress reached for her husband's hand. "We're going to have a baby."

In the hush that followed, the only sounds came from beyond the deck, where a few bathers, buffeted by the surf, screamed delightedly.

Christopher seemed dumbstruck by his wife's admission. But then, so did everyone in the room. Even the self-important assistants who were always tiptoeing around behind the cameras, exchanging urgent notes, came to a rest, as if frozen by a magic wand. Deborah, feeling her three-by-five cards slip out of her lap, let them fall to the floor. No one dared to do anything that might influence the course of the next few minutes.

The actor and actress seemed lost in a private dream-world—the crew, invisible; the lights and cameras, forgotten. A rush of emotion had seized them both. It heightened their beauty, further elevating them above the common mortals who watched with the growing realization that they were privy to an exceptionally intimate moment in the stars' lives.

Jennifer's eyes glistened, and the corners of her mouth turned up in a Mona Lisa smile that blended contentment and mischief so thoroughly there was no distinguishing one from the other. Christopher lifted his wife's hand slowly into the air, then bent forward and pressed his lips to her palm. It was an old-fashioned gesture that recalled the romance of the silent movies, of sheiks and vamps swept up in secret passions.

Accustomed as she was to celebrity revelations, Deborah felt her heart racing, too. She could never have hoped for this. It was better than that sportscaster, who-ever he was, asking that actress to marry him right in the middle of a broadcast. Better than Michael Jackson and Lisa Marie Presley admitting they had a sex life. The nation's most voluptuous movie star had just told the nation's handsomest movie star that he was about to become a father, and it was a Deborah Myers exclusive!

Talk about headlines! Ratings! Deborah allowed herself to luxuriate in the unexpected triumph. She had wanted a special moment, and boy did she have one now! Hollywood history in the making. Her viewers would be riveted. It was perfect.

Too perfect. Somewhere, in the back of Deborah Myers's mind, a doubt began to form. Why, she wondered, had Jennifer Osborne taken this occasion to break the news to her husband? And was she really breaking it to him? Something about the way she'd tilted her head as she smiled at him, and the gallantry with which he had kissed her hand made Deborah think they were both performing.

Well, they *were* actors, and actors performed all the time. Getting carried away with their emotions was one of the hazards of the job. So what? Deborah sensed that wasn't the whole truth, though. Jennifer Osborne and Christopher Knight knew what they were doing, knew instinctively the value of gestures and the significance of head angles. If they were caught up in the drama of the moment, they were also shaping it. But to what purpose?

"I'm speechless," she said, breaking the silence. "I couldn't be happier for you both."

For once, she didn't know what else to say.

15

Brent's eyelids flickered, then sprang open. *I* was the first thing he saw, hovering above him.

He blinked several times, fearing he was hallucinating, but when he looked again, it was still there, like a big, black exclamation point on the white plaster. The capital letter *I*.

He was lying on a bed in a dark room, the covers pulled up to his chin. The curtains were closed, but some light from outdoors spilled over the top of the curtain rod, illuminating part of one wall and a corner of the ceiling. And there in the patch of brightness—no mistaking it—was the *I*.

He stared at it for a while, expecting it to disappear suddenly or start writhing like a snake. Then he'd know it was just one of the bizarre dreams he'd been having lately. But the letter didn't move. What's more, he realized, to one side of it, loomed an equally large *H*. And on the other side, a *J*. His eyes raced back and forth. The whole alphabet was strung out along the top of the wall.

"*H, I, J, K,*" he mumbled, trying to make sense of what he saw.

Then he heard the breathing.

Another person was in the room with him, standing in

the shadows, not moving at all. The figure registered only as an indistinct shape, but without turning his head, Brent knew he was being observed. He could feel the eyes boring into him. The breathing was barely detectable, that of someone trying hard not to be noticed, but in the darkened room, it sounded to Brent like the puffing of a bellows. He fought the urge to sit up and cry for help.

Then a tiny voice piped in his ear. "I knew the alphabet when I was three. Want to hear me recite it? *A, B, C, D*..."

He lifted his head and found himself face-to-face with a small girl with long, brown hair and brown eyes fringed with feathery lashes.

"Who are you?"

The girl blithely ignored his question. "This is my room. I slept with my mom last night. I wish I could sleep in her bed all the time, but she won't let me because she says I'm six and I have to learn to stay in my own room now."

"Oh."

"Actually, I'm six and three months. My mom said you were in an accident and not to bother you because you needed to rest. But you've been sleeping a very long time." She rolled her eyes dramatically. "I've never seen anyone sleep so long as you. My mom kept looking in the door and saying, 'Rip Van Winkle is still dead to the world.' I thought you would never wake up, Mr. Winkle."

"What time is it?"

The little girl skipped over to a bureau and picked up a plastic *Beauty and the Beast* alarm clock, the hands of which were shaped like eating utensils. "The fork is on the seven and the spoon is on the two," she announced authoritatively. "So it's ten minutes after seven. I've been able to tell time since I was four, you know."

"Have you?"

"Yes. And you've been sleeping for . . ." Her mouth dropped open. She put the clock down and began counting on her fingers. "You came here at three o'clock, so that's one, two, three—"

"Four hours," he interrupted her.

"No, silly. Three o'clock *yesterday*." She giggled and began to count all over again. "One, two, three, four five—"

"You mean I've been sleeping for sixteen hours?"

"Wait. I'm not done yet." She pretended to make a quick mental calculation, then said, "Sixteen hours. Wow! I'll get Mom." She skipped out of the room and her voice echoed down the hall. "Mom, he's awake. Mr. Winkle is up."

As Brent's eyes became accustomed to the gloom, the room came into focus. It was a child's room, filled with the clutter of an exuberant childhood—dolls of varying sizes, stuffed animals, a small easel with a finger painting thumbtacked to it. Drawings and photographs were taped everywhere on the walls, and along the top, the letters of the alphabet served as border paper. His mother never would have permitted that, when he was young.

Ma, he remembered calling her. Always Ma. Never Mother or Mom.

He rolled over onto his side and felt a throbbing in his head. He reached up and touched the bandage and it came back to him that he had been in the hospital recently. His body was drained of energy, and sitting up required a conscious effort. Once his feet were on the floor, he let his head dangle between his knees and the rush of blood helped.

Other needs began to assert themselves. He was thirsty and had to go to the bathroom. He brought his head back up and examined his surroundings. Hanging on a clothes tree in the corner was a green suit. He recognized it as the one he'd been wearing before all the confusion began, when? Yesterday? Two days ago? A full-length mirror on the back of a door reflected the image of a man in a white T-shirt and underpants. With a shock, he realized he was looking at himself.

He tried to study the reflection objectively and saw someone who was coming off a weekend bender. The bandage signaled a bad fall or a fight. Although the face was unbruised, it gave off an aura of exhaustion. The body seemed in good condition, though, still youthful and resilient. He inflated his chest and flexed his biceps. Yes, the body was bearing up. He ran his hand through his hair, brushing it off his forehead, when the door opened and the image flew away.

Tina stood in the doorway, hand on hip. "He lives!"

Behind her, the little girl giggled and picked up the refrain. "He lives . . . he lives . . ."

"That's enough, Angelina. So finally decided to rejoin the human race, have we? How about something to eat?"

"Some coffee, maybe?"

"Let me see what I can do. Angelina, do you want to set another place at the table?"

The girl clapped her hands enthusiastically. "Hooray!" she squealed as she raced down the stairs. "Mr. Winkle is coming to breakfast, everybody."

* * *

He didn't think he was hungry, but with each bite of French toast, his appetite increased and his strength returned.

"Did I really sleep sixteen hours?"

"Straight through. I wasn't even sure you were going to make it here. You started fading on the subway."

"I remember running to catch it."

"I think that nearly did you in. We had to put you to bed, when we got here. Don't worry. I didn't undress you. Johnny did. In fact, Johnny wanted to lock the bedroom door, just in case you woke up in the middle of the night and turned out to be an ax murderer."

"Johnny?"

"My brother. Works the late shift. Gets up around nine. You'll meet him."

"I guess I've put you through a lot, huh?"

"Not that much."

"I appreciate all you've done for me."

"You'll return the favor someday . . . Hey, stop playing with your food, Angelina, and eat up."

"I am eating. Do you like French toast, Mr. Winkle? It's my favorite. I don't like eggs. Mom says it's just a phase I'm going through, but I don't think so."

"It's not Mr. Winkle. It's Mr. Stevens." Tina refilled the coffee cups and took her place at the kitchen table. She had on an oversize T-shirt that listed to the side, exposing one shoulder, and navy blue sweat pants. Without makeup and in the soft light filtering through the kitchen window, she came across as younger and more vulnerable than Brent recalled. The tough, Queens facade was, apparently, armor for the outside world.

"I just want you to know I'm grateful, that's all. Not everybody would have bothered."

Tina shrugged off the compliment. Thank-yous made her uncomfortable. "Blame my grandmother, bless her soul."

"Your grandmother?"

"Long story. She used to prepare these big pots of spaghetti and meatballs. Then she'd put it on paper plates and cover them with tinfoil, and take them down to the bums on Grand Avenue. When she was in her seventies—I must have been about nine or ten—it was hard for her to carry all that food by herself. So I started helping. The first time, I was scared shitless. These were guys who looked like they'd kill you for a dime. But you shoulda seen their faces light up when they saw my grandmother coming. They called her Saint Ida. And she was, too.

"She told me if anybody needed help, you gave it, because that person might be Jesus. She was convinced Jesus would come back any day, if he hadn't already. I said, 'Norna, these men aren't Jesus.' And she said, 'Oh, Miss Smarty Pants! And how do you know that?' I never had an acceptable answer, of course. She talked to Him all the time like He was in the room. She'd say things like, 'Do you believe the lip this granddaughter of mine is giving me, Jesus? What are we going to do with her?' She'd wait for an answer, which only she could hear, of course—and then whack me on the wrist with her knitting needle. In the name of Jesus, of course. The whole family thought she was crazy."

Brent smiled. "I'm not Jesus."

"I kinda gathered that already. But Saint Ida wouldn't have ruled it out."

Angelina set down her fork with a clatter. "Look, everybody. Clean plate club! Can I be excused now?"

"Yes, honey. Get your backpack and don't forget to brush your teeth."

Brent watched the child skip out of the kitchen. "I guess you'd like me to leave, too."

"Relax a minute. I'm not going to push you out the door. I told you I'd take you to the airport. You got a ticket to L.A., remember? You do remember what happened yesterday?"

"The emergency room and the hotel, yeah, although it seems like a dream now."

"No dream. That was real. Do you have any idea who that guy might be?"

"What guy?"

"The guy you thought was after you."

"No."

"I was kinda hoping everything would be clear when you woke up today. My brother's theory is that you're screwing around with somebody else's wife, but that's only because Johnny has a little too much experience in that department himself. He says a handsome guy like you—young, no wedding ring—has ladies' man written all over him. 'Just look at him, Tina,' he said. I told him you can't always believe what you see. Anyway, be logical. Someone isn't going to trash your hotel room just because you're messing with his wife . . . They'd shoot you in the nuts first."

Brent's back stiffened.

"You really don't get my sense of humor, do you?"

Before he could reply, the little girl padded back into the room. She'd put on a blue jacket with a giraffe appliquéd on the back and dragged a backpack behind her. "Megan's here. I have to go now, Mr. Win—Mr. Stevens." She offered a tiny hand for shaking, gave her mother a peck on the cheek, and was gone.

"Off to school?"

"First grade. Megan is her best friend. Megan's mother and I take turns dropping them off and picking them up. The school's only two blocks away, but you have to be careful with kids these days. I used to walk to the same school by myself. My mother would stand in the front doorway and watch until I reached the corner. Times have changed."

"She's beautiful."

"Thanks."

"And smart."

"We say she's gonna be the first in the family to graduate Harvard."

"Where's her father?"

"Oh, boy. Long gone. But that's another story. It's always been one of the bigger mysteries that out of that sad, fucked-up marriage came the joy of my life. Go figure."

For a moment, they both sat in silence.

If Tina had managed to put a stamp on the other rooms, the kitchen seemed anchored in a time warp. The cabinetry, the Formica dinette set, even the appliances harked back to the early 1960s, when for about fifteen minutes they had probably been judged the height of modern. Their chief distinction now was to serve as reminders of the people who'd bought them—members in good-standing of the immigrant class, striving to put the old world behind them and be part of the new.

Brent's own past was a blur, but here the identities of people long gone seemed vivid to him. Tina's mother, he thought, must have regularly waxed and polished the linoleum floor. The dinette set, worn by the years of constant use, had surely been witness to countless conversations and arguments. It wouldn't have surprised him to learn that the skillet Tina was using to make French toast had belonged to Saint Ida. Brent tried to picture his own house, but heavy clomping coming from the stairway distracted him and he gave up.

A burly man, wearing only a T-shirt and boxer shorts, poked his head into the kitchen. His eyes were puffy from sleep and his dark hair was an uncombed tangle. Although he was still in his twenties, his body had already begun to settle into middle age.

"Yo, Rip. How'd you sleep? What'd you fix me for breakfast, Tina?" Still on automatic pilot, he poured himself a mug of coffee.

"That's his majesty," Tina explained. "Our mother spoiled him rotten and he expects me to do the same. The equality of the sexes is still a radical notion here in Queens. You want some French toast, Johnny?"

"Yeah, sure. Just don't burn it this time." Mug in hand, he shuffled into the living room and switched on the TV.

Tina raised her voice so she could be heard over the racket. "Johnny, gimme the car keys, will you?"

"What for?"

"I have to take Brent to the airport."

"He can't take a cab? I got things to do."

"What things?"

"*Things!*"

"You don't have diddly-squat to do, Johnny. Gimme the keys."

"Yeah, yeah, yeah" was all that came back. Then, "This coffee's freezin' cold."

"So heat it up. You a cripple?"

"I don't want to cause any more trouble," said Brent.

"Don't worry. He always talks that way. Basically, he's a good guy. He's just a lazy fuck. Anyway, forget about him."

"So it looks like I'm going to California."

"Unless you got a better idea. You're already booked, and the airlines sock you with big penalties whenever you change your flight. We know your address. To make sure, I checked with information in Los Angeles last night. You're listed. When I called the number, I got an answering machine. Sounded like your voice to me. As soon as you're back in familiar surroundings, I bet everything will fall right in place. If not, you should see Doctor Park."

"Doctor Park?"

"Name on the prescription bottle."

"You don't miss much, do you?"

"Since you're staying in my house, I figured I was allowed to pry a little. By the way, we should leave early for the airport so we can check out that locker key." She collected the plates off the table and rinsed them under the faucet.

"You make it sound like everything will work out just fine."

"Everything usually does, doll. Not always right away. In time. Nothing is ever the huge drama we think it is at first."

16

*S*teve pressed the "pedal to the metal," as the guys liked to
say. This was his favorite strip of highway—everyone's
really—because for two solid miles, it stretched out straight
and flat. The policeman who patrolled it on Friday and
Saturday nights (and sometimes parked his car behind the
crumbling billboard touting the majesty of Howe Caverns)
was certain to be elsewhere at this hour. Weekends, the high
school kids used the highway for drag racing, but at seven-
fifteen on a Monday morning, the traffic was nonexistent. A
few cars and pickups were traveling in the opposite direction
toward town, and an occasional tractor, lumbering from one
field to another, clung self-effacingly to the shoulder.

He watched the speedometer climb from fifty-five to sixty,
then to sixty-five. When it hit seventy-five, the Impala
started to shimmy. Still, he kept his foot on the accelerator.
The thought went through his head that all he would have to
do was give a sharp pull on the steering wheel one way or
another and he could end this nightmare.

Because that's what it had turned into—a real nightmare. It had begun with Linda's teary admission that she
was pregnant and continued through the ridiculous family
meeting yesterday. And now he was only hours away from

walking into the courthouse, where he and Linda would fill out the necessary papers for a marriage license under the watchful eyes of their parents.

Steve glanced at the clock on the dashboard, which read seven-twenty. In less than two hours, they would be expecting him at the town hall. Well, maybe this was the fate he deserved. The guidance counselor at the high school had told him more than once that he was a drifter who "let life happen to him." Sooner or later, the lecture went, he was going to have to make "a few hard decisions about his future." If not, "someone else will make them for you."

The fields to either side of the road were a buttery green under the morning sun, but he didn't notice them or the Daisy Farm milk truck, which gave a friendly honk of the horn as it approached from the opposite direction. People recognized Steve's red Impala.

He passed a yellow sign, warning that the highway took a series of dangerous curves ahead, and knew that he would have to slow down and turn back before long. The speedometer fell to fifty-five miles per hour, then to forty-five, and then dipped below thirty-five. It was as if he had come to the end of his rope and now the rope was tightening around his neck and someone was pulling him back. His mother was probably wondering at this very instant where he was. She had given his white shirt a quick pressing the night before. As she had returned it to his closet, she'd reflected, "Sometimes things do turn out for the best, even if it doesn't seem so at first." But then she had always been so grateful for small favors. Hadn't she had any dreams of her own once? He realized that he had never asked her.

The highway shook free of the curves and straightened out briefly as it came to an intersection and a cluster of road *signs. This was as far as the high school crowd usually drove on Saturday nights, and the shoulders of the road, worn down and dusty, showed where they parked their hot rods or made skidding U-turns. The milkweeds hid a multitude of beer cans.*

Steve couldn't count the number of times he had shuttled between town and this intersection. And yet this morning he seemed to be viewing it all for the very first time. He pulled the Impala off the pavement and let the motor idle while he looked at the familiar landscape—the ruts in the dried mud, the abandoned phone booth that hadn't worked for as long as he could remember. And the signs, stacked one on top of the other—a jumble of arrows and names and numbers that was guaranteed to confuse any tourist passing through.

Then, he saw it, so clear and bold it could have been the only sign, not one of a dozen, weathered by the elements and bent by the wind. Funny, it had never stood out before. ALL POINTS WEST it said, with a black arrow underneath. From the rusted holes in the metal, it appeared someone had used it for target practice.

As Steve stared at the sign, the letters seemed to jump out at him, telling him to take charge, showing him the way out. He could be anything he wanted to be. Anybody. But not here.

The hands of the clock on the dashboard were coming up on seven-thirty. His heart pounding, he edged the Impala off the dirt and onto the pavement. The intersection was empty and no cars were coming in either direction.

He hesitated for only a second, then gave an easy turn to the wheel and pointed the Impala west, as the sign had instructed him. Slowly, the automobile picked up speed. The sun glinted off the silver hood ornament and Steve heard himself laughing. He was going to Hollywood.

17

Like most of the major arteries knitting the boroughs of New York together, the Brooklyn/Queens Expressway was not calculated to lift the spirit. To the west, the Manhattan skyline invited admiring glances, but the immediate landscape was one of fast-food joints, flickering neon, and drab brick housing projects. The road's only virtue was its convenience—if it wasn't rush hour, that is, and the weather was good. Both being the case, the Jeep Cherokee—with Tina Ruffo at the wheel and Brent Stevens in the front seat beside her—sped in a northeasterly direction toward La Guardia Airport, unencumbered by the traffic that would start building up in a few hours.

For the past couple of minutes, Tina had fallen uncharacteristically silent, aware that their odd adventure was nearing its end. Brent would get on his plane shortly and she would never see him again. Oh, he would phone to say that he had arrived safely—she'd made him promise that—and he would probably write her some kind of thank-you letter, maybe send a Christmas card. But she had no doubt that his old life would come back to him. He would step back into familiar patterns and come to view the last few days as an aberration—like the vacation horror story that with each recounting grows less horrible and more humorous.

She stole a glance at him and caught him staring out the window. "Do you believe they called it Fun City once! Part of some big tourist promotion. Not much fun for you, huh?"

"I was just thinking I don't want to go."

"You don't? Why not?"

"Who knows what I'll find in California. It's strange, but I'm sorry to have to leave."

"After all you've been through?"

"Not the place . . . no. Sorry to leave you. You're different."

"Tell me!" Tina cackled.

"I didn't put that very well . . . you're special. Do you believe that people come together for a reason?"

"Yeah, to annoy one another."

"That's a joke, isn't it?"

"You're catching on . . . Ida used to tell me that angels turn up in the lives of people in distress to help them change. You don't know they are angels, though, because they look and dress like everybody else. Then once their mission is achieved, poof, they up and disappear."

"So you're an angel?"

Tina gave a snort. "I wasn't referring to myself. After I drop you off at the airport, I don't disappear. I go home to make supper for my brother and Angelina. Then there's the nightly struggle of getting a six-year-old to bed. Tomorrow, the whole cycle begins again. No, if anything, I'd say you were the angel in my life."

"How's that?"

"Last night while you were sleeping—this is gonna sound dumb—I began to envy you. Makes no sense, I know. I'd go out of my mind if I was in your shoes. Nevertheless I started to think that some sort of selective amnesia would make my life a lot better right now. I wouldn't get so upset about my ex-husband. All my anger toward him would vanish. I could forget the disappointment I had in my mother. Just start all over. No bad stuff. Why not? Who wouldn't like to begin a fresh life?"

She pulled the Jeep into the left lane and passed a slow-moving beer truck belching waves of black smoke.

"You make it sound like I should be the happiest person alive."

"I don't mean it that way. But I'd like to take a big eraser to parts of my life sometimes . . . erase all the people who told me how stupid I was, growing up. Or what a fool I was to get divorced. 'Nobody wants secondhand goods!' My mother actually said that, when my divorce papers came through! To her, I was secondhand goods! So you can understand how your situation might seem enviable from the outside . . . theoretically."

"I don't know if my past was any happier. It seems so fuzzy now. Except for odd details that stand out sharply. Like I can picture the gray runner on the staircase going up to my bedroom and the brass rods that attached it to the risers. Sometimes my mother is as clear to me as if she was sitting right here, but my dad—I can't tell you the color of his hair."

"You have to get in touch with a doctor as soon as you get to California, even when things start coming back.

Make sure you have yourself checked out. I've got a feeling you're going to be just fine."

"What if I'm not? What if the past never comes back and I *never* remember the color of my dad's hair? Or I start forgetting new things? Like they said in the hospital. What if I forget you?"

"I'm unforgettable. Didn't I mention that? . . . You're already a lot better than you were. You were acting like a crazy person yesterday. Look at you now—calm, cool and respectable-appearing. If I didn't know any better, I would swear you were a TV star. Yeah, one of those cute guys who do the weather."

Brent searched her face for a sign that she was putting him on. All her attention seemed concentrated on her driving. He burst out laughing. This woman he'd hardly gotten to know had a way of defusing his fears and making him feel happy.

"Come to California with me," he said impulsively.

"And join the rest of the weirdos?"

"No, I'm serious. I have the money from the hotel. I'll buy you a ticket. You'd like it out there."

"And what do you do when you open the door and find a wife and three kids waiting for you?"

"I doubt it."

"Your hunky surfer boyfriend, then."

"I doubt that even more."

"For some reason, so do I. Well, I'm flattered, Brent. Really. First time anyone's asked me out in ages, and it's to go three thousand miles. Some date! But aren't you forgetting that little person who'll be getting out of school soon? And the brother, who can't boil an egg for himself? Not to mention, a couple of bubblebutts, who have got to be pissed as hell at me for taking the morning off."

"You said you wanted to start over."

"It's just a fantasy. We all have responsibilities and obligations that tie us down. You do, too."

"So how come you said I was an angel in your life?"

Tina thought for a while. "You made me realize something important, that no one's gonna hit me over the head and make the past magically go away. I'm the one who's gotta put it behind me and get on with my life. That sounds pretty basic, but I needed the reminder."

A silver limousine cut sharply in front of them, putting an end to her musing. "Sonavabitch!" She pounded on the horn, which responded with a series of angry bleats. Up ahead, where the road split, airport traffic bore to the right.

"Would you mind if I called you?" Brent said.

"I told you I want to hear you got home in one piece."

"No, more than that. Can we be friends?"

"Back in first grade, Rita Salvo marched up to me on the first day of school and asked me the same thing. 'Why not?' I said. We've been best friends ever since. Funny, nobody ever asked me that question again."

"You didn't answer. Can we?"

"We already are."

The line at the American Airlines counter was already a dozen people long—most of them burdened with too much luggage, which they slid forward with their feet each time a space opened up. Tina had insisted on parking the Jeep and accompanying Brent to the gate.

"What's another five hundred feet? I've come this far, haven't I?" she remarked when he told her it wasn't necessary. Secretly, he was glad to spend a few more minutes with her.

"Now, you got your ticket? You can check the suitcase. How about something to read? You want a magazine or a paper? Gum?" Tina was rambling, but she couldn't help it. Flying made her nervous, even when it was someone else who was getting on the plane.

"Next."

Brent handed his ticket to a woman with poofed-up hair, purple eye shadow, and the petrified look of a 1970s beauty contestant, determined to ignore the encroachments of time. "Flight forty-six to L.A. with a change in Chicago," she confirmed. "Could I see a picture ID, Mr. Stevens?"

"I beg pardon."

"I need to see a piece of identification with your photo on it." She flashed a broad, perfunctory smile.

"I don't have one."

"You don't have a driver's license? A passport, then?"

Brent shook his head.

"Something from your work, maybe?"

"Nothing."

He appealed for help to Tina, who intervened with an explanation. "You see he was mugged recently and his wallet was stolen."

The agent eyed Tina coolly. "I'm terribly sorry about that. But we can't let anyone on the plane without a photo ID. It's the rule. Surely you must have some piece of identification."

"Lady, I just told you. He was robbed and beaten up.

What's he supposed to do? His name's on the ticket. Isn't that enough?"

"I'm afraid not. Tickets get lost or stolen. We'll need some kind of additional proof that it's his."

"Whose do you think it is? Donald H. Duck's?"

"Perhaps I should get a supervisor." The ticket agent picked up a phone and gingerly pressed it to her ear, so as not to muss her hairdo. A frost had come over her features, suggesting that if she ever had won a beauty title, it wasn't Miss Congeniality.

The balding man who quickly joined her behind the counter had a more conciliatory air. They conferred in hushed tones, then the woman stepped back and let him take over.

"Mugged?" the supervisor said. "Hope you weren't too badly hurt. Let me see what I can do here." He punched a few buttons on a computer keyboard and studied the screen.

"Traveling to Los Angeles today, Mr. Stevens? Leaving at eleven. Transferring at O'Hare. You wouldn't be a frequent flyer with us, would you?"

Brent didn't know. There was a chance he was. He had flown before. Lots of times. Frequent flyer sounded right. "Yes," he said.

"Well, that's going to help. Let me just ask you a few questions and I'm sure we'll be able to speed you on your way. Could you give me your home address and zip code, please."

"My address?" He threw a sidelong look at Tina.

"It's something like . . . Mayfair," she prompted.

"Madam, I'd prefer that the gentleman answer the question himself."

LEONARD FOGLIA AND DAVID RICHARDS

"Sure. I live at . . . um . . . I wrote it down. I have it right here on a slip of paper in my bag. It'll only take me a second to get it."

The supervisor's face registered mild surprise. "You don't know your own address, sir."

"Not right off the top of my head, no . . . I . . . just moved there."

"I see. Perhaps we still have your old address in the computer, Mr. Stevens. Can you give me that?"

"No . . . I can't."

"A phone number, then?"

"Um . . ."

"No phone number, either." The skepticism on his face was growing. "Under the circumstances, I don't see how we're going to be able to let you on this plane."

Tina was unable to keep silent. "Am I hearing correctly? This man has a ticket that he has bought and paid for, and you're telling us that he can't board your plane."

"Madam, he has a ticket that *someone* paid for. If he can prove to me he is that person, we'll be more than happy to serve him. All our passengers must have a photo ID to pass through security. We do this for their protection. Certainly, you can appreciate that. Sir, don't you have anything you can show us? Even a letter addressed to you would help?"

"No," Brent replied weakly.

"I'm sorry, then. There's nothing I can do." He handed the ticket back to Brent. "If you require some kind of assistance, I'd be glad to call the airport police for you. Or you'll find a traveler's aid desk in the next terminal. Now if you both wouldn't mind stepping aside, there are people who have flights to catch."

A few travelers, who had overheard the confrontation, watched Brent and Tina suspiciously as they walked away from the counter. "What an asshole!" Tina muttered. "Next thing you know they'll demand a vaccination certificate." Traveling had sure changed dramatically from the days when you just walked on a plane and took a seat.

Brent came to a halt in the middle of the terminal and let his suitcase drop to the floor. "What am I supposed to do now?" His voice was loud with frustration, and several of the people in line turned around to convey their disapproval one more time.

"Well, you said you didn't want to go yet," Tina said, breezily. "Now, you don't have to. These things happen for a reason. So you'll come back to the house, have a nice dinner, and we'll figure out what's next. No big deal. We'll get some identification somehow."

"Wait!" He fished around in his pockets.

"What?"

"This!" Brent showed her the key with the orange plastic tip. "Let's see if we can find where the lockers are. If there's any identification with my stuff, I may still have time to catch the plane."

"A name tag would probably be enough for that supervisor."

A skinny black man in a green jumpsuit two sizes too big for him passed in front of them, his shoulder pressed up against a cart of cleaning supplies. "Excuse me," Brent said. "Where are the lockers in this terminal?"

The man straightened up. "What you need a locker for?"

"I don't need one. I was just wondering where they are."

"I can tell you where they used to be."

"What do you mean, 'used to be'?"

"They took 'em out. Lordy, been no lockers in this airport for five or ten years now."

"There haven't? Why not?"

The black man chuckled to himself. Sometimes white people asked the dumbest questions.

"Ain't you never heard of terrorism, mister?"

The return drive to Tina's house would have passed without conversation had it not been for her attempts to remain upbeat. On days like this, she felt her real occupation was cheerleader, not aerobics instructor. "You want to know somebody who's going to be deliriously happy?" she said, taking a hand off the steering wheel and patting Brent on the shoulder.

"Who?"

"Angelina. This morning, she told me that she found you 'very intriguing.' Yup! Her very words."

The remark failed to elicit a response, and even Tina had to admit that she was forcing things. There wasn't a whole lot to be upbeat about. Right now Brent was suppose to be over New Jersey in a plane headed west. Not in a Jeep, going south in Queens. They weren't quite back where they'd started—but almost. What, she wondered, would she do with him? She couldn't just drop him off on a street corner. Ida wouldn't approve. Johnny would go through the roof, though, when they pulled up in front of the house.

As if reflecting their mood, the surroundings seemed drabber than before. Litter lined the sides of the road, and on buildings of no character, graffiti provided the rare

spot of color. Every now and then, a tidy house and garden testified to its owner's will to resist the encroaching
ugliness. But it was the exception in a landscape that
breathed resignation and neglect.

On the right, a billboard loomed above dreary row
houses. *In the Beginning,* it trumpeted in flowing silver
script. Several times the size of life, a naked Jennifer
Osborne and a naked Christopher Knight hid from the
wrath of an unseen God, but there was no mistaking the
lustful expression in their eyes. Only a few well-
positioned palm fronds and a couple of the ornate letters
prevented the sign from being indecent. Along the bottom, read the teaser: THE FIRST MAN, THE FIRST WOMAN,
THE FIRST SIN.

"You see that!" Tina whistled. "How many pileups do
you think that's caused already?"

As the Jeep got closer, Jennifer Osborne and
Christopher Knight grew bigger still—her streaming hair
like a golden waterfall, his limbs massive as tree trunks.
Mesmerized, Brent studied the images.

Tina swerved to avoid a truck that had drifted across
the white line, as if inexorably drawn to Jennifer Osborne's
gargantuan curves.

"Hey, cool it, buster," she shouted out the window and
tooted the horn. "What did I tell you? That billboard is an
accident waiting to happen. And I thought those Calvin
Klein ads were a menace!"

Brent broke his silence. "I know those people."

"Who?"

"On the billboard."

"I wouldn't exactly call that a breakthrough, doll.
They're only the biggest stars on the planet, that's all. The

ads for that movie are everywhere. Even Angelina has started to ask me about it. Try explaining original sin to a six-year-old."

Eager to get off the highway, she pressed down on the accelerator, and the Jeep leapt forward. Brent turned in his seat and watched the billboard shrink on the horizon.

"No, I know those people," he said firmly after it had disappeared from view. "I really do."

18

The camera started out on her toes and then traced a path up Jennifer Osborne's naked form, moving slowly over her feet, her ankles, her calves.

Deborah Myers watched the monitor in fascination and asked herself how many actresses had bodies that could withstand such scrutiny. She assumed that everyone had at least one flaw that, magnified for the wide screen, would give the viewers (and the makeup artists) pause, even if it was only a bunion or a nagging patch of eczema. From the evidence, though, Jennifer was the glorious exception.

This was the first time Deborah or her crew had seen an actual scene from *In the Beginning*. The studio had purposefully kept the film hush-hush, leaving the columnists and commentators to speculate How Far Will They Go? The tactic had doubled the prerelease publicity, and the two-minute clip, which would be aired in the final segment of her television special later this week, would provide America with its first hard answer to the question.

From Jennifer Osborne's calves, the camera advanced to her knees, round and dimple free. It occurred to Deborah that what they were watching was a fetishist's delight. She knew there were plenty of leg men in the world, but were there knee men, as well? No doubt! The clip seemed to be intent on exploiting a body part for every possible taste.

If Jennifer and Christopher were nervous about how the scene was playing, the dispassionate expression on their faces gave no indication. They had both settled back in the couch and seemed to regard the naked image on the monitor as that of a distant relative, whose conduct, while a bit scandalous, didn't really reflect on them. The crew, on the other hand, had once again relinquished any claims to worldliness and displayed a prurient curiosity more characteristic of adolescent boys.

Pete stood riveted to his spot behind Deborah's chair.

The camera was now on Jennifer's thighs, avoiding, but only just, her pubic hair, which registered as a passing shadow before caressing her stomach and the swirl of her navel. An "innie," Deborah noted despite herself. She kept waiting for a cutaway to interrupt the camera's epic journey—or a blurry special effect, at least—but no! Then, suddenly they appeared—the celebrated Osborne breasts in all their perfectly formed majesty. Not so much as a fig leaf covering them! No golden tresses, artfully arranged, either. The erect nipples, surrounded by their dark pink areolas, pointed toward the sky. The art department was going to have to do some fancy camouflage work to get this by the censors, but no one was thinking about that problem for the moment.

No one was thinking at all. Just staring.

The camera had reached Jennifer's face, which was tilted backward, her eyelids closed, as if she were in a deep slumber. A man's hand reached into the frame and stroked her cheek lovingly. Her eyelids flickered open.

Then the hand, cupping the back of her neck, gently pulled her up out of her sleep, until she was face-to-face with Christopher. The two stars gazed at each other admiringly as the camera pulled back to reveal that he, too, was naked.

They were kneeling opposite each other in a natural arbor, dotted with white and blue blossoms. His body hovered gracefully over hers—the arms strong but not overly muscled; the stomach flat and hairless; the buttocks compact. The shot was in sharp focus, but somehow the overall impression was gauzy and dreamlike. As the camera continued its retreat, the two figures became smaller and smaller until they disappeared in the lush greenery. Then, the clip ended and the monitor turned to gray.

The crew, suddenly jolted back to reality, shifted uneasily, as if they'd just been caught outside a neighbor's bedroom window, peering in. The two worshipful minutes of footage bordered on the voyeuristic. "Well," Deborah said, taking a deep breath and exhaling it audibly, "I'll buy a ticket." That helped defuse the awkward mood, and even Pete relaxed enough to laugh. "It will certainly be interesting to hear what Reverend Greenway has to say about that."

"How could he object?" Christopher replied disingenuously. "The creation of woman? As the Bible says, 'And God saw everything that He had made and, behold, it was very good.' "

"Well, I can't say I've ever seen either of you look better. And so much of you, too! So . . . epic!" Deborah said. "Shall we wrap this up?"

The crew took their places, and the red light on the television camera flicked on.

The hostess paused, wrinkled her brow ever so slightly, and asked, "Why? You two can make any film you choose. So why *this* film? Why the Bible?"

Jennifer jumped right in. "Christopher has always loved to read the Bible. Yes, I was even taken back a bit myself, when I met him. What's more, he likes to talk about it, which at times can be a real conversation stopper. But one night, Franco Festi, the director, came to dinner, and the two of them got into a fascinating discussion about Genesis."

"It's really an account of man's first encounter with God, you know," Christopher said. "And Franco and I thought that would be something worthwhile to explore on film—the beginning of what has grown into a very complex relationship over the centuries. We didn't just sit down and say, 'Oh, wouldn't it be fun to play Adam and Eve!' Our film is about Adam and Eve and *God* . . ."

Oh, please, not God, Deborah thought. Her viewers would put up with a lot—violence, incest, betrayal and anguish—but not discussions of God, unless He had just cured a twelve-year-old child with terminal asthma in a trailer park. She let Christopher Knight's ruminations run on a while longer, reassuring herself that the good stuff was on tape already.

"I can't talk for Jennifer," he was now saying, "but Adam was one of the hardest roles of my career. If I'd known how hard, I'm not sure I would have agreed to do it. Dropping all the trappings of civilization, getting back to that state of pure innocence, that requires enormous effort and . . ."

Deborah felt weary. Why did actors talk about acting, as if it required the same effort that real life demanded and exacted the same toll? Surely, it was easier to be a make-believe convict or a make-believe prostitute than the real thing. Not to hear actors talk, though. Roles "took so much" out of them. Who were they fooling? In the end, they were all engaged in a great big act of pretending. Nothing easier.

Even Deborah herself was pretending to be interested this very instant. She'd had to get up too early this morning, after a bad night's sleep, too. Her shoulder blades ached. Out of the corner of her eye, she saw Pete making a twirling gesture with his index finger—a sign to wind down the interview. None too soon.

"So what's next for you two?" she asked, in a last burst of official curiosity.

"A rest for me," Jennifer said, stroking her stomach.

"I guess so," Christopher agreed. "The next thing for us both is going to be . . . a child. I'm still reeling from Jennifer's announcement."

"So it looks as if Hollywood's first couple is about to become Hollywood's first family."

"I guess it does." He gave out with a schoolboy laugh.

"Well, I wish you both well. Thank you for letting us into your home and your hearts today. Thank you for your frankness, and nothing but success with *In the Beginning*."

She turned to the camera and the legion of viewers who would be watching in several days. "And thank you, for being with us tonight. Remember, we keep up so you don't fall behind. God bless, and we'll see you next time."

Deborah held her weary smile until Pete indicated it was okay not to.

* * *

A half an hour later, the crew had packed their equipment into two vans and driven away. A limousine waited for Deborah, who lingered at the front door of the house with Jennifer, while Christopher changed his clothes upstairs.

"The interview went fabulously," Deborah said. "I don't need to tell you the look on Christopher's face, when you told him about the baby, was priceless. Has he recovered yet?"

"I hope you didn't mind."

"Mind? It's only one of the great moments of television."

"I had this idea that I wanted the moment preserved. Especially Christopher's reaction. He was surprised, wasn't he? The dear. I hope he forgives me. The only alternative was to have someone with a video camera lurking in a closet. I thought this was the preferable solution. Not to mention that the lighting would be more flattering! Of course, the tabloids will be furious that they weren't informed first!"

"Believe me, whenever you want to do anything like that again, you're welcome to come on my show."

Christopher had on blue jeans and a short-sleeved shirt when he joined them on the front stoop. Even dressed down, he seemed dressed up, Deborah reflected. She kissed each of them twice on the cheek, European style, and then, once she was inside the waiting limousine, rolled down the window and waved.

Christopher Knight and Jennifer Osborne stood in the doorway holding hands and waved back. Like some exalted version of the couple next door, they seemed to be an advertisement for the goodness of the American life.

Well, they'd all come out ahead today, Deborah thought as the limousine inched down the narrow lane between the extravagant "beach houses," wedged unceremoniously up against one another like the shacks in a Mexican fishing village. Pete was convinced the show would be a ratings bonanza. Her own reputation for getting scoops was intact, even if the "special moment" had been handed to her this time on a silver platter.

Jennifer and Christopher got what they wanted, too: a big, fat hour of prime time on network television that would coincide conveniently with the opening of their new film. After all, $100 million was on the line, and no car chases, either. For all their highbrow talk about the Bible and the creation of woman, they were banking on the enduring appeal of raw flesh. The two-minute clip had been shrewdly chosen. No fools, those two.

And the public? What did the public get from all this? Deborah sighed as the limousine joined the ribbon of traffic, heading south to Los Angeles on Route 1. Normally, the answer came to her automatically. Her viewers got an intimate look into the hearts and minds of their most cherished idols. They got more fuel for their fantasies. They got to feel "included."

But today, perhaps because she was tired, she wasn't so sure. Maybe she just encouraged envy and discontent. Maybe she was a meddlesome snoop, fighting to stay ahead of the competition. The inner lives and passing tribulations of the pretty people? Really, what did it matter?

She struck the thought from her mind.

19

"Tah dah!" Tina announced triumphantly. "This is your life, Mr. Brent Stevens, from Los Angeles, California."

With a sweeping gesture, she indicated the items spread out on the coffee table in the living room. Coming from anyone else, the remark would have sounded like a snide joke.

All they had to go on was there on the table, and it wasn't much: an amber prescription bottle with Brent's name and address on the label; a plane ticket to L.A. (useless for the time being); an orange-tipped locker key (equally useless, it seemed); a ticket stub to a performance Brent couldn't remember seeing; the bill from the Mayflower Hotel; a brief letter from somebody called Lisa; and finally two notes, scribbled on hotel stationery.

Brent had written the note with the phone number on it and Tina had found it in the pocket of his jacket at the hospital. On the other piece of paper were the notations she herself had made when they had played back Brent's phone messages at the hotel.

"Somewhere on this table is the clue that is going to unlock the mystery to your life. I just know it!" she said, her enthusiasm undampened by the paltry evidence. "The hotel bill itemizes all of your charges. Well, it seems the day before yesterday you made four telephone calls. The numbers are listed here. Two local numbers and two long-distance numbers with a 518 area code. See? And here's what's interesting. You wrote down one of the local numbers on the piece of paper that was in your jacket. So you must have phoned it after you left the hotel, the night you were attacked. Or else you intended to."

Brent examined the hotel bill, but the telephone numbers said nothing to him. "What's it mean?"

"One of those numbers could belong to someone you know. Better still, someone who knows you."

"So what do I do now?"

"Well, I guess you start calling. What else?" She handed him the white Princess phone on the end table.

"And say what?"

"I dunno. See if the voice is familiar. Sound the person out."

Brent hesitated.

"Tell them your name and see what reaction you get," Tina insisted. "What can you lose?"

The first number rang four times before Brent got a recorded message that informed him he had reached the automated information system of the MTA Metro North Railroad and then laid out the various options for obtaining train schedules and fares.

"Metro North Railroad," he said, hanging up, puzzled.

"Oh, yeah? That's Grand Central Station. You must have been planning to go someplace. That's probably what those long-distance numbers are about. Dial one and see."

The woman who answered was all efficiency. "Good afternoon. Dover Plains Savings and Loan. How may I help you? . . . Hello? . . . Hello? . . . Is anyone there?"

"Just a second please." Brent covered the receiver with his hand. "It's a bank. Dover Plains. What should I ask now?"

"A bank? Huh! Ask them where they're located."

"Excuse me, ma'am, could you tell me where the bank is located?"

"We're at 251 Main Street, next door to the pharmacy."

"No, in what city?"

"I beg your pardon?"

"What city are you located in?"

There was a pause before the woman replied, "The Dover Plains Savings and Loan is in Dover Plains . . . as the name indicates."

"Of course . . . Well, I telephoned the bank two days ago and I was wondering if, uh, anyone there remembers talking to me? Brent Stevens?"

"I'm sorry?"

"That's my name, Brent Stevens. I'm calling from New York City on the chance that someone there remembers having a conversation with me the other day. Would you mind asking—"

His voice trailed off. "She hung up."

"Ida wouldn't go near a phone for that very reason. 'If people are going to be rude to me,' she'd say, 'they'll have to be rude to my face.' She believed that if you couldn't see a person's lips when they were talking, you couldn't trust them . . . Hey, don't get discouraged yet. You just started. Give the other long-distance number a ring."

It was a man who came on the line, this time. "Law offices of Lobel and Lobel."

"Mr. Lobel?"

"Which one? Father or son?"

"Er . . . son?"

"Speaking."

"This is Brent Stevens calling."

"What can I do for you, Mr. Stevens?"

"Do you know me, Mr. Lobel?"

"Should I?"

"I phoned the other day."

"I'm afraid I don't recall offhand. Perhaps you can remind me what the call was about."

"That's just it. I'm not sure. I was hoping you'd be able to provide me with some details."

"Is this some kind of a joke, Mr. . . . what did you say your name was?"

"Stevens."

"I never talked to anyone of that name."

"Could it have been your father then?"

"That's unlikely. He's been away on vacation for the past few weeks. Sorry. Now if you'll excuse me, Mr. Stevens, I have business to—"

"Before you hang up, Mr. Lobel, could you tell me one thing. Is this Dover Plains by any chance?"

"It's not Paris, France. Good day, Mr. Stevens."

The lawyer's sarcasm gave way to dead air. Another hang-up! Brent put down the phone. He'd managed to reach a train station, a bank somewhere, and now an irritated lawyer. None of it added up. They were getting nowhere.

"That was Dover Plains, too. A lawyer," he mumbled to Tina.

Without explanation, she left the room. When she returned, she was studying a road map. "Well, I'd say this is definitely a piece of the puzzle. Dover Plains is about an hour and a half north of here. I thought I'd heard of it. And you called for information about trains. So you must have been intending to go there."

"Why?"

"That's a piece we're still missing. But a lawyer and a bank? Sounds like business to me. Funny, you don't look like a businessman."

The front door burst open and there was a clatter of feet in the hall, then a small voice sang out, "Mom, I'm home."

"Oh, shoot! Is it that late already?" Tina checked her wristwatch. "In here, honey."

Swinging her backpack, Angelina skipped into the living room. Her face brightened as soon as she saw Brent.

"Mr. Stevens! Are you going to stay with us?"

"For a while," Tina answered.

"Hooray! Would you like to see the drawings I did in school today?" She dug into the schoolbag and proudly produced a notebook. "This is my best friend, Megan, and this one is my teacher, except that I made her hair wrong. If you want, I'll draw you, but you have to sit very, very still."

"I'd like that," Brent said. "Will you sign the picture for me?"

"Okay, okay, you two. Do you think you could hang up your jacket first, Angelina? Then come give me a hug? Then you can draw Mr. Stevens." For Brent's benefit, she added, "I've got to get my things together for work."

"Work?"

"Mrs. Shriver. My client in the Dakota. She was so upset when I canceled this morning that I rescheduled her for this afternoon. Don't worry. You can hang out in the house. Johnny should be upstairs, taking a nap. The night shift has thrown him all off. But I'll be back before he goes to work. I'm sorry. I thought you'd be on a plane by now."

Angelina plunged her hand into her backpack again and withdrew a box of Crayolas. "Ready!" she announced. "My teacher says you have to look real close at what you're drawing." She rumpled her nose and squinted. "Don't move now."

"Maybe I should find myself another hotel room."

"Don't be silly. We'll sort all this out tonight."

"Mr. Stevens, you're moving! Mom, don't talk to him."

"Excuse me, Picasso. I'll get changed and check on Johnny."

The living room fell silent—Angelina absorbed in her drawing, Brent, sitting motionless and wrestling with his thoughts. He had no business being here. He barely knew these people, and he'd disrupted their routines. Not that Tina had said anything. Even the little girl, who was drawing him now, had accepted him, as if he were a family friend or a long lost relative.

He wasn't, though. He was an outsider.

He wondered what would have happened if Tina hadn't helped him out. Would he still be in the hospital? Or dead on a street somewhere? Or just running, running aimlessly. And from what?

He had to get control of things. Tina couldn't continue to do everything for him. She'd done enough already. For no reason he could tell, except that he needed help badly and she was a helper. But they all had lives to get on with. He didn't belong here.

The doctor had used such a fancy term to describe his condition, "temporary global amnesia," whatever that meant. It was like moving through a thick ocean fog. Now and again, an island would come into view, an island of memory. And for a moment everything on the island—the vegetation, the homes, the people going about their business—would stand out bright and clear. Then the fog would roll in again, obliterating the details at first, then the island itself, and he found himself back in the enveloping whiteness.

"Mr. Stevens, you moved," Angelina scolded. "But that's all right, because I finished." Spotting her mother coming down the stairs, the child said, "Look, what I made."

The person in the drawing was little more than a stick figure that listed badly to one side, with arms and legs like twigs and a head like an oversize pumpkin on a pole. The eyes were round and staring . . . more lopsided, Tina noted, than round. But something about the portrait was absolutely right. The sadness. How had Angelina captured that? Maybe it was just the inadvertent effect of a child's unsteady hand or the colors she'd chosen, blue and black. But the sadness was there.

"Why, it's beautiful, isn't it, Brent? Why don't you tape it up on the refrigerator, honey?"

She waited until the child was gone, then said, "Our very own Leonardo H. daVinci, eh?"

"Did you tell Johnny I was back?"

"No, he's out for the count. These nighttime hours are killing him. I set the alarm clock to make sure he wakes up in time."

"I can't impose on you anymore."

"You're not imposing. I'll let you know when you are."

"No. While you were upstairs, I got to thinking that maybe I ought to check out this Dover Plains. See what's there. The name seems familiar somehow."

"Good idea. I could rearrange some of my clients tomorrow."

"No, Tina. You've put yourself out enough. I'll go myself. I can manage. I've got to begin sooner or later."

"Well, I'm sure you can. It's just that New York's a scary place. You gotta keep your guard up."

"You didn't."

She cocked her head. "What do you mean?"

"Keep your guard up. With me, you didn't." As he looked for a reaction, he was struck by how delicate her features were. She was soft, physically. It was the defensive attitude that made her seem hard. As soon as she dropped it, she seemed another person.

Tina felt his gaze and reddened. "Okay, I made an exception. Big deal! Are you fishing for compliments or what?"

"No, just trying to figure out Tina Ruffo."

"Me, now! I thought we were trying to figure you out."

The arrival of a pint-size ballerina in purple leggings and a pink tutu broke the mood. Angelina, who had abandoned art for the dance, twirled vigorously across the room, careened off the leather armchair and then, still twirling unsteadily, positioned herself dramatically in front of the coffee table.

"My, what do we have here?" said Tina.

"This," the child proclaimed, "is my spinning dance."

"Oh, yeah? Where did you learn that?"

"I made it up."

Suddenly, the movements changed. With each twirl, the child also gave a sharp kick with one of her legs—which made her appear rather like a wobbly top throwing a temper tantrum. "This is the leg dance," she announced breathlessly.

"Did you make that one up, too?" Brent asked.

"Yup." She was working very hard to keep up to a beat that only she could hear.

"Do you know any other dances?"

"Oh, I have hundreds of dances in my head," she answered, as if everybody did, then spun out of the room, a blur of pink and purple.

"Wow! What energy!" Brent said. "She takes after her mother."

"Are you kidding? She exhausts me. You'd think aerobics would be the perfect training for having a kid, wouldn't you? Wrong! Boot camp, maybe."

"How does her father handle her?"

Tina didn't answer right off. "You mean, the scum-sucker? Not very well. If you want to know the truth, he hasn't been around for more than two years now."

"So he's never seen the leg dance, then," Brent said with disbelief.

"Afraid not. No reflection on Angelina. It was me he couldn't stand."

"I don't get that, either."

"What can I tell you? The guy was a scum-sucking S.O.B. who only thought about himself and made the world miserable for everybody else."

"Oh . . ."

"Johnny says I attract the scum-suckers. I am a regular

magnet for scum-suckers. Don't ask me why. Every two-bit low-rent loser manages to find me one way or another."

"Does that include me?" Brent asked.

"My God, you're taking me seriously, aren't you?" She reached out and grasped his hand. "No, doll, that does not include you. You're one of the good guys. I've been around the other kind enough to know the difference. I was just mouthing off. I do that sometimes. You may have noticed."

Yet she did believe it, did think the world could be split down the middle into the users and the used, the takers and the taken. The odd thing was, though she could spot the scum-suckers a mile away, see right through their manipulative ploys, she ended up falling for them anyway. That rashness had caused her a lot of heartache, and a few times she'd also paid dearly with her purse. Angelina's father had been the worst. He had left her with a deep reservoir of anger that still hadn't abated, even though it was nearly three years now since he had decamped.

From the moment she'd seen Brent on the sidewalk before the Dakota, she told herself he was different, although if she'd been asked to cite hard evidence for her feelings, she wouldn't have come up with much. He seemed childlike to her—all his emotions were right there on the surface for anyone to read. Just now, his joy at watching a six-year-old dance awkwardly around the living room had been so full and unapologetic. In her experience, most men came wrapped in layers of swagger and bluff. Brent didn't. Nothing was hidden with him. He was almost naked in that respect.

She found him attractive, too. She'd thought so from

the start, although that had merely been a fleeting impression, supplanted in her mind by a sense of emergency. Now that the danger had ebbed, the thought returned, more insistent this time, not so easily dismissed. She liked the contrast of his strong features and his hesitant manner. He was definitely a man, but part boy, lost boy, too, and the two were hard to separate, like two negatives superimposed one upon the other.

She became aware that she was no longer holding his hand. They were holding each other's hands and had been for some time now. Neither of them felt any need to speak.

The intimacy was pleasurable, but once Tina became conscious of it—his fingers exerting the pressure on hers now, her hand more passive—she grew uncomfortable. She knew what Johnny would say, if he caught them, and she pulled her hand away.

"This is what I think we should do," she said, trusting she wasn't changing the subject too brusquely. "There's no point in your just sitting around the house all afternoon, moping. You can come into Manhattan with me. Maybe something will jog your memory. Angelina can come with us. I've been promising to take her to the zoo forever. I'll work out Mrs. Shriver and we'll go to the zoo afterward. It's a beautiful spring afternoon. Maybe it will help clear your head."

"The zoo?"

"Yeah. There's a little zoo right there in Central Park. It'll be a lot more fun if there's three of us. You'll be doing me a favor. What do you say?"

"If you put it that way . . ." And he realized she'd done it again, pulled him away from the edge and put him back into their lives. She wouldn't let him feel lost. Had she read his mind earlier?

"Before we leave, there's one more phone number for you to call. It will only take a sec."

It was the number he'd written on the hotel stationery. "Nothing ventured, right?" she said as she passed him the phone. He dialed the number and listened to it ringing. He was prepared to hang up when a recording machine clicked on:

"I'm either on the other line or not in right now. But your call is important to me. Let me know who you are and the time you called. I'll get in touch as soon as possible."

"Er . . . hello . . . I'm Brent Stevens and it's about one-thirty." He couldn't think what else to say. Then he noticed the number on Tina's phone. "You can reach me at 718-759-7311 . . . Good-bye."

He tried not to show his disappointment. "It was a machine."

"Man or woman?"

"A man. It sounded like he had a British accent."

Johnny found the last Coke in the refrigerator and plopped down in front of the television set. Naps really knocked him out and the jolt of caffeine was a necessary part of his wake-up routine, followed by one of the television talk shows, which represented for him a halfway point between slumber and consciousness. He had trouble dealing with real people right after he got up. The idiots on the tube were challenge enough, and he could yell at them without fearing any consequences.

The day's topic on the *Jenny Jones Show* was "Teenage Lesbians Who Want to Get Married," and Vicki from

Maine was telling Jenny that her really close friends called her Vic.

"Okay, Vic," Jenny obliged. "That's okay, that's cool."

Vicki was wearing overalls, a flannel shirt, just like one Johnny had upstairs in his closet, and what looked to him like high-heeled work boots. Where did these people come from? Oh, yeah, he remembered, Maine.

The camera moved in on Jenny. "Now, let's welcome Vic's fiancée, Trixie, who says she wants it all—a church wedding, bridesmaids, and a honeymoon in Bermuda." The studio audience erupted in wild applause, so Johnny didn't hear the phone ringing right away. Trixie was waif-like, and her leather miniskirt rode high up on her thighs when she sat down next to Vic.

Without taking his eyes off the set, Johnny reached for the phone. "Yeah?"

"Brent Stevens, please."

"Who?"

"Brent Stevens."

"You got the wrong number."

"Is this 718-759-7311?"

"That's the number, but there ain't nobody here by that name . . . Wait a minute. You mean that blond guy? He's gone."

"What do you mean he's gone?"

"Don't you understand English? He ain't here."

"He left a message that this was where I could reach him. When do you expect him back?"

"He's not coming back. Tina took him to the airport."

On the television, Trixie was showing the camera her pierced tongue, and Johnny found himself distracted. He was about to hang up when the caller spoke up.

"Where was he going?"

"Sorry. Can't help ya."

"This is extremely important. Is there someone who can?"

"Like who? Tina's not home."

The voice turned cold and clipped. "Who is this? Whom am I speaking to?"

"Hey, wait a minute, buddy. You're the one who called this number. Why don't you tell me who you are instead?"

"Enough of these games! You just let Brent Stevens know that the longer this goes on, the worse it will get for him."

"Did you hear me? Who are you?"

"Tell him that he'll have no one to blame but himself. He'll know who this is. He'll know what I'm talking about."

"Oh, yeah? Well, let me tell you something, asshole. If you ever phone this number again, I'll shove this phone so far up your butt that each time you fart, it'll be a toll call."

Johnny slammed down the receiver and turned back to the *Jenny Jones Show*, where a marriage ceremony was about to take place.

He watched in disbelief as Vic and Trixie joined hands before a makeshift altar, decorated with roses. Vic sported a white carnation in her overalls and Trixie had on a veil. (At least it hid her tongue.) "Dearly beloved," intoned the round-faced pastor, whom a close-up revealed to be a woman with short-cropped hair.

"The world has gone fuckin' nuts," Johnny muttered, as he pressed the remote control and changed the channel.

20

As Tina and Brent emerged from the dingy light of the subway station at West Seventy-second Street, a perfect spring afternoon was well under way. Angelina bobbed happily between them. (So did Angelina's Madeline doll.) The police had blocked off the entrance to Central Park, barring the roadway to automobiles, and a lively collection of dog walkers, roller-bladers, and joggers had taken possession of the pavement.

On the subway ride into Manhattan, Angelina's excitement had mounted steadily, and the sight of so many people did nothing to calm it. The three paused on the corner to get their bearings. Behind them, the Dakota rose like a fortress.

"Recognize where you are?" Tina asked Brent. His attention was drawn to the iron railing around the building with its stern figures and sea monsters, but he couldn't say why. He looked at it for a while. It was unusual. Maybe that's all he was responding to.

"No," he said.

Tina led them down West Seventy-second Street in the direction of a bronze sentry box. A uniformed man stepped out and called to her in a loud voice.

"Tina, where were you this morning? You're the only reason I keep this lousy job, you know. The day you quit coming here is the day I put in for retirement."

"Come off it, Joey. You could hang the wash on a line like that. I been busy taking care of Brent here."

The doorman took a closer look at the man beside her, unable to differentiate him from the hordes who showed up outside the Dakota every day, cameras in hand, expecting to be able to march right in and take photographs.

"You remember Brent, don't you? You called 911 for him yesterday."

The doorman's face lit up. "Holy mackerel! You telling me this is the same guy? You look about a hundred percent better, mister. I swear, you got magical powers, Tina."

"When did you doubt it? And this is my daughter, Angelina."

The doorman whistled appreciatively. "Pleased to meet ya. You're even prettier than your mother, if that's possible." In a rare display of modesty, Angelina shrunk behind Tina's leg.

"Okay, guys, I got to get cracking. Mrs. Shriver calls. I'll meet you in one hour in Strawberry Fields, just inside the park. Don't wander off. There are benches. Wait for me there. Okay?" She pointed down Seventy-second Street in the direction they had just come, gave Angelina a pat on the bottom, and hurried inside the Victorian lobby.

"So what happened to you?"

It took Brent a second to realize that Joey was addressing him.

"Oh, my wallet was stolen. I got mugged by somebody."

"Well, they did a real number on you. When you went down, I didn't know if you were dead or alive."

"I blacked out. I forgot a lot."

"I know what you're saying. Blacked out a couple of times myself back in the days when I was drinking. Fact is, I thought that was your problem, the way you came weaving down the sidewalk, clothes all rumpled, eyes looking like two pools of tomato juice. There's somebody who's had one too many, I said to myself, recognizing the old symptoms. When you got here, you were sure determined to go inside, though."

"I was?"

"Had your mind all made up. Pushed right by me like you knew just where you were headed. Didn't stop to ask for anybody. I figured you must have been here before. Then your knees buckled, and well, I guess Tina filled you in on all the rest. Anyway, it's good to see you're all right."

The chatter of approaching tourists put an end to the conversation. A group of Asian tourists had spilled out of a double-decker bus and were making a beeline for the entrance. "Before John Lennon was shot, they all wanted to see where *Rosemary's Baby* was filmed," Joey said, bracing for the onslaught. "It's always something with this damn place. All right folks, let's keep to the sidewalk. This is an apartment building, not a museum. I'll have to ask you to keep the entrance clear."

Dodging the tourists, Brent took Angelina by the hand and walked back toward the park. By a low stone pillar at the entrance, an ice cream cart had opened for business, and not far beyond, an Indian merchant was arranging a display of cheap sweatshirts and T-shirts on a pushcart shaded by a striped awning.

The tear-shaped oasis that was Strawberry Fields attracted a steady stream of sight-seers for whom it was an obligatory stop on their John Lennon pilgrimage. But nearby residents also used it as an outdoor reading room, mindful that the grounds were better maintained than the surrounding parkland. Brent and Angelina found themselves a place on one of the benches. Angelina propped up her Madeline doll beside her and was soon engaged in an animated discussion with it. Under no necessity to entertain the child, Brent mulled over the encounter with Joey.

Something the doorman had said intrigued him.

A flash of light went off nearby and he jumped, but it was only a young woman in a granny dress with a camera. The tourists were out in force today, snapping indiscriminately. The woman in the granny dress had just taken a picture of a bunch of flowers that someone had left on the ground. Two months from now, Brent thought, she'd look at the photograph and have no idea why—or where—she'd taken it.

Several minutes later, a man came up and pointed a Leica at the same wilted bouquet. His curiosity piqued, Brent stood up and took a few steps forward to get a better view.

The flowers lay about twenty feet in front of him and Angelina on a circular mosaic, made out of small black and white tiles. People were approaching it with a kind of reverence, and he overheard a woman explain that it was "a memorial to the Beatle that got shot." In the center of the kaleidoscopic design, an inscription urged passers-by to "Imagine."

A shock ran through him, and he fell back on the bench. He had been in this very spot, facedown on those tiles. But it had been cold out, not warm like today, and the sky was dark. It had been night.

He tried to force his mind back two days. He had been grabbed from behind and immobilized in a choke hold. Someone must have been tailing him. He never saw the face of his assailant, but he had felt the man's lips up against his ear and heard a sharp, hissing voice, saying his name and telling him to "wise up."

Somehow the man had known his name.

He had managed to wrestle free of the man's grip and had started to run . . . Then came the blow to the back of the head and . . . blankness. The blow had put an end to his memories.

No, not an end. Things were coming back, submerged fragments rising to the surface of his mind. He had to believe they were real. He told himself to hold on to them so he could put the whole picture together, the way the little squares making up the mosaic in front of him went together. He had to be vigilant with his thoughts and feelings and intuitions even. Couldn't let them slip away. Fix each thought, he urged himself. Cement it into place.

Beads of sweat pearled on Brent's upper lip.

"What's the matter? What are you looking at?" Angelina asked.

He could tell the child sensed something was wrong and tried to hide his unease. "Nothing. A squirrel over there."

"I can read what it says on the ground. It says 'Imagine.' "

"Oh, yeah? Do you know what that means?"

"Sort of. It's when you make things up in your head the way you want them to be."

"Right. Like pretending."

"Sometimes I imagine that I live in Paris with Madeline."

"Who's Madeline?"

"My doll, silly. Mom says I have a big imagination. What do you imagine, Mr. Stevens?"

"Me? Nothing."

"Nothing ever ever?"

"You don't imagine as much when you're grown up." Seeing her disappointment, he added, "Okay, sometimes I imagine what it would be like to have a nice young girl like you someday."

Angelina's pout conveyed her dissatisfaction with his response. "Not *some*day. What do you imagine this very minute?"

"Let me see. I can imagine eating a big chocolate ice cream cone. How about that?"

"She squeaked with delight. "Chocolate is one of my favorite flavors, too, but not pistachio."

"Let's go, then."

He reached over and took her hand and was struck by how tiny it was. He knew he must have held a child's hand before, but no memory of it came to mind. Today seemed to him like the very first time.

Angelina's fingers were delicate against the roughness of his palm, so soft that for a moment he felt larger than he was, almost lumbering. The sense of disproportion prompted a thought: Because he was so very big and she was so very small, he somehow had an obligation to protect her, although exactly from what, he couldn't specify. Harm took many forms.

Someone had to have protected him, when he was

Angelina's age. His father or a friend or a neighbor. Someone taller and stronger, at any rate. Angelina's head barely reached his chest, and her fingers seemed to him as fragile as spider legs.

"Ouch," Angelina protested. "You're holding my hand too hard."

"Oh, I'm sorry, honey." Brent bent over the child nervously. "Did I hurt you? Here, let me make it better."

"No, I'm fine now," she said, turning all her attention to the Madeline doll. "You don't have to hold my hand anymore."

"I didn't mean to squeeze you so hard. I'm a clumsy old bear. I just didn't want anything to happen to you, that's all."

Even though her face was turned away, he sensed the child was taking in his apology, weighing it. Suddenly, she looked up at him, her eyes bright with inspiration. "I've got an idea."

"What?"

"I'll hold *your* hand. Okay?"

"If you want to."

She grasped his fingers gently. "There," she said. "Now nothing will happen to *you*."

They retraced their path under the canopy of trees out to the street and the ice cream stand they'd passed earlier. Angelina studied the glossy pictures on the front of the vendor's cart and opted for a pink and white concoction identified as Raspberries 'n' Cream. Brent paid the vendor, then picked up the child and sat her on top of the stone pillar, out of the stream of pedestrian traffic. She kicked her legs contentedly and proceeded to chip away at the frozen dessert with a plastic spoon.

"I'm imagining that I'm a princess, sitting on my throne," she announced. "What are you imagining?"

"I dunno . . ." The child's pout prompted him to revise his answer. "Okay, how about I'm a prince from a faraway land?"

"Where?"

"Egypt?"

"I know what. You're lost, so you come to my castle and ask me to help you find your way back home. And on the way we meet some dragons."

"Who breathe fire out of their noses?"

"No, friendly dragons, who give us a ride on their backs. And we go across a big ocean and over a high mountain and down a winding road."

"Whew, what a long, long trip." Brent huffed and puffed, acting the journey for her benefit. "I'm getting tired."

Angelina giggled.

"But look," he said, pointing across the street to the Dakota. "We found it. There's my palace. We've arrived. We're home."

"Hooray!"

"Yes, of course, I'm sure it's him. He's with a little girl. He's pointing right at me."

The silver-haired man stood back from the window as he talked into the phone. He wasn't even attempting to control the shrillness in his voice. All morning his nerves had been on edge. This had put him over the top.

"I thought he'd gone. When I called the number he left on my machine, that's what I was told. 'He's no longer here. He's gone to the airport.'"

"Obviously, he hasn't," replied Spiff. "Whoever answered that phone was lying to you. Or else they haven't got their stories straight."

The silver-haired man took a drag on his cigarette and felt the heat of the burning tobacco on his fingers. Not only was he smoking more, he was smoking the rotten weeds right down to the filter now. Angrily, he ground out the stub in an ashtray before continuing.

"I spotted him in front of the building about half an hour ago, talking with one of the doormen. I told myself it couldn't be him. Then I happened to look out the window later, and there he was—right across the street. For some reason, he's hanging around this place." A quick glance out the window verified that the situation hadn't changed. "I don't know what the hell is going on here."

"So what do you want me to do?"

"Get over here fast. He's not going to stay there forever. Oh, and one other thing, Spiff. This is your second chance. Do I need to point that out? Don't blow it. It's the last one you get."

"You haven't been listening to me." Angelina tugged at Brent's sleeve. Lost in thought, Brent was staring at the window on the third floor, his eye attracted by the rustling of the red curtains.

"Are you imagining now?" asked the child.

"Yeah, I guess so. I was trying to imagine who lives inside that great big building."

"Mrs. Shriver lives there."

Brent thought he saw the curtains move again. A figure, partially hidden in the deep set of the window frame, seemed to be watching them. It was someone with white hair, but the brightness of the sun and the darkness of the window made it hard to see the person's features.

"Are we going to go to the zoo?"

"What? Yeah, in a little while."

"How long?"

"Not long now. The time it takes your mother to get here. You've got to finish your ice cream first."

The child plunged her spoon into the cup with renewed enthusiasm. When Brent turned back to the third-story window, no one was there. The curtains were still. He must have mistaken a reflection in the pane for a person.

Then Joey's words came back to him. "You were sure determined to go inside . . . I figured you must have been here before." Maybe he did know someone in the building. Someone appeared to know him. The white-haired person up there in the shadows.

"There's Mom," shouted Angelina.

On the far side of the street, Tina waved at them while she waited for the stoplight to change. "You two been having fun?" she called out as she approached. "How come you got ice cream on your mouth, Angelina? What's up with you two?"

"Over there," Brent said. "I think someone's been watching me."

"What are you talking about?"

"Observing me from one of those windows."

"Really? Did this person wave or acknowledge you in any way?"

"No, but I had this funny feeling."

"Show me the window, Brent."

"Third floor, on the corner. The one with the red curtains."

Tina hooded her eyes with her hand and looked where he was pointing. The window was empty. So, for that matter, was the one beside it and the one below. The whole building seemed to give off an air of stately indifference, like a wealthy dowager ignoring the riffraff swirling at her skirts.

"I don't see anyone."

"They're not there now."

"Well, whoever it was, must have gotten bored and found something better to do."

"You don't believe me?"

"Of course I do. But this is New York, Brent. People stare at people. It's a pastime. Why, half the people who live on this park have telescopes in their apartments just so they can spy on the people who live on the other side. If you want, I'll ask Joey if he knows anything."

A series of gentle tugs on Tina's dance bag diverted her attention and a youthful voice piped up. "Mom! Mr. Stevens! Can we *please* go to the zoo now?"

Brent glanced up at the empty window one more time. "No. You're right. It was probably nothing."

"You must have imagined it," Angelina said brightly.

21

Spiff spotted them ambling along the pathway, like any young family on an outing. The white bandage on the back of Brent's head caught his eye first, then the woman at his side. The sprayed-on exercise gear she was wearing made her hard to overlook.

A few seconds later, he became aware of the kid, who kept skipping ahead of them. A regular bumblebee. That complicated things, but Spiff figured it also worked in his favor. The kid would keep them distracted.

"We're back in business," he said.

He didn't like talking to himself in public. Old folks and psychopaths talked to themselves, and he was neither yet. More to the point, someone could overhear him, and in his line of work that could be an inconvenience. Sometimes, he couldn't help it, though.

"Back in business," he repeated more softly, and slipped on his sunglasses.

Brent was behaving normally enough, not like before, and the woman seemed quite smitten by him. A girlfriend from appearances. Spiff had seen her somewhere before. He probably could have marched right up behind them without attracting their attention, but he wasn't so foolish as to try. Following a couple of hundred feet behind them like this was fine right now, just so long as he was prepared to deal with changing circumstances.

Because circumstances would change—that was for sure. Who could have predicted this turn of events? Brent had given him the slip twice yesterday—at the hospital and later at the hotel. Then, he'd vanished altogether. Not a trace of him anywhere and not a hope in hell, either, of finding him in this overpopulated burg.

And what happens? He turns up in front of the Dakota, milling about like nothing's wrong. The client sees him and can't believe his eyes. Well, it *was* a stroke of good fortune. Spiff chuckled. Either this Brent fellow was asking for it, or he was nuts.

There was a third alternative, of course. The guy was up to something that none of them had figured out yet. Spiff didn't like that scenario. It meant that Brent was shrewder than they suspected. It meant he was playing them for fools.

At least the client wasn't screaming for the moment. That was a blessing. It seemed as if he'd been spending as much time pacifying the client as doing the job. But things would come to a head soon, and then he would collect his fee and blow. But there he was, thinking of the future, and he knew he had to stay focused on the present.

The man and the woman and the kid were approaching an open promenade that bordered the grassy expanse called the Sheep Meadow. The crowds were thicker here. A couple of volleyball games were in full swing and clusters of roller-bladers were skating in circles, like schools of fish, around a boom box that was blaring a samba.

The kid stopped to watch a Labrador retriever chase

after a Frisbee, pluck it out of the air, and bring it back to its master. Now the man and woman were watching, too. That was fine by Spiff. There was no reason to rush. He had all the time in the world. After all, he wasn't going anyplace today they weren't going.

He stepped off the path, leaned up against a tree, and allowed himself to appreciate the splendid afternoon it was turning out to be.

This, he thought, was the fun part.

The mood in the park was one of happy coexistence. Stretched out on the grass, the indolent quietly soaked up the sun while nearby fitness freaks did push-ups or ran vigorously in place. Joggers threaded artfully among pedestrians, who regarded them with no more concern than they might an errant butterfly.

"I can't imagine New York without this place," Tina said. "Everybody jammed into apartments, driving one another crazy. They say Central Park is a big safety valve. I believe it."

She looked around to check on Angelina, who had struck up an acquaintance with an elderly painter with a paisley kerchief knotted around his neck. His easel was positioned near a clump of lilacs, and he was trying with more labor than inspiration to transfer their essence to his canvas. Angelina was offering advice.

"Don't bother the nice man," Tina called out. With a gesture, the man signaled that the child was no bother.

"I recognized the mosaic in Strawberry Fields," Brent said.

"What do you mean?"

"That was the place where I was attacked. While

161

Angelina and I were waiting for you, it came back to me."

"I was hoping that would be the case. The doctor said there would be all kinds of triggers."

"I don't remember much more. It was dark when I went into the park. I'm sure of that, though. I must have passed out for a long time, because the next thing I knew, the sun was coming up and I was lying flat on the ground. My head was killing me . . . It's so strange. Most people try to forget the bad things that happen to them. Here I am, trying to bring it all back."

She put her arm around his shoulders and gave him a consoling hug.

At the ticket booth for the Central Park Zoo, Tina paid for three admissions and pushed Angelina ahead of her through the turnstile. Although small, the facility packed a variety of exhibits into the limited space, and in several instances a real effort had been made to duplicate the animals' natural habitats. In a large tank, polar bears bobbed among huge plastic cubes, meant to simulate chunks of arctic ice, while snow monkeys roamed on an island studded with tree branches to encourage their proclivity for leaping and swinging.

Angelina darted to the edge of a large pool where sea lions, as if mindful of their status as crowd pleasers, shot out of the water, hung in the air for a second, then fell back with a splash, drenching anyone standing too close. The people shrieked and the sea lions honked. Soon Angelina was adding her cries to the mix.

The atmosphere was that of a state fair, with penguins and pandas in place of cows and pigs. A clown moved among the crowd, handing out free balloons with pictures of endangered species on them. Children on a school trip clustered in front of a portable stage, where a puppet troupe was performing an ecological morality play.

On an impulse, Brent ran over to the clown, took a balloon from him, and bowing formally, presented it to Tina. They sat down on a bench under a vine-covered trellis, newly in leaf, and watched the people, neither quite sure what to say next. Tina could sense the closeness of Brent's body.

"Jesus H. Christ. Here I am, a divorced mother with a six-year-old daughter, and I feel like I'm on my first date or something!"

"Is that so? Do your parents know about me?" he asked.

"Huh? Oh, not yet," she said, playing along. "I thought I'd see how it went first before telling them. I wouldn't want to get their hopes up."

"Or yours?"

"Or mine!"

"Smart of you." He took her hand. "And how is it?"

"How is what?"

"The date? How *is* it going?" He leaned in to her, smelling her fresh scent.

"Okay."

"Only okay?"

"I mean, pretty well, actually."

"Pretty well?"

"Brent! What do you want from me? It's going fine. *There!* Are you satisfied? What do you think?"

"I think it's going fine, too," he said. "Could I kiss you, Tina?"

"In front of the animals?"

He didn't let her say any more.

Ten minutes later, Angelina had tired of the sea lions' antics and was clamoring to see another part of the zoo.

"Let's go over there," suggested Tina, pointing to a redbrick building that housed The Tropic Zone, according to the lettering above the door.

The temperature inside was twenty degrees warmer than it was outside, and banks of thick mist hung in the air like filmy curtains. The interior had been landscaped to resemble a rain forest, and the luxuriance of the vegetation—massive palm fronds, feathery ferns, and spiky vines lacing the trees together—was vaguely oppressive. The place gave off the sultry odor of a rich compost heap. A boardwalk zigzagged through the lush greenery, its planks slick with condensed moisture.

As they moved forward, the mist lifted in spots to reveal people up ahead, then settled back in again, reinforcing the illusion that they were all alone, sealed up in cotton batting. Birds in the foliage emitted squawks and whistles, and a waterfall somewhere cascaded down a ladder of artificial rocks. The sounds were as exotic as the colors.

At the top of a flight of stairs, a dark passage beckoned. Once their eyes adjusted to the gloom, they realized that the tunnellike area housed the bat population. The light was kept low to simulate night, and in a long, glass-fronted case, the mammals whirled and swooped back and forth in a mad frenzy of wings, narrowly avoiding collision. A half dozen people stood in the darkness, watching. Brent and Tina joined them and were soon fascinated by the intricacy of the flight patterns. They didn't see that Angelina had ventured on ahead.

As the child skipped out of the tunnel into the muggy

rain forest, she nearly collided with a man standing in the mist.

"What's in there?" he asked.

Angelina looked up at him. "Bats."

"Bats? That so? I haven't seen a bat in a long time. Are they scary?"

"No. I've seen them before."

"You're a brave little girl."

"I know."

"How about snakes? You afraid of them?"

"Nope, not snakes, either." Angelina reached up her hand to caress a swatch of low-hanging Spanish moss.

"What are you scared of?"

"Nothing."

Spiff took a step closer to her. "Do you live nearby?"

"No."

"Far away?"

"Queens."

"That's a nice place to live. Is that your mummy and daddy in there?"

"My mom. Not my daddy."

"Your uncle?"

"No."

"Who then?"

"Someone who's staying with us."

"A friend of your mom's, huh?" He took another step. "What's your name?"

Angelina could see her reflection in the man's dark glasses and wondered why he was wearing them. It wasn't sunny in here. She no longer felt like conversing, but the man wouldn't look away, and she was afraid to move.

Tina's voice echoed from within the passage. "Angelina? Where are you, honey?"

Spiff noticed the girl's head turn slightly. "Angelina? Is that it? Is that your name? That means little angel, doesn't it?"

"Yup."

"You hiding some wings under there?"

"I have to go now." The child spun around and ran back into the darkness.

"Queens, eh?" mumbled Spiff. "Well, that shouldn't be a problem. That's no problem at all . . . Angelina."

The semidetached brick house was nothing special. There were thousands just like it in the working-class neighborhoods of Queens. A little patch of grass out front, concrete steps leading up to the front door, and inside, rooms not much larger than large packing boxes.

The house probably still had old-fashioned steam radiators for heat, lace doilies on the armchairs, and a porcelain Jesus on the wall. Spiff didn't want to be snooty about it, but he'd been in enough of them to imagine the decor. A few family heirlooms, sprinkled among the modest furniture. A braided rug somewhere. A grandfather clock, someplace else. Nothing of value, though. Never anything worth stealing.

Earlier, there had been a flurry of traffic in the street as men and women returned from work, some of them carting groceries for supper. He'd had no difficulty following Brent, his lady friend, and the kid the five blocks from the subway stop. They were so engrossed with one another they hadn't paid much attention to anybody else. He'd more or less hung back until they'd disappeared inside.

The kid had gone upstairs shortly afterward, and he'd caught a glimpse of her in the window with the bright yellow curtains. That had to be her bedroom—*Angelina's* bedroom.

A light went on in the living room and he saw people moving behind the lace curtains. He was tempted to cross the street for a closer look but decided against it. Wisely, because just at that moment, a burly man emerged from around the side of the house and climbed into the Jeep Cherokee in the driveway. The motor throbbed to life and the backup lights came on, throwing a reddish glow onto the pavement. Spiff turned away so the driver couldn't see his face. But the vehicle drove off in the opposite direction.

There probably wouldn't be much more activity until the morning, he surmised, when parents dragged themselves out of bed and headed back to work and kids were packed off to school. In neighborhoods like this, once dusk descended, most people stayed behind closed doors to watch television, fight, or have sex. Sometimes all three.

The bluish flickering in the living room window of the brick house meant the television had been turned on. The street was quiet, and Spiff was beginning to feel conspicuous. There was no reason to stand here much longer.

He walked to the end of the block and entered an alley to see if he could approach the house from behind. Here, all was pretty much as he expected—clotheslines, trash cans, weathered lawn furniture. The postage-stamp gardens hadn't yet recovered from the hard winter and had a beaten-down appearance. Where there were trees, they were short or stunted. Power lines ran down the alley.

He noticed that the basement windows of the house were barred, but the storm door to the back porch seemed to be sprung. The door hung at a slight angle and didn't shut tight. He could make out the kid's bike and a Webber grill in the clutter on the porch. A back door opened onto the kitchen, as he had suspected. That's how the man driving the Cherokee had left the house minutes ago.

The two windows over the porch belonged to the master bedroom, he guessed. They were dark for the time being. Neither of them had bars. In the yard, there were a redwood picnic table and a deflated plastic wading pool that looked as if it had sat out all winter.

As he moved closer, he brushed up against a chain-link fence surrounding the neighboring property. Suddenly, a black shape sprang out of the darkness and hurtled up against the mesh. Instinctively, Spiff recoiled. Behind the barrier, a German shepherd bared its teeth and growled menacingly. Without warning, the animal lunged a second time, throwing itself at the fence with such force that Spiff feared it might actually give way.

"Keep your fucking eyes open!" he scolded himself. He'd been so intent on casing the house that he hadn't seen the crazy dog coming at him. He backed off into the shadows and waited for it to quiet down. But the barking only grew louder. Feeding on its own frenzy, the animal prepared to jump again. A dull clank rang out as it hit the fence with its full weight, followed by a scraping sound. Spiff realized that the dog was tearing at the mesh links with its teeth.

Afraid the commotion would bring one of the neighbors to the back door, he quickly retraced his steps to the street. He'd seen all he needed to see. The house presented no challenge. It was a piece of cake. And as for the dog, forewarned was forearmed.

If it leaped at him the next time, he'd simply slit its throat.

22

*T*he Andersons arrived at the town hall at quarter to nine, even though the offices didn't open for another fifteen minutes. Their tan sedan was the only vehicle in the parking lot that Monday morning. Linda's parents, resigned to what lay ahead, occupied their usual places in the front. Linda sat in the back and tried to contain her eagerness until Steve Carroll showed up.

In less than three weeks, she would be Linda Carroll. Mrs. Steven Carroll. Mrs. Linda Anderson Carroll. She tested the various names in her mind, wondering which sounded best. She'd always known Steve would be her husband one day. She'd pictured their marriage differently, of course, but their love was what counted—not engraved wedding invitations or pastel bridesmaids' gowns or a surprise shower, which she would probably have to forgo now.

The early arrival at the town hall was prompted by Mr. Anderson's wish "to get this matter settled as quickly as possible." After he and his wife had recovered from their initial shock, they had accepted the fact that their "little girl" was neither little nor a girl any longer. They voiced their disappointments and recriminations out of her hearing.

Linda felt a sudden swelling of affection for her parents. "I'd like to thank you both."

Her mother turned around in the front seat. "Whatever for?"

"For sticking by me. For not abandoning me."

"We would never do a thing like that, dear."

"I didn't want it to be this way, Mother. Honest."

"Naturally, you didn't. When you've lived a little longer, you'll learn that things don't always happen the way we want. All of us make mistakes and sometimes those mistakes can have serious consequences. But the sun comes up every morning just the same, and that's when you show the world what you're made of. That's when you show people your character."

Mr. Anderson interrupted. "It's nine-ten. Where's Steve?"

Linda looked out the car window at the vacant lot. "Oh, Daddy, you know how he likes to primp."

"Not exactly a time for primping."

Five minutes later, a dusty Ford turned off Main Street and pulled up alongside the Andersons' car. Kate Carroll rolled down her window and leaned out. "Isn't Steve here?"

"We've been waiting for him. Wasn't he at home with you?" Mr. Anderson's tone conveyed his growing displeasure.

Kate Carroll knitted her brow. "He got up early. I could tell he was real nervous, because he wasn't talking a whole lot. He said he wanted to go out for a drive and that he would be back. But that was a couple of hours ago. When I noticed it was nine o'clock and he still hadn't returned, I figured he'd come directly here. I brought a freshly ironed shirt for him."

No one knew what to make of Kate Carroll's disclosure, so

they sat a while longer in silence. Whenever a car passed by, Linda glanced up hopefully. Finally she pushed open the door and walked over to the steps of the town hall, which commanded a better view of Main Street. The sinking feeling she had experienced at the doctor's was coming back. Before he'd informed her she was pregnant, she'd known it, just as she instinctively sensed now that something was wrong.

She sat down on the top step. Her parents and Mrs. Carroll got out of their automobiles and joined her.

"You don't think that car of his broke down?" conjectured Mr. Anderson. "I've just been waiting for that old rattletrap to go on him. I swear, first thing I'm going to do is get the two of you a good secondhand car. Something more reliable."

Mrs. Anderson, who had been fighting not to check her watch, capitulated at nine-forty-five, and then wondered aloud if Steve hadn't got the time wrong. "At one point, we did say ten o'clock, didn't we? Then we all decided on nine. Maybe he got confused and is coming at ten. That must be it."

But ten o'clock came and went with no sign of Steve or the red Impala.

At ten-twenty, Linda stood up. "Let's go home."

"Maybe we should wait a few more minutes, just in case something's happened?" Mrs. Carroll suggested weakly, although she offered no elaboration of what that might be. Everyone seemed to be avoiding the obvious explanation, for fear that once it was mentioned, it would be irrevocably true.

Linda thought back to the night she told Steve that she was pregnant. He had been uncharacteristically quiet, but his silence had seemed understandable at the time. Now she realized how little they had spoken to each other in the days that had followed. Her father had made his feelings clear. So had her mother. Even Mrs. Carroll, in her effacing way, had eventually expressed her point of view. But it occurred to Linda that she had no idea what Steve really felt.

She looked at the three adults, who had mapped out the future for her. "Did Steve say he would be here?" she asked, an edge creeping into her voice. "Did anyone actually hear him say he would be here this morning?"

"Linda, sweetheart, we all agreed," said Mrs. Anderson.

"We did. But did he?" Feeling her knees buckle, she grabbed the metal railing on the steps for support. Her world was slipping out of control. These past three years, she'd given Steve everything—all her attention, her love, herself! She had held herself back in class just so as not to outshine him. She had begged and badgered her parents until they had agreed to accept him as one of the family. What had she gotten back?

She sank to the ground.

Her mother rushed to her side. "Are you all right? You had better get out of the sun, dear. We'll take you home right away. Paul, give a hand."

But Mr. Anderson, sensing his usual Olympian composure deserting him, stomped down the town hall steps instead.

Linda brushed her mother's help aside and put her head in her hands. "What am I going to do now?" she moaned. The older women made fluttery, ineffectual gestures and stared helplessly at each other.

In the parking lot, Paul Anderson paced in circles, vowing over and over in a knotted voice that "someone is going to have to teach that boy a lesson he won't forget, a lesson he'll remember for a good, long time."

23

"Dover Plains," the conductor called out as the train pulled into the station, which consisted of a small waiting room with worn wooden benches and a ticket window, staffed only on weekdays. Brent stepped down onto the platform and took in the town or what little was left of it. Across the tracks lay the remains of a once thriving commercial district—a pharmacy, a five-and-dime, and a savings and loan, on which a vintage clock advised passers-by it was "Time to be Thrifty." A lot of the stores were boarded up and had FOR RENT signs plastered on the windows. Commerce had fled to a mall on the outskirts of town, and the main street had a desolate air.

As he crossed the railroad tracks, Brent realized the bank was the one he had telephoned. He didn't see a sign for the law offices of Lobel and Lobel anywhere, but reasoned there couldn't be too many lawyers in a town this size. It sounded like an old, established firm. The person on the phone had mentioned something about a father and son.

Earlier that morning, Tina had reiterated her offer to

accompany him, but he'd turned her down. How difficult, he'd argued, would it be for him to catch a train to Dover Plains, do a little exploring, and return home? It was obvious that he had business of some kind in Dover Plains. He'd been planning a visit before he was attacked in Central Park. Once he was on the scene, perhaps that purpose would become apparent again. Anyway, he had to start putting some of the puzzle pieces together himself. She had her own life to get on with.

The main street did, in fact, look vaguely familiar, he thought as he paused under the savings and loan clock. The sidewalks were deserted, and only a few cars and battered pickup trucks were parked at an angle to the curb. Without people bustling about, the town seemed to be mired in the 1950s. Brent glanced up at the clock. It registered just a few minutes past noon. Lunch hour. That explained the empty sidewalks.

Impulsively, he entered the savings and loan. Except for the hum of an electric fan and the murmured conversation between a teller and a woman in a plain print dress, the bank was eerily still. A secretary looked up from her metal desk, and Brent imagined for a moment that he saw a glint of recognition in her eyes. But then she turned away and pulled a file from her desk drawer and contact was broken. The teller seemed to be involved in a drawn-out transaction with the woman in the print dress. Otherwise, there was nothing much to see, and Brent couldn't think what to ask the teller. When the secretary looked up at him again, he patted his pockets and pretended that he had forgotten something and quickly left.

The flaked gold lettering on the window of the pharmacy next door identified it as BLECKNER'S, EST. 1924.

Brent paused in the doorway and looked around. The interior had been modernized in the 1970s, but the original soda fountain had been preserved, and a few people were having the luncheon special—tomato soup and grilled cheese sandwich—advertised in chalk on a blackboard. The stools at the counter were upholstered in shiny red vinyl, and a ceiling fan revolved gently overhead. At the back, a pharmacist with a green eyeshade was busy filling prescriptions.

Just as Brent made up his mind to go in, a young girl got up from the counter, waved good-bye to the waitress, and came toward him. She was about seventeen or eighteen with long, straight hair that was parted in the middle and fell dramatically away from her face. She wasn't pretty in any conventional sense, but her eyes were piercingly blue and her skin had a healthy outdoor glow. Brent felt his heart begin to race. He knew that face. He'd seen it hundreds of times. Even the lithe body in tight jeans seemed familiar to him. She must have been the reason he had been intending to come to Dover Plains.

She looked directly at him as she approached, and he waited for the telltale sign of recognition. Any second, he felt, she would speak his name, then she would tell him hers, and clarity would come into his life at last. He was on the verge of experiencing one of those clicks the doctor had talked about.

She was standing right in front of him now. "Excuse me?" she said, smiling fetchingly.

He recognized that smile, too. "I know you, don't I?" he said, barely able to rein in his excitement.

"Do you?" She cocked her head, the expression on her face less startled than quizzical.

"Yes, I do. I'm sure of it."

"Maybe you do. I'm afraid I don't remember, though."

"No, you don't understand. This is very important to me."

"Well, I've never seen you before. I'm sorry. Would you mind letting me by? You're blocking the door." She smiled again to show that she was accustomed to men wanting to pick her up and nurtured no animosity toward those who tried.

He watched her open the door of her beat-up Dodge, slide behind the wheel, and drive off. What about her had provoked such a reaction? The shape of the face? The lustrous black hair? His thoughts racing, he walked over to the luncheon counter and took a place on a stool at the end. A name was all he needed. The girl's name was the key. If he could just come up with it, he had the impression that all the rest would fall in place.

A heavyset waitress was tapping her pencil on the Formica before him.

"You want to order something or not?" The plastic tag pinned to the bib of her apron was more welcoming than her demeanor. HI, it read. I'M SANDY.

"A cup of coffee, please. Black."

"Anything else?"

"Can you tell me who that young woman was?"

The pencil came to a rest. "Local girl, that's all."

"No, her name."

Sandy eyed him suspiciously. "What are you asking for?"

"She's . . . I think I met her once."

"You and every other male over twelve in the county. Tell me about it! . . . So? Something with that coffee or not, mister?"

177

"Nothing."

Sandy went off and busied herself with a gleaming coffee urn.

As he waited for her to return, he sensed a stirring in the depths of his consciousness and told himself to concentrate. The name was coming back. He couldn't articulate it yet, but it was there in one of the dark vaults of his memory. He could feel it rising up toward the light, the letters more distinct with each passing moment. He could almost make them out now. And then it was there—on the tip of his tongue.

Linda!

He spoke it out loud. As he did a smile broke across his face. The young woman was named Linda.

"What are you smiling about?" Sandy placed the coffee cup and a metal pitcher of half-and-half on the counter.

"Linda! That's her name, isn't it?"

"You still going on about that?" She cackled to herself.

"I'm right, aren't I?"

"Well, I guess you'll just have to ask her the next time you see her."

"Tell me where she lives and I will."

"You expect me to do that? Men! Honestly!" She gave out with another of the throaty cackles. "How about you? You look sort of familiar. Why don't you tell me what your name is."

"Brent Stevens."

"Brent, eh? Can't say I ever heard that one before. Sounds like a movie star. I don't suppose you've been in any movies?"

He shook his head.

"Too bad. I saw what's-his-face once. That guy on *Law*

and Order. He was passing through town and he came in for a package of Rolaids or something. Where are you from?"

"Er . . . California."

"Long way from home."

A mechanic in bib overalls took a place at the counter and called out, "What about some lunch, Sandy. I only got a half-hour break."

"Hold your horses, Hal. I'm coming."

She threw one last look at Brent. A faraway expression had come into his eyes. It sounded as if he was murmuring "Linda" to himself.

"Odd bird," she said to Hal.

"The world's full of 'em," Hal agreed. "My wife and mother-in-law to name two."

As she rustled up the luncheon special for Hal, she kept glancing back at the stranger, trying to figure him out. At first, he had struck her as simply one more man on the make for a pretty girl, but now she was less sure. Something seemed to be weighing on his mind. He was a nice-looking man, or would be if he unfurrowed his brow. The air of preoccupation made him slightly forbidding, but his features had a chiseled strength and his—.

She nearly dropped a bowl of tomato soup when the revelation came to her.

Of course, that's who he was! He had changed some, matured, but not so much as to be unrecognizable. The square jaw was the giveaway. And the hair! That had always been his pride, she remembered, and it was still thick and blond. My god, how many years had it been? Her head was swimming.

Brent caught her eye and asked, "Can you tell me where the offices of Lobel and Lobel are?"

"That's over on Oak. You take a right out the door. Then go five blocks and take another right. Big Victorian place. There's a sign. You can't miss it . . . You don't want a refill first?"

"No, thanks."

"Sure now? It's on the house," she said, trying to delay him.

He took a dollar bill out of his wallet and put it on the counter. "Oak Street, right?"

Sandy waited until the pharmacy door had shut before she ran over to the plate-glass window and pressed her nose against it. The man who called himself Brent Stevens was walking slowly and seemed to be drinking in everything, like a tourist on his first trip to the big city. For a moment, she almost believed that he had never seen the place before. Then he passed out of her sight.

She trotted over to the pharmacist's station. From the apron pocket in which she kept her tips, she fished out a quarter, dropped it into the slot, and dialed a number.

"Pick up the phone, honey!" She tapped her pencil nervously on the wall while she waited for someone to answer. "Pick up the damn phone!"

A few blocks west of the pharmacy, Main Street split to go around an ungainly concrete monument, commemorating the town's World War II casualties, then it came back together. A gas station and a vacant lot marked the transition to a residential area—a few large frame homes, built before the turn of the century, when the town had

enjoyed a period of prosperity, but mostly a lot of bungalows and ranch houses of newer vintage and unexceptional
appearance.

The lawns were neatly mowed, and a couple of oak
trees arched over the sidewalk, shading Brent as he
walked.

A blue Toyota passed him, slowed down at the intersection, and then pulled over to the curb. A woman with
dark sunglasses and short-cropped hair stepped out and
looked back at him. She was in her thirties, dressed in
slacks and a blouse, with a gray sweater over her shoulders. Brent expected her to remove a bag of groceries
from the trunk and disappear into one of the bungalows,
but instead she stood by the car door and waited as he
came up beside her.

The street was as deserted here as it had been in the
center of town. There were just the two of them, and the
woman was staring hard at him now, her mouth tight with
disapproval.

He nodded tentatively and mumbled, "Good afternoon."

"I never thought I'd see your face here again, not until
you were famous . . . or dead."

The vehemence of her response startled him. "I'm not
dead. Not yet."

"What a pity!"

"I'm not famous, either . . . I guess you recognize me,
anyway."

"You haven't changed that much. Sandy didn't have any
trouble. She called me up and said I'd never believe who
was back in town. She was right. I don't."

"Sandy?"

"You don't remember her? She's put on a lot of weight the last few years, but still . . ."

"I guess that's it." Brent told himself to play along. This woman knew him, too. She'd certainly needed no encouragement to talk to him. If he could just keep up the conversation a while longer, her name would come to him, the way the name of the young girl had come to him in the pharmacy.

"Was Sandy . . . that surprised to see me?"

"Are you kidding? From her tone, I thought she'd seen a ghost. Well, in a way, she had. You might as well be a ghost. 'Are you sitting down, Linda?' she asked, 'because if you're not, I think you better.' "

"What did she call you? Linda? You're Linda?"

The woman took off her sunglasses and glared at him. "Yes, I'm Linda. Who the hell did you think I was?" The anger in her eyes was tempered by flashes of something softer—disappointment, maybe hurt.

"I didn't know that. I really didn't."

"What kind of game is this?"

"It's no game at all, I swear."

She exhaled loudly. "Did you think you could just slip into town? Do whatever you had to do and then leave without anyone noticing? We're not that dumb around here, although you certainly thought so once."

"But if you're Linda, then who is . . . I'm sorry. I'm all mixed up. This isn't what I expected when I came here this morning."

Linda turned away.

"Me, neither," she said flatly. "I was all prepared for this meeting last year, well, because of your mother and all. I asked myself what I would feel when I saw you. Would I still be angry after all these years? What was I going to say to you? More importantly, what would I say to Melissa?"

"Melissa?"

"Yes, my daughter . . . I told myself I was ready for you to come breezing back then. I could handle it. But you didn't show. Nobody could find you. 'What else is new?' I thought. After that, I figured the prodigal son was gone forever. Missing in action. I even thought you might be dead. It had been so long since anyone had heard anything from you."

"Was I really gone that long?"

"Now you are joking! That's what I accused Sandy of doing. 'No joke,' Linda,' she assured me. 'Believe me, he was sitting right here at the luncheon counter. Steve Carroll has come back to Dover Plains.'"

Steve Carroll!

All at once, the pent-up images started to cascade through his mind, a blizzard of them. He saw a frame house with a bay window and a kitchen table covered with yellow oilcloth and a woman in a housecoat sitting at the table drinking coffee. Behind the house, he saw a yard with a sandbox and—this part was less distinct—a man tossing a child up in the air playfully while the child shrieked, delight mingled with fear.

Then daylight turned to dusk, and in his mind he had a picture of the woman in the housecoat standing at the back door and calling out, telling him it was time to come in for supper.

They were images from childhood, Brent realized. His childhood in Dover Plains. He had a past here. It was all around him. He had bicycled up and down this very street, probably climbed those oak trees. The soda fountain at

Bleckner's Pharmacy was where he and his friends had gathered after school. No wonder he'd felt at home there when he had walked in an hour ago.

"Are you all right, Steve? What's come over you?" Linda reached out a hand.

"You've got to help me. I'm in trouble."

"I should have known if you came back, it would be for no good."

"When was the last time you saw me? How long has it been?"

"Why are you acting so strange?"

"How long, Linda?"

"You know perfectly well, Steve."

"No, I don't. I had an accident. No . . . not an accident. I was attacked. In New York. They hit me on the head. I just lost my . . . No, I don't mean that. I couldn't remember things. Lost my bearings . . . for a while, I didn't even know my name—"

"Steve? You didn't know you were Steve Carroll?"

"I was in a hospital. I thought my name was Brent Stevens. That's on the bottle of pills. But that doesn't matter now. Because you can help me."

"Help you? What kind of a screwy story is this?"

"With the pieces. Putting them together. When I saw the young girl in the pharmacy, it seemed as if I had known her all my life. That's why I spoke to her. But she brushed right by me. Afterward I thought, 'That woman is Linda.' But now you say that she isn't."

Linda's voice was stern. "You left before she was even born. *I'm* the one you know, Steve. *I'm* Linda. The question is, why did you come back?"

More images flooded his head. He could see a red

Impala, filled with teenagers, speeding down a highway. He was at the wheel, and they were all laughing and shouting into the night, and then the car pulled into a dusty lot and made a U-turn and raced back toward town as the raucous laughter redoubled. Yet there seemed to be no happiness attached to the image, no joy, just a kind of defiant bravado. The speed was borne of a reckless need to escape.

"I came because I'm lost and I need to find out who I am."

"And you expect me to help you?"

"Can you . . . please?"

Linda leaned up against the car door, the strength suddenly drained from her limbs, and tried to compose herself. She had imagined this meeting hundreds of times—the excuses he would make, the complicated reasons he would give for leaving so precipitously. She hadn't imagined it like this, though. He barely remembered anything! Her name alone had been a big surprise to him.

The preposterousness of it all took her breath away.

"What a thing to ask me!" she murmured, as much for her own benefit as his.

But if it was just a made-up story, she had to admit he was a convincing actor. Why bother, though? Why come all this distance just to play such an outlandish role? It made no sense. Unless he was telling the truth. She tried to detect a sign that would give him away—a twitching of the mouth or a darting movement of the eyes. But his confusion seemed genuine, and that realization slowly quelled her indignation. How could she be furious with him for something long ago, when he was having such difficulty remembering it? It was like being angry with a child. With a pet!

For so many years, she had blamed herself for everything that had happened! She had been too possessive, she hadn't paid enough attention to his dreams, her parents had looked down on him. Then, after Melissa was born, the self-recriminations had been replaced by the fear that he would show up and lay claim to their daughter. She'd lived with that fear for years and years, too. Even after she married Ted Beckley.

Ted had adopted the child, given her his last name, raised her as his very own. When Melissa was in grade school, she had been told that she had two daddies. Her real daddy, the one who had "made" her, had gone away. But Ted was the daddy who "chose" her and loved her very much and would never ever leave. The child had accepted the explanation with no questions and grown up happy and adjusted.

And finally Linda's fear subsided, too. Steve lost his power over her and her imagination. The photographs she had saved of him faded with time, and one day, when she stumbled on them in a drawer, she realized that they probably bore little resemblance to the person he had grown up to be. That was the day he ceased being a real person and became a figment of her youth.

Now he was standing there, pleading with her to resurrect a time that she had put behind her. He had been part of a girlish fantasy back then—he had even had the starring role—but she'd never really known him. She'd made up the relationship and he had gone along with it. Eighteen years later, nothing had changed: He was still a mystery to her.

24

"And one and two and one and two and . . . don't drop the head . . . and one and two . . . you're looking good, Mrs. Shriver."

Tina clapped out a steady rhythm as Mrs. Shriver struggled to keep pace. But jumping jacks were not the woman's strong suit, and her feet hit the floor with an alarmingly heavy thud. Her hair hung in damp ringlets about her face, which was very nearly the color of her purple jumpsuit and streaked with rivulets of sweat. Tina stole a quick look at her wristwatch—another ten minutes to go—and redoubled the vigor of her clapping.

"And one and two . . . don't stop now, Mrs. Shriver. We want to keep that heart rate elevated . . . and one and two . . ."

Mrs. Shriver landed on the floor with the full force of her 154 pounds—down 15 pounds since she'd begun exercise classes four months ago, but still 35 pounds short of her goal. Right now she looked ready to collapse on the chintz sofa behind her, but it was Tina's policy to push her clients for the full hour. They hated her the last five minutes, but they invariably thanked her once the session was over. Tina noted that Mrs. Shriver had just entered the hate phase, then let her thoughts go to the apartment below them.

All through the workout, she had been able to think of little else. While Mrs. Shriver had grunted through her push-ups, moaned through her sit-ups, and puffed her way loudly through a set of agonizing fanny tucks, Tina was busy constructing and reconstructing scenarios in her head. Brent knew someone in the building or someone in the building knew him. The morning after he was attacked in the park, he was trying to get inside. Joey's impression was that he had been here before. Unless this was simply the first building Brent had come upon, after stumbling out of the park, and he was looking for help from anybody, which was possible, too.

Part of Tina clung to the idea that he was the victim of a random mugging.

But what about the face in the window? Brent was persuaded that someone had been observing him yesterday. The window he had pointed at belonged to the apartment right under Mrs. Shriver's. Granted, Tina hadn't seen anyone herself. But maybe if she'd arrived a few seconds earlier, she might have. Brent's conviction was real enough at the time. Maybe the man in the window was the person who had threatened him in the hospital. No, she thought, that was stretching things.

If there was a connection, though, a big clue to the mystery lay just beneath the floorboards that were currently bearing the punishing impact of Mrs. Shriver's jumping jacks.

"I hope the people downstairs don't mind all this jumping up and down," she said as Mrs. Shriver heaved a sigh of exhaustion and fell back onto the chintz sofa, utterly spent.

"He's . . . never . . . complained . . . before," the woman puffed, struggling to bring her breathing under control.

"It's just, well, that you've been jumping so, so vigorously lately."

Mrs. Shriver beamed at what she took for a compliment, reached for her glass of Evian water, and drained its contents.

"I suppose I really should ask . . . Mr. Reed . . . if the noise bothers him . . . Actually, that's not a bad idea . . . It would give me a chance . . . to find out if he's married. He's a rather attractive type, you know."

"Mr. Reed? Tell me more?" Tina noticed Mrs. Shriver's eyes light up. The opportunity to gossip seemed to have momentarily revived the woman's will to live, and her huffing slowly diminished.

"Oh, yes. Very attractive. In a distinguished way. Older man. He came up once and knocked on my door to tell me that he was having a few people over and he hoped I wouldn't be disturbed. He was so polite about it. But you know how the British are. Everything sounds civilized with them. Even the insults."

As the woman nattered on, Tina collected her exercise gear—the stretch bands and the hand grips that lent variety to her workouts and kept her clients from getting bored—and packed them in her dance bag. An idea had taken shape in her mind.

"Good job today, Mrs. Shriver. See you Monday? Same time, same place." Mrs. Shriver managed to lift a plump arm and wave it limply by way of agreement.

"Let yourself out, dear. Do you mind? I think I'll just sit here for a moment."

Instead of waiting for the elevator, Tina took the stairs to the third floor. The thickly carpeted landing was decorated with a Parsons table and several easy chairs to look as if it were an actual room, not a common foyer shared by two apartments. The door marked 3-G corresponded to Mrs. Shriver's. Tina pressed the door button and heard a deep chiming sound within.

She didn't know exactly what she would say, if he let her in, but getting a good look at him would be enough. Her first impressions of people, she liked to think, were pretty reliable, and she hadn't forgotten the face of the businessman who had terrified Brent at the hospital, even though she'd only brushed up against him. There was "a nasty piece of goods," as Ida put it.

She listened for the sound of approaching footsteps, but none came. Perhaps it was a silly idea. It was already late in the morning, and most people were at work by now. Just to be sure, she sounded the chimes a couple more times. Still no answer. Readjusting the strap of her dance bag on her shoulder, she prepared to leave when the door swung open. There stood an elegant silver-haired man in an expensive suit and silk tie.

Mrs. Shriver hadn't been wrong to call him attractive. A certain pinched quality, however, robbed his features of generosity and prevented him from being truly handsome. His nose was too sharp to be judged aquiline and his chin too small to be assertive. But he still gave off an air of class and breeding. It didn't take a second glance for Tina to know that he wasn't the businessman at the hospital. So much for that theory.

"Yes, may I help you?" he asked.

"Hi! I'm sorry to bother you like this. I work out Mrs. Shriver in 4-G and she just wanted to make sure that we weren't disturbing you."

"I beg your pardon?"

"Mrs. Shriver. Your neighbor upstairs. I'm her physical trainer." Tina thought she detected a flicker of recognition in the man's eyes. "I've got her doing a lot of jumping jacks these days."

"And? . . ."

"I thought if any cracks had appeared in your ceiling, we owed you an explanation." The quip momentarily melted the man's reserve. He allowed a smile to cross his lips. For an instant, Tina felt as if he were checking her out, not the other way around.

"No serious damage, yet. Thank you for inquiring, Miss . . . ?"

"Ruffo . . . It's Italian."

The ringing of a telephone interrupted them. "Drat!" the man said. "I'm afraid you'll have to excuse me. I'm expecting a call." He reached to shut the door, then changed his mind. "Actually, I do have something I'd like to ask you. I don't suppose you'd mind waiting just a moment while I take this call?"

"Go ahead. I don't have—"

"I'll be back in a jiffy." She watched him hurry down the hall in the direction of the ringing phone, then heard his muffled voice answering, "Hello. Is that you? . . . Sorry, there was someone at the door."

The apartment appeared to be a duplicate of Mrs. Shriver's. The long hall in which Tina stood bisected it in half. To the right, were the living and dining rooms, sunny, high-ceilinged spaces that overlooked the park. The bedrooms—or what in this case seemed to be an office—lay farther down the hall to the left. Tina hesitated to take a seat in the living room. The man hadn't invited her in; he'd just asked her to wait. From the entranceway, she craned her neck, seeing what she could see. Tasteful antiques, mostly. A grand piano. Two large sofas, upholstered in a bold stripe.

Then she noticed that the walls of the hall were hung with photographs—dozens upon dozens of them. Almost every photograph had someone famous in it, posing with the man who had just opened the door. Tina recognized Elizabeth Taylor in one, and she was pretty certain that was Whitney Houston in another. Hillary Clinton and somebody. The photographs seemed to have been taken at galas or balls or some such high-society function, because the women all wore fancy evening gowns and jewels, and the men had on tuxedos. Everybody was smiling radiantly, as if it were the stroke of midnight on New Year's Eve or their taxes had been rescinded.

One photo stood out because it was so different from all the others. It had been taken outside on a beach, and the three people in it, casually dressed, were fooling around for the camera, rather like giddy adolescents. The man who had just gone to answer the phone was in the middle, grinning foolishly, his arms around the other two. The blonde woman to his left had on a man's white shirt, much too big for her, that hung down to her midthighs and made her look like a street urchin.

With a start, Tina realized that it was Jennifer Osborne, the movie star. The other man in the photo, with the exceptionally trim body, had to be Christopher

Knight. She leaned closer. Yes, that's who he was. Even in an informal shot like this, taken without the benefit of studio lighting, they made a dazzling couple. And right there between them was the inhabitant of this very apartment. She noticed the inscription: "For His Lordship, with love from his humble servants." Unlike the lacquered people in the other photographs, these three seemed to have been caught at a moment of real happiness. Tina speculated that it was a vacation shot, but the landscape was too blurred for her to identify it with any accuracy.

The resident of 3-G, whoever he was, obviously led a glamorous life. The dark thoughts Tina had entertained at Mrs. Shriver's began to strike her as a bit stupid. The man hardly seemed the type to slink around in the dead of night, whacking people over the head or stalking them in the city streets. The circles he moved in were more exalted, lethal probably only for the amounts of booze that was consumed in them.

She was wasting her time. Joey would have a good laugh at her expense when she told him. Maybe, she'd keep it to herself.

She heard the man's voice, rising in the far room, but she couldn't make out what he was saying. A moment later, he reappeared in the hall.

"Sorry for the interruption, Miss . . . what did you say your name was?"

"Ruffo," replied Tina.

"Ah, yes. Italian, right? So, wrestling Mrs. Shriver into shape, are we?"

"Four times a week. Anyway, she just wanted me to check with you. If we've been making too much noise—"

"Heavens, no. The walls and floor are so thick you

could strangle her and I'd be none the wiser." He smiled—an oddly wide smile that revealed part of his upper gums.

"The jumping jacks are torture enough, I guarantee you. She'll be reassured to know you can't hear anything." Tina turned to go, but the man stopped her.

"For some reason, you look awfully familiar. I don't suppose we have met before, have we?"

"Er . . . Not to my knowledge. You could have seen me coming in and out of the lobby."

"That must be it."

"I'm here all the time. If you ever need a workout, let me know. I can always use the extra business."

"As a matter of fact, I've been thinking about it." He gave a little pat to his stomach. "My clothes have started to feel a little snug. You wouldn't happen to have a card?"

Tina fished around inside her dance bag. "Somewhere in here . . . Where the hell are they? . . . Ah, here." She selected the one that was least creased and handed it to him. "My phone number's on it."

"Very good. I may give you a ring soon, Miss Ruffo. My name's Reed, by the way. Geoffrey Reed. English!"

"Pleased to meet you, Mr. Reed."

So much for her galloping suspicions, she thought. Although her immediate impression of Geoffrey Reed had been one of aloofness, he seemed to have a great deal of charm underneath. But then, he would have to, in order to socialize with so many famous people. She backed out the door and into the hall and punched the elevator button several times. If she had picked up a new client today, it was worth the embarrassment she was feeling.

As she stepped into the elevator, Geoffrey Reed gave

her a friendly nod and called out, "Tah." Then he turned back into the apartment and studied the card she had given him.

TINA RUFFO
Physical Trainer
718-759-3311

He was positive he knew her from somewhere. That hadn't been a line he was feeding her. He had seen her recently, but not in the lobby of the building. He tried to concentrate, picturing the oversize dance bag slung over her shoulder, the taut figure, the shiny black hair. Then, he knew. She had been with Brent Stevens yesterday. They were standing at the entrance of the park with a little girl. He didn't think he had dreamed it up. The telephone number on the card jumped out at him.

He ran down the hall to his office. He rarely threw anything away and on his desk was a stack of papers—bills, invitations, personal correspondence, memos to himself, even restaurant menus that had been slipped under the door in flagrant violation of the building regulations. He had to go through the stack twice before he found the piece of yellow lined paper. It was the paper on which he had jotted down the messages left on his answering machine yesterday.

As he suspected, right at the very top, he had scribbled in pencil: B. S.—718-759-3311. The number Brent had left was the same one on the card the Ruffo woman had just handed him.

He got to the bay window just in time to catch sight of her on the sidewalk below. She seemed to hesitate for a second and look up in his direction, before rounding the corner and trotting down the steps into the subway.

His hand shot to the package of Benson & Hedges in his pocket and he fumbled for a cigarette. Then he had to strike his pocket lighter several times before it ignited. The woman who had just left the apartment was a friend of Brent Stevens! That whole business about not wanting to disturb him with her exercise class had been a pretext. But for what? What were the two of them up to? He felt as if he were caught up in the plot of one of his clients' movies—one of the more absurd ones.

His whole career had been based on planning and control. He was supposed to be the unflappable one, handsomely paid to get other people out of tight situations. So how had he managed to land in this mess? Leaving a trail of smoke behind him, he strode back to his office, snatched the receiver off the hook, and dialed a number. With each ring, his nerves tightened. Finally, someone picked up.

"Yup?"

"Spiff? It's Geoffrey. The girl was just here."

25

Reduced to the bare facts, theirs was, Linda realized, a simple story. Almost banal without the emotions that had given it weight and color in her mind for so long. But anger would have been wasted on Steve—or Brent, as he now called himself. There wasn't even the satisfaction of drawing herself up tall and asking him to explain himself—the customary stance of the aggrieved woman confronting her seducer with the baseness of his actions.

Irony of ironies, she was having to tell *him* what happened.

She hadn't even proposed going anywhere private to talk. The front seat of the Toyota was good enough, and that setting, too, struck her as appropriately banal. Few vehicles went by at this time of day—and even fewer pedestrians. Those who did took little notice of the two adults conversing in the parked car.

"You just left that morning without telling anyone," Linda said. "We waited for several hours at the town hall and then gave up. Everyone believed you were scared and acting impulsively, and that you would have a change of heart and show up later. You didn't. You phoned your mother the next day and said you weren't coming back."

"You have every reason to hate me, don't you?"

"Not anymore. But I did for a long time. It was cowardly, what you did. Once I realized that, once I understood the problem was with you, not me, it became easier."

"Did my mother ever say where I was?"

"No. She never told us much of anything. She was always so . . . mortified by events. She stayed to her house a lot after that, didn't like people dropping in. I tried to go by, but I don't think she was comfortable around me. She never knew how to react. She was always apologizing for the way things had turned out."

"It wasn't her fault."

"I know, but you couldn't convince her of that. Melissa's birth only made it worse. There was so much gossip in town at the time, and your mother never acknowledged that the child might be her granddaughter. That was all right. No one was insisting. After I married Ted, it mattered less. Ted's parents were happy to be grandparents."

"When did she die, my mother?"

"Last July."

"What was it?"

"Cancer . . . Don Lobel tried for a long time to get in touch with you about your mother's estate."

"She had an estate?"

"Well, that's the word they use. I don't suppose the house is worth much. Not in the shape it's in. She stopped driving a year or so before her death and sold her car. There are the furnishings . . ."

"Well, that explains one thing, at least. Why I was coming to Dover Plains. To settle the family estate! Sounds like a big deal. It's Chestnut, isn't it? Our old address is 412 Chestnut! How do you like that? Maybe I haven't forgotten as much as I thought . . . Where is she buried?"

"Out at Woodbridge . . . with your father."

"One of America's ten most beautiful cemeteries . . . Isn't that what they used to say about it?"

"Something like that, yes."

"I must be getting better . . . my memory, that is . . . Did anybody show up for the funeral?"

"A couple of distant cousins. My parents . . . Melissa. About a dozen people in all . . . It was a nice ceremony . . . I'm sorry, Steve. Nobody knew where you were. Nobody knew for years." She was tempted to reach over and pat his arm but resisted the impulse.

Finally he gave a shrug. Did it mean that he was overcome with emotion or simply that he had no more questions to ask? Linda experienced no need to decipher the gesture. She could almost be objective about their situation. Funny, detachment was the one response of which she would have never thought herself capable.

"Would you like me to drive you over to Don Lobel's?" she inquired.

"Will he be in his office now?"

"If not, he'll be out back with his kids. He works out of his house."

They rode the three blocks in silence. Linda brought the car to a stop in front of a white Victorian mansion with a wide front porch. She left the motor running. He started to get out, then ducked his head back.

"Are you going to tell Melissa I was here?"

Linda shifted uneasily. "No, Steve. I don't see the point."

"I'm her father."

"Ted's her father now. He loves her. He brought her up. Someday, if Melissa wants to look you up, that will be her choice. Not yours, not mine. I've given this a lot of consideration. It's got to be that way, Steve."

She looked to him for a fight or at least a protest, but mild confusion was all she saw on his face. Maybe that's what she would have to settle for after eighteen years: His life baffled him. If he had suffered, as she had, he bore few traces of it. Perhaps remorse would come later, when the fullness of his memory was restored. But not necessarily. Maybe he'd never been bothered by what he'd done. Maybe he would always be cut off from others.

Suddenly, she felt weary. All the emotions she had carried around for so long—the outrage and the righteousness—no longer meant anything to her. Whatever Steve had been to her once, he was a stranger now. She would let him sort out the past for himself and by himself. She had only one request to make.

"Promise me you'll say nothing to Melissa and that you'll leave as soon as possible."

"I promise."

The silence reasserted itself.

"Well, I'm glad you came back. For your sake." She managed a slight smile in his direction. "Take care of yourself, Steve."

"You, too, Linda."

The Toyota pulled out into Oak Street, turned left at the first intersection, and disappeared from sight.

Linda was right—his mother's estate amounted to precious little. Two accounts totaling a few thousand dollars in the Dover Savings and Loan, and the house, which needed extensive repairs, before it could even be put on the market.

"The taxes on it are up-to-date," explained Don Lobel, a ruddy-complexioned man in a seersucker suit. "That's about all I can say for the place. You'll probably want to have a look-see yourself." Out of his desk drawer, the lawyer took a small manila envelope, checked that there was a key inside, and passed it over to Brent.

"Your mother left a few outstanding bills, nothing major, which were paid out of the funds in her checking account. A small insurance policy covered the funeral expenses. Other than that, I think you'll find everything pretty cut-and-dried." He ran his eyes over a sheaf of papers. "I'll have to get you to sign a few forms, Brent . . . It's Brent now, is it? Around here, I'm afraid we still think of you as Steve. Well, I'm sure you'll forgive us."

Brent signed "Steve Carroll" to the forms and assured the lawyer he would stay in touch this time. Don Lobel breathed a sigh of satisfaction, pleased to be able at last to start clearing up Kate Carroll's dossier, insignificant as it was.

"Now that we can set everything in motion, probate will take about six or seven months. We ought to be able to wrap it up by January or February. You'll tell me what you intend to do about the house." He leaned back in his chair, not ready to terminate the meeting yet.

"So, what's it like out there in Tinsel Town? Is it really like they show it in the movies?"

"Oh, well . . . yes. It's pretty much like you would imagine it to be."

"All the women look like they do on *Baywatch?*"

"Not all . . . Some, though."

"A lot different from Dover Plains, then." Don Lobel chuckled. "You always had a way with the ladies. I remember that. I bet that hasn't changed. You're doing well for yourself?"

"I have no complaints . . ." When the salacious details the lawyer expected were not forthcoming, he stood up and extended a plump hand across the desk.

"A real pleasure to see you back home, Steve."

The frame house on Chestnut Street came back to Brent as soon as he caught sight of it, although it was smaller and shabbier than he would have wished. The yard was overgrown and the fence was missing some pickets. He had to jiggle the key in the lock for a while before the back door opened with a creak. Flicking a switch on the wall, he discovered the electricity had been turned off.

The kitchen had a familiar odor of dankness, but when he tried one of the faucets, nothing came out. The water had been cut off, too. A chipped tea cup with a brown stain still sat in the sink, and he wondered if it had been the last cup his mother had ever used. He remembered her sitting at the table with the yellow oilcloth, nursing her coffee, staring at a half-completed picture puzzle and trying to stave off her disappointment with life.

He wandered into the living room, which gave off a similar sense of exhaustion. The furniture looked so old and forlorn it seemed unlikely there had ever been a time when it was considered new. The Magnavox TV console deserved to be in a museum. On top of it sat a yellowed lace doily and several framed photographs. He blew the dust off one. It was Kate Carroll in a sunsuit, gardening on her hands and knees and smiling up at the photographer. It had to date from the 1950s, when she was still young and hopeful.

The other showed a man tossing a baby playfully in the air. The shutter had clicked the instant the baby had left the man's hands, so the child seemed to be floating in space. From the expression in his eyes, he was either startled or frightened. As Brent examined the image closer, he realized he was the child. It was his father, Bill, who was tossing him in the air. The father who had left them.

No, not left them. Died. Died when Brent was still in junior high school. Now he remembered. But wasn't that a form of abandonment? One day Bill was there, the next day he wasn't. His mother had changed afterward, lost all her sense of fun and embraced the sour stoicism that hardened her features into a mask. Bill represented the high point of her life. Everything that came afterward was a spiraling off, a diminishment. How often had she said so?

And eventually Brent had left her, too.

Not the way his father had, although in the end, it amounted to the same thing. One absence had been just as final as the other.

Brent climbed the staircase with its worn, gray runner to the second floor and automatically entered the door to the left, knowing in advance that it was his old bedroom, seeing in his mind's eye the felt pennants in maroon and gold, his high school colors, before he saw them on the wall. A thick layer of dust covered the bureau, but the bed was made and his schoolbooks were still lined up along the back of the desk. Several of his old sports shirts still hung in the closet.

All those years, his mother had kept the room the way he had left it. Did she eventually realize he would never return? Or had she held out hope to the very end? What need, he wondered, had driven him so far from this house, had put him at such an emotional remove that he had never been prompted to come back?

He must have wanted something very desperately from the world. This bedroom, this house, Dover Plains—they'd been too small to contain the dreams. On the bed-side table, he saw a leather-bound book, almost the size of a scrapbook, with silver embossed lettering on the cover. He picked it up and leafed through the pages. It was *The Beacon*, his high school yearbook. He went to the index at the back and ran his finger down the names:

> *Capson, Steve, (22, 36, 49)*
> *Carlisle, Angela (24, 51)*
> *Carlson, John (25, 39, 43, 57)*
> *Carroll, Steve (26, 44, 61)*

Excited, he sat down on the bed and turned to page twenty-six. Sure enough, there was his graduation picture in a cap and gown. To meet the deadlines of the yearbook, it had been taken in midwinter, he recalled. The gradua-tion ceremony was a blank in his mind. Then it occurred to him why. He hadn't gone to it. He had fled from town several weeks before. A ridiculous question entered his mind: Had anyone bothered to pick up his diploma for him?

On page forty-four, there was a photo of the basketball team. He was second from the left in the third row and had his arms around the players on either side of him. He hadn't actually played in all that many games, but the cocky tilt of his head was no indication of his minor athletic status.

The photograph on page sixty-one gave him a jolt. The caption identified it as "a scene from *Double Trouble*, the Masque and Dagger Society's spring play." In it, two women were tugging a brash young man in different directions. The women wore the coy expressions of those who know they are posing for a camera, but the man had a natural charisma about him.

Brent had no trouble recognizing himself as the man in contention, or recollecting what he had felt so overpoweringly at that moment. That was when he'd discovered the visceral thrill of acting and sensed that there was a way out of the measly life that had been dealt him. In that instant, his penchant for pretending was exonerated. It had ceased being a moral flaw and become a calling, the key to his future. And the turning point was captured right there in the photograph. He regarded it with amazement and dismay.

He went back to the index, found "Anderson, Linda," and flipped to a picture on page twelve and stared at it for a while. Then he closed the album and lay it on the bed. His eyes slowly filled up with tears. The young girl in the photograph barely resembled the woman who had just deposited him on Oak Street. She was so much younger and prettier. All the radiance had gone from the older woman.

The girl in the photograph had a wealth of possibilities ahead of her. She shone. She looked exactly like the person who had passed him today in the pharmacy.

Melissa. His daughter.

26

As the train pulled out of the station at Dover Plains, Brent Stevens had an odd thought. He wasn't just leaving his hometown behind, he was leaving Steve Carroll there, too. It was almost as if his younger self was another person entirely, a distant relative with whom he shared certain family traits, but not a lot more.

Is that why he'd changed his name? To mark the difference, to say, "Hey, world, that's not who I am anymore. I'm a different person now." It seemed likely to him.

The doctor at the hospital had been right when she'd said the pieces would come together. The visit to Dover Plains had proved that. Dover Plains didn't explain everything. It didn't explain what he was doing in New York or how he came to find himself facedown in Central Park. But it had brought back some of his past.

He could remember clearly now how he once was—wanting so much more than the paltry life of his mother and straining to get away. And Linda, he remembered her, too. Not the tired, middle-aged woman, but the pretty, impulsive girl she'd once been.

He told himself that what had happened between them no longer mattered. It was so many years ago. She had become a different person, just as he had. Their lives had diverged. He'd gone to California, changed his name, started all over. Doing what, though? That part of it was less clear.

Not to worry. It would come back. The missing answers no longer terrified him with their remoteness, as they had several days ago in the hospital. He sensed they were within reach now. He settled back in his seat, let himself be lulled by the clickety-clack of the wheels on the train track, and fell into a light sleep.

The train deposited him in Grand Central Station at six-forty-five. By the time he'd caught the subway to Queens and walked the five blocks to Tina's house, it had grown dark.

Coming around the corner, he noticed that all the lights in the house were blazing. The Jeep Cherokee was parked in the driveway, which struck him as unusual. Johnny should have left for work by this time.

He climbed the concrete steps to the front door and rang the bell. Tina was in the kitchen, washing up the supper dishes. At the sound of the doorbell, she jumped. She looked over her shoulder with a startled expression, then reached for a towel to dry her hands.

"Oh, it's you, Brent," she said as she unlocked the door to let him in. "You scared me." She turned back and called up the stairs, "It's just Brent, Johnny."

"You were expecting somebody?"

"What? On, no, nobody. So how was the trip?"

"Fine . . . What's the matter? Why are you so nervous?"

"Am I? I thought I had it under control. We had a little problem today, that's all."

She locked the door behind him.

"What kind of a problem?" He hovered awkwardly in the entryway.

"Come in and sit down, at least," she said and waited until he had taken a seat on the sofa. "The house was broken into."

It was his turn to be startled. "When?"

"This afternoon, far as we can tell. Johnny was here all morning. Around noon, he says he took the Jeep down to the service station to get the oil changed and run a few errands. I picked up Angelina at school directly after work and arrived home before he did. It was about two-thirty when we got here. So it must have happened sometime in between."

"Did they take anything?"

"That's the strange part. It doesn't look like it. Maybe something will turn up missing later. Johnny says he can't find his high school ring. But I think he lost it a long time ago. I mean, who would want an old high school ring?"

"Nothing else is gone?"

"Nothing . . . odd, isn't it? But I'm certain someone was in here. As soon as I walked in, I felt it. You know how it is—when things aren't quite in the right place. The cushions of the sofa were askew and the doors to several of the kitchen cabinets were open. At first, I thought Johnny had been looking for something. He's not the neatest person in the world. But later when I went upstairs, my bedroom wasn't the way I'd left it, either. The closet doors were open and so was one of the bureau drawers. The pillows on the bed—well, this is nuts, but I swear to God they'd been fluffed up and rearranged. Johnny might tear up the living room, if he'd lost his keys or something, but he never ever goes into my room."

She was trying to maintain her composure, but Brent could see the effort it required. "Did you call the police?"

"I waited until Johnny came back, just to make certain it wasn't him. He was as surprised as I was. So, yeah, then we called the police. They just left about an hour ago. I don't think they took us very seriously. I mean, we couldn't tell them anything that was actually stolen. There were no signs of forced entry. Whoever it was probably came in by the kitchen window. The lock's been broken for months."

She got up and started pacing nervously. "It's my own fault. I've been wanting to get those burglar-proof windows installed for a long time. I just should have done it. But we haven't had the money. It's a big job. These are the original windows from when Ida bought the house. Anyone could get in, if they wanted to. A pair of tweezers is all it would take."

Before she had a chance to go on, Johnny clomped down the stairs.

"Well, look who's returned," he said as soon as he spotted Brent on the sofa. "Where the hell have you been?"

"I told you, Johnny," Tina said. "He went upstate."

"Well, did you? Did you go there?" Johnny asked.

"Yes. Dover Plains. I just got in. Tina told me what happened."

"You didn't come back in the middle of the day, by any chance? To get something you forgot, maybe?"

"No. I was gone all day." Johnny didn't look convinced. Brent was tempted to show him the stub of his train ticket but didn't. "Besides I don't have a key," he said.

"Yeah, well neither did the asshole who busted in here." Johnny shuffled over to the coat closet and yanked his jacket off a wire hanger, which came off the rod and fell to the floor. He left it there. "Tina, I gotta get to work. I can't afford to take the whole night off."

"It's okay. You can go now," she said. Then to Brent: "I asked him to wait until you came back. I wouldn't feel safe all alone."

"Where's Angelina?" Brent asked.

"Upstairs in her bedroom."

"How's she doing? Is she all right?"

"Well as can be expected. She was a little freaked out by the police. After they left, she asked if we could turn all the lights on in the house. I was kind of relieved she did. I would have done it anyway. When she realized how upset I was, she got pretty upset herself. That's the way it is with kids. They pick up on your mood. They're like these little blotters. She'll be happy to see you."

"I'll be happy to see her, too. Anything I can do, Tina?"

"Maybe you could tuck her in bed tonight. Tell her a story."

"Sure."

Johnny held up his key ring and jiggled it. "Hate to break up this party, but I'm late, Tina. Mind if I have a quick word with you in the kitchen before I scram?"

"Sure, Johnny." She gave Brent a weak smile. "Family conference. Only take a second."

Brent let them go. It was pretty clear Johnny didn't trust him, and he'd probably been giving Tina a rough time about it. That was no surprise. There *was* something traumatic about a break-in. Even if nothing had been stolen, as seemed to be the case, the space had nonetheless been violated. Somebody had gone through the rooms of the house, pawed over personal possessions.

Brent was the outsider. Why wouldn't Johnny think that he was somehow responsible?

He wasn't, of course. He'd been miles away—a whole world away—in Dover Plains, caught up in his own past. He was pretty confident that Tina believed that. She'd trusted him from the start, even when he was out of it and unsure of his name. Why would she start doubting him now? She was the one who had invited him to Queens. He hadn't invited himself. She had asked him in the hotel room . . . *the hotel room!* . . . His mind flashed back to the disorder—the stripped-down bed, the cushions out of place, his things pored over.

At first, the voices coming from the kitchen were too soft to hear, but as Johnny grew angrier, Brent could make out the conversation.

"You just can't pick up people off the street like stray animals."

"Johnny, the guy didn't have anyplace to go."

"So why is that our problem? What was wrong with the hospital? Does it ever occur to you that that's where he belongs?"

"No, he doesn't. He was just confused. And he didn't want to stay there. He's a lot better now."

"You said he's got money. He can go to a hotel."

Tina's voice rose in pitch to match her brother's. "Oh, yeah! In this city, it'll be gone in two days. Then what? Then what's he supposed to do?"

"Quiet down and listen to me. We don't know this guy. Who knows what he's up to? What if this memory thing is all a big act?"

"It's not an act, Johnny."

"So you're suddenly a big expert, are you? And what about today?"

"You're not going to blame the break-in on him. He was in upstate New York."

"How do you know? Because he told you! I swear, Tina! How do you manage to end up with so many losers?"

"One, he's not a loser, and two, I haven't 'ended up' with anybody. There's nothing between us. He's a stranger. I'm helping him out. Period."

"Exactly, a *stranger.* Don't forget that. All I'm saying is, Brent Sevens better figure out who he is and what he's doing damn quick, because this isn't a Holiday Inn we're running."

"Well, I'm glad he's here. I don't exactly relish the idea of Angelina and me being in this house all by ourselves."

"Okay, okay. I gotta go. We'll talk about it tomorrow. One other thing . . ."

"What?"

"Just make sure he doesn't eat all the pastrami."

The kitchen door clacked, feet thudded down the back steps, and a car motor growled in the driveway. With a squeal of tires, Johnny was gone.

A moment later, Tina emerged from the kitchen. "You must be hungry. Want something to eat?"

Brent looked up at her. She seemed wan and tired, as if bled of her usual energy.

"I heard what Johnny said."

Tina forced a causal shrug. "Oh, don't give it another thought. He's just upset. We all are. In all the years my family has lived in this house, nothing like this ever happened. We take our safety for granted around here, but I guess we can't anymore, especially with a kid. The old neighborhood is disappearing. Bound to sooner or later. But look on the bright side. Maybe Johnny will let me get those new windows now. Anyway, enough of that. I'll make you a pastrami sandwich."

They went into the kitchen and she busied herself at the counter. "I'm ready for some good news," she said, spreading mustard on two slices of rye. "Did you find out anything today?"

"Matter of fact, I did."

"Tell me, tell me."

"My name's Steve Carroll," he said.

She put a plate and paper napkin in front of him. "What are you talking about? You're not Brent Stevens?"

"Steve Carroll is the name I was born with. I changed it." He bit into the pastrami sandwich.

"Who told you this?"

"I saw the lawyer. Don Lobel. He knew me."

"Wow! That's great!" She pulled out a chair from the kitchen table and sat down opposite him. "What else did he say?"

"That's where I'm from. I grew up in Dover Plains. I even went by the old house. It doesn't look like I thought it would. Pretty run-down by now."

"That's exciting, Brent . . . Do I still call you Brent?"

"I guess so. It seems right." He took another healthy bite of pastrami.

"So you did remember some things. Like the doctor said?" She'd struck the discussion with Johnny from her mind, and her energy was flooding back.

"Some things. Quite a few things. But I left there a

long time ago. Eighteen years. I'd never been back until today. The old soda fountain hasn't changed. You know, where we hung out in high school. It's the same as it always was."

"What do you know! . . . Are your parents still there?"

"No. They're both dead." His voice dropped. "That's why I was planning to go there the other day—to settle my mother's estate. What little there is of it. It's not much. I signed some papers at the lawyer's."

"I'm sorry, Brent."

"That's all right. It happened a while ago."

"Did you see anybody else? Neighbors? Old friends?"

He paused, wiped his mouth with the paper napkin.

"No, I didn't," he said. "Everybody's gone. There's no one left."

Buoyed by the account, Tina pushed back her chair and began cleaning up. "Well, it's still encouraging news." She took his plate to the sink, rinsed it under the faucet, then wiped down the table with a sponge. "I bet this is just the beginning. You'll see. I feel it in my bones. Don't you?"

"I hope so. Well, yeah, I suppose I do."

She opened the cabinet under the sink, took the plastic garbage bag out of the container, and tied the drawstrings tight. She was halfway to the back door, when she stopped. "Brent, would you mind?"

He jumped up from the table. "Sure. Where do I put it?"

"Just come with me. It's silly, but I'm still a little spooked by what happened this afternoon."

"Give me the trash bag. I'll do it."

"No, if the neighbor's dog doesn't know you, he'll go

214

nuts and wake up the whole neighborhood with his barking. Just come with me, okay?"

Brent followed her down the porch steps. A chain-link fence separated the yard from the one next door. The garbage cans sat in a cluster at the end of the lot on the cement alleyway. Clouds had settled over the night sky, masking the stars, but the light spilling from the porch made a narrow corridor of illumination, bright enough for them to see their way.

"Be careful you don't trip on all this junk," Tina said. "We should have taken in Angelina's wading pool this winter. We're going to have to get her a new one." In the darkness, it looked rather like a large fish that had washed up on the shore and expired.

The trash cans had been thrown around cavalierly by the sanitation men and had the dents and scrapes to prove it. Tina had to tug to get the lid off one of them, but it finally came free with a clank. Brent deposited the trash bag in the empty receptacle, and with another clank, the lid was clapped back on. "Good thing these things aren't made of china," Tina cracked.

She turned to go back inside the house when she noticed the trash bag on the other side of the fence. It had been just pitched there, where it could attract rats, if it hadn't already. What was the point of garbage cans, if no one used them? Johnny was bad enough, but if she was going to have to start picking up for the neighbors, too!

"People are such slobs," she said to Brent, and let out a martyred sigh. "Look what they've left on—"

She cut herself off. It wasn't a bag of trash there on the ground. It was the German shepherd, sprawled on its side up against the fence, fast asleep. She was surprised the animal hadn't been roused by the noise she and Brent had been making.

"Prince?" she called out and made a cluck-clucking sound with her tongue. When the dog didn't respond, she bent down to take a closer look. "Hey, boy! Is Prince being a good pooch tonight?"

The dog was lying in a pool of blood, its head twisted to one side, its eyes glassy. Someone had slit its throat. In the dim light from the back porch, it appeared to be wearing a bright red collar.

27

The cabin of the Lear jet was outfitted with swiveling leather armchairs, a large television screen, and a mobile bar. On a small scale, it successfully evoked a plush Las Vegas cocktail lounge. As the plane streaked eastward, the sky deepened from navy blue to black. The occasional cluster of twinkling lights indicated a farm town below, but such signs of habitation were like haphazard punctuation marks on a vast scroll of darkness.

Jennifer lifted a champagne glass to her lips.

"Tut, tut."

She looked across the aisle at her husband.

"One sip is all. Remember the baby."

"Right as ever, darling. Not even a sip from now on."

She put down the glass, gazed out the window at the blackness, and let her thoughts go to the future.

Tomorrow night the *Deborah Myers Special*—one full hour devoted to Mr. and Mrs. Christopher Knight and *In the Beginning*—would be aired and the world would hear that she was a mother-to-be. The prospect of setting a few tongues wagging was one that she contemplated with delight. The following night, the film itself would have its premiere in New York. That thrilled her less, but it had been their publicist's idea, and when His Lordship had an idea . . . !

The Ziegfeld Theater, where the premiere was to be held, was a big drafty picture palace decorated with an excess of red velvet. But it occupied a site not far from where Ziegfeld's own theater had stood until the wreckers had knocked it down in the 1960s, so it meant glamour in Geoffrey Reed's mind. With klieg lights in front sweeping the Manhattan skyline and crowds massed on bleachers, screaming at the stars as they emerged from the limousines to parade down a red carpet, it would be a good, old-fashioned premiere, he argued. Jennifer's fears, precisely! Old-fashioned and out-of-date.

But that was Geoffrey. He should have lived back in the 1930s, when movie stars were thought of as royalty and the press played along with the charade. The 1990s were trickier to negotiate, and she and Christopher knew it. What they called "the Geoffrey problem" would have to be resolved soon. After the premiere, though. There were pressures enough with the film, which would be opening on a whopping 2,500 screens.

Already, controversy was coming to a boil. In yet another fulminating article that asked "Is it Art or Is It Blasphemy?" the Reverend Greenway had declared his belief that Satan clearly had a hand in the film. A number of religious groups were threatening a boycott. The studio, counting on the enduring power of human curiosity, was trying not to be nervous, but $100 million were on the line. If *In the Beginning* failed, it would fail big. Jennifer banished that unpleasant scenario from her mind and brought her attention back to the other passengers in the jet.

The attractive couple in their early thirties, Dolly and

Ned Hobart, were the stars' closest friends and could some-times be spotted in the paparazzi's shots, standing in the background, slightly out of focus. The large sixtyish woman was Eleanor Osborne, Jennifer's mother, a dour and conser-vative person by nature who rarely passed up the chance to attend a premiere or visit her daughter on location. Apart from the two pilots, the only other person on board was Jim Perkins, Christopher's personal assistant, who was currently in charge of keeping everyone's champagne glass full and was doing a good job of it. He was still new enough in the position, Jennifer mused, to be a little starry-eyed.

"Chris, dear, did you return Geoffrey's call?" she asked her husband, who was perched casually on the edge of Ned's chair, regaling him and Dolly with show business anecdotes.

The actor let out a groan. "Did you have to bring that up? Just when we were all starting to have fun." He tilted back his glass and drained it. "Jim called him before we left, didn't you, Jim?"

"Yes, sir," the assistant replied. "He wanted to know what time you were getting in tonight."

"I hope you didn't tell him."

"I'm afraid I did. Then he asked if dinner tomorrow night at the Four Seasons would be all right?"

"What did you say?"

"That I would get back to him."

"Good man! You're learning," the actor said, clapping his assistant on the back.

"He seemed rather annoyed that I was returning the call, not you."

"Yes, well that's our Geoffrey in a nutshell—seriously annoyed!"

"Chris," spoke up Jennifer. "I won't sit there at dinner and listen to him try to change your mind."

"My mind's made up, dear. You know that."

"Then why can't we make a clean break now?"

"Because now's not the time. We're Adam and Eve this week. Remember? You can be Salome and ask for his head soon enough."

"Very funny!"

"I do wish you two could be more serious," piped up Eleanor Osborne, who was feeling the heightened sense of righteousness that alcohol brought out in her.

"I take everything seriously, Mother, except life."

"What kind of remark is that?" sniffed the older woman.

"A clever one? . . . Oh, never mind."

"And this film of yours. Adam and Eve! I've told you what I think."

"Yes you have. Several times."

"Well, some things are sacred to people. You don't fool with them."

"Mother, it's just a movie."

Eleanor Osborne's readiness to mount a soapbox with little or no encouragement was not so easily checked. "I read where there may be protests. I can tell you right now I'm not going to walk by a bunch of people who are yelling at me. I'd rather stay at home. There are so many things you could have made a movie about. Why on earth did you have to pick this?"

Jennifer rolled her eyes and sent a silent plea of help across the aisle to Dolly Hobart. Do something, it said, before my mother and I get into one of our rows. Dolly had seen it before and promptly intervened.

"Mrs. Osborne, I never showed you the pictures from the wedding, did I?"

"What wedding?"

"Ours. Ned's and mine. Hand me my bag, Ned."

"I told you all about it, Mother," Jennifer said. "Chris was the best man and I was the maid of honor."

"*Matron* of honor. If you are a married woman, you are the *matron* of honor."

"Matron of honor? It sounds like a prison guard at her retirement ceremony," said Christopher blithely.

Disregarding the quip, Dolly handed a stack of photographs to Eleanor Osborne. "Here."

"They look like vacation pictures to me," noted the older woman, disapprovingly, an observation that was not entirely unfounded. In several of the pictures, Dolly, Ned, Christopher, and Jennifer cavorted in an aqua blue ocean while others showed them hiking in luxuriant tropical vegetation. In still others, they lounged poolside and toasted the photographer with exotic drinks the color of a violent sunburn. They all had the carefree spirit of models in cigarette ads that try to equate the fresh taste of tobacco with the invigorating spray of the ocean.

Dolly and Ned were every bit as photogenic as Christopher and Jennifer. Dolly, with her short dark hair, well-toned body, and one-piece bathing suit could have been the captain of an Olympic diving team. Ned, slighter than Christopher, came across as a bright young intellectual by way of Princeton, especially when he wore his wire-rimmed glasses.

"We were married on Virgin Gorda. It's part of the British Virgin Islands." Dolly explained. "There are some photos of the actual ceremony at the bottom." She reached over and shuffled through the pack until she came to a shot of her and Ned, in flowered shorts, standing in front of a bamboo altar. The minister—a round and ebullient black man—beamed at the camera. On either side, were Jennifer and Christopher, she with a pink hibiscus pinned in her hair, he with one tucked behind his ear. "An hour after the ceremony, we all went in swimming."

Eleanor Osborne was unimpressed. "Marriage is a holy sacrament. It shouldn't be mocked."

Jennifer could sense another argument on the horizon. "We were just having a good time."

"Don't you two work?" The question was directed straight at Dolly and Ned.

"Mother!"

"I was just wondering. They seem to be able to pick up and go anywhere at the drop of a hat."

"We're lucky to have good friends who like to spend time with us," Christopher said.

"Well, they always seem to be around, that's all."

"I'm an architect, Mrs. Osborne," offered Ned, who had grown used to Eleanor Osborne's presence on official outings and took no offense at her outspokenness. "Dolly's a freelance writer. Our schedules are pretty flexible."

"That's very nice for you, I must say. In my time, work meant nine to five. Five days a week. And sometimes on Saturday, too. Nothing flexible about it."

"Times have changed, Mother," Jennifer said, her patience coming to an end. "One day, you'll understand."

Eleanor Osborne sat upright and her face, flush from the champagne, registered a sudden change. "Don't get fresh with me!" she said in a voice sharp with anger.

"Oh, Mother, please!"

"I understand plenty, young lady. I understand a lot more than you think."

28

The following morning, Tina was back to her usual cheerful self. Her energy was up, her face had color, and she looked as if she had enjoyed a restful night's sleep. She had called a window company and they'd promised to send out a salesman the following week. In the meantime, Johnny had nailed the kitchen window shut. If she was still upset about the break-in or the neighbor's dog, she gave no signs of it. Brent wondered how she managed.

He'd lain on the living room couch for hours, tossing, fidgeting, unable to fall sleep. Around three, he'd stopped trying and had sat up in the darkness for a while, thinking. His mind wouldn't shut down. The trip to Dover Plains had awakened a lot of long dormant memories, but it wasn't the past that troubled him. It was the present.

Only a few hours earlier, the house had been gone through, just as his hotel room had. Maybe it was a coincidence. Robberies were not exactly unknown in New York. Except that nothing had been taken in either case. The intruder appeared to be searching for something specific. And if it wasn't a coincidence, in all probability that "something" was Brent's. But there he came up against a blank. His personal belongings were without value. And his wallet and papers had already been stolen. So what could it be?

He was sure he had gotten away from the thug, who had threatened him at the hospital. Anybody asking for him at the hotel would be informed he'd checked out abruptly and, presumably, left the city. There was no reason for anyone to think he was in Queens. Until he'd met Tina, Brent had never been there! Yet he had the unsettling feeling that he was being watched.

Whoever it was, whoever *they* were, they were observing his comings and goings, observing Tina and Johnny, too. When the house was empty, they'd come right in with hardly any effort at all and searched it from top to bottom. What would they do next?

He chose not to discuss his thoughts with Tina at breakfast. Having clearly got out of the right side of the bed, she was seeing only the positive side of things. The break-in had not been forgotten, but it had been relegated to a separate part of her mind and she refused to dwell on it. Instead she wanted to talk about "the discoveries" Brent had made in Dover Plains. She had gone back over their pile of evidence that morning—the various notes, the locker key, and the ticket stub—and devised a plan of attack.

She had to work out several clients, but her early afternoon appointment was on the Upper East Side. She could meet Brent afterward and they could look into the Lisa connection. In one of the angry messages the woman had left for him at the hotel, there was mention of a Madison Avenue address. Number 635. It was worth checking out.

They could also go by the theater where *Crime and Punishment* was playing. Who could tell what would come of that? And maybe the Port Authority Bus Terminal. That, Tina admitted, was a long shot. But the terminal had to have public lockers, and the orange-tipped key could well have come from one of them.

A quick phone call was all it took to arrange for Angelina to spend the afternoon at her friend Megan's house after school.

"You'll see. We're going to unlock the rest of the mystery that is Brent Stevens," Tina announced, slapping her hands together enthusiastically. Brent tried to echo her enthusiasm, but he wondered if there wasn't something behind it. He had invaded their house and disrupted their routines. Johnny hadn't bothered to hide his displeasure last night.

Maybe Tina just wanted to clean up the mess that was Brent Stevens, so they could get back to their normal lives without him.

Madison Avenue remained one of the civilized streets of New York, at least the section that stretched north from Fifty-ninth Street. The buildings, which were fairly low to the ground, housed art galleries and exclusive shops, and the windows were filled with luxury goods alluringly displayed. The pedestrian traffic was less frantic here, slowed by the window-shoppers who, like birds to bits of aluminum foil, were drawn instinctively to bright and shiny things.

The west side of the avenue lay in shadow, but the afternoon sun warmed the east side, where the odd numbers were located. Tina and Brent scoured the doorways for 635.

"We'll just have to ask for Lisa and see what happens,"

she said, switching her dance bag from one shoulder to the other. "A last name would help. But how many Lisas can there be at one place? It's not like Christy or Amanda. Half of Angelina's classmates are named Amanda or Christy. I think there's even a Christy-Amanda! . . . So I wonder if Lisa ever got over her snit?"

As soon as they came upon 635, Brent's hopes melted. It was one of the sleek new office buildings, forged of steel and glass, that were slowly creeping north and altering the scale of the neighborhood. The impersonality of the two-story marble lobby told him that few of the tenants were likely to be known by their first names. Identification cards were probably required to get in.

They pushed through the revolving glass doors only to run up against a uniformed security guard, who gave them a cursory glance. "Can I help you?"

Tina started to ask him if he knew anybody called Lisa and quickly thought better of it.

"Oh, we were just checking on an address," she improvised. Spotting the directory on the far wall by the elevators, she pointed to it and said, "Do you mind if we take a look?"

"Go ahead."

Their heels clicked sharply on the marble floor. "Been here before?" Tina whispered to Brent, knowing even as she asked the question that the antiseptic lobby was no different from hundreds of lobbies in hundreds of cities. The negative nod of his head did not surprise her.

More than thirty firms were listed on the directory, starting with the Allure Model Agency and ending, three columns over, with J. Witherspoon & Associates.

"I don't suppose you were coming here for a modeling

job," Tina said. "What's this? The Society for the Advancement of Inner Peace? I've been searching for inner peace all my life. Who knew you could find it right here on Madison Avenue?" The stab at humor failed to revive their hopes.

Two floors of the building were given over to the Informer News Agency.

"What do you know! My mother's Bible!" said Tina.

Brent looked at her blankly.

"Obviously you don't spend much time in supermarket checkout lanes. The *Informer* is one of those rags that tells you how to lose twenty pounds in two days or how many members of Congress are really aliens. For some reason my mother ate it up. It was her main source of news. I'd tell her they just made those stories up, but she insisted they would never do such a thing. That would be against the law . . . Pretty classy address for a scandal sheet!"

Most of the names on the directory were those of companies or associations. They sounded respectable and important, but what business they were engaged in was impossible to tell. J. Witherspoon and his associates could have been dealers in fine art or white slavers. Only half a dozen individuals were listed, their names followed by cryptic initials that probably meant they were doctors or lawyers. There was a sole woman: Gertrude Blau, a dermatologist.

No Lisa.

"Hey, it was worth a try." Tina shrugged. The click of their footsteps followed them to the revolving door. Her mind seemed to be elsewhere.

"I think my absolute favorite headline of all times was 'Michael Jackson to Wed Chimp,'" she said. "For some reason, that one I had no trouble believing!" She let out a guffaw that bounced off the marble walls as they exited into the sunlight.

The city's major performing arts groups were housed in the sleek marble and glass buildings that opened on to Lincoln Center Plaza. But much as people were drawn to the spot by the heady delights of culture, they also came for the plaza itself. The edge of the circular fountain in the center was a popular place to sit and take the sun, especially when a breeze was blowing and a cooling mist came off the jets of water.

In the summer, a section of the plaza was actually turned into an open-air ballroom at night. A live band played pop hits from decades past, couples did the fox-trot and the mambo under the stars, and New York didn't seem like New York at all, but a friendly provincial European city.

As they crossed the pavement, Brent's eye was attracted to the Chagall murals in the windows of the Metropolitan Opera House, luminescent in the afternoon light, and he felt a stir of recognition. Unlike the office building they'd just left, he knew he'd been here recently.

The Vivian Beaumont Theater was tucked off to one side, at the end of a reflecting pool that resembled a low-slung coffee table. In the glass wall, fronting the pool, neon script advertised the current attraction. The acid green letters that spelled out *Crime and Punishment* shimmered in the glassy water.

Brent stared down at the reflections, and the stirring in his head turned into a certainty. "I *was* here before. I remember how bright those reflections were. It must have been at night."

"That makes sense," Tina said, perking up. "Your ticket was for an evening performance. It would have been dark out."

Just outside the entrance, two large sandwich boards had been set up in an effort to woo undecided theatergoers. One was a poster for the show and depicted a celestial white light, shining through an open door. MATINEE TODAY, read a banner, pasted across the top. At the bottom, in alphabetical order, were the names of the cast members and the various designers.

"Look. There's a Lisa Littlejohn in the show," Tina said, pointing to a name in small print. "Could she be Lisa?"

Brent thought for a while. "I don't think so."

The names on the poster meant no more to him than those on the directory of 635 Madison.

The other sandwich board was a blowup of a favorable review the play had received in one of the daily newspapers. "Dostoievsky Sings!" trumpeted the headline. As they combed it for clues, the double doors leading into the auditorium burst open and theatergoers began to spill into the lobby for intermission.

An irate woman paused near them to scan the review while she angrily tugged on her coat. "I'd like to know what show *he* saw!" she sputtered, then stormed off across the plaza. By the dazed looks on many faces, it seemed that her reaction was not an uncommon one. Before long, the lobby had filled up and the concession stand was doing a brisk business in wine and other anesthetizing beverages.

"Let's take a look inside, while we can," Tina suggested. Together, they pushed though all the bodies toward the auditorium doors. The two ushers, engaged in conversation, paid little attention to the crowd, figuring that no one was going to crash the second act of this show. Brent and Tina slipped past them.

Unlike most Broadway theaters, which were old and cramped, the Vivian Beaumont had been designed with a view to comfort. Beyond the auditorium doors, a wide corridor wrapped around the back of the orchestra. Lockers lined both sides of the corridor so that patrons didn't have to take their coats with them to their seats or queue up at an overcrowded hat check window.

Four quarters, deposited in a slot, opened the locker and freed the key, which the spectator kept until reclaiming his affairs at the end of the show. Because of the nice weather, few lockers were in use. Most of them still had the plastic-tipped keys in their slots.

It took a moment for Brent to realize the tips were orange.

"Tina . . . look."

"Mother of God! You don't suppose . . ." She let the sentence die while Brent thrust his hands in his pockets and withdrew his key. The number 102 was stamped on the end.

They were in front of 608, which meant that 102 was at the other end of the corridor.

He took off at a trot with Tina in close pursuit.

"If it's drugs, remember, I warned you," she called out to his back. "On the other hand, if it's just a raincoat, I'm going to be really disappointed."

But it was neither.

Locker number 102 was empty except for a large manila envelope sitting on the shelf where hats and gloves would normally be stored. Brent reached up and gingerly took it down. There was no writing on the outside and the flap was tightly sealed with masking tape.

He was about to open it when they heard a chiming of bells, and one of the ushers announced, "Ladies and gentlemen, take your seats, please. The second act of *Crime and Punishment* is about to begin."

There were some scattered grumbles and the human tide that had washed out into the lobby minutes earlier reluctantly began reversing itself.

Fighting the crowd, Tina and Brent inched their way back into the lobby.

"Open it, Brent. I can't stand it any longer," she urged when they finally got to a clearing.

The tape came off with a dry rip. Inside the envelope were two smaller envelopes. The first one contained a plain, unmarked video cassette. Brent turned it over several times. "What do you think this is?"

"A movie?"

"Of what?"

"You're asking me?"

The second, thicker envelope posed no mystery. In it were a stack of about thirty eight-by-ten glossies and two strips of negatives. When she saw the glossy on top, Tina automatically sucked in her breath and checked to make sure nobody was looking over their shoulders. Brent flipped through the pile, not quite believing what he was seeing either, then quickly slid the photographs back in the envelope, wishing he'd never opened it.

"I hope you have an explanation for this," Tina said. "Come on, Brent, say something."

But he just stood there, dumbstruck, as a few stragglers in the lobby polished off their drinks before hastening back to their seats.

"Well," she continued. "If nothing else, I think we have a clue to what the fuss is all about."

The manila envelope sat on the kitchen counter in Queens while they had dinner and cleaned up the dishes. By unspoken agreement, Tina and Brent were waiting until Angelina had gone to bed before reexamining its contents. All during the meal, the child chattered enthusiastically about art class at school (she'd made a teddy bear out of an oatmeal box) and Megan's new doll, which grew hair.

"Well, it doesn't actually *grow*," she explained. "You have to pull it to make it longer. But it's *like* growing."

The mood was uneasy just the same, and Tina found it hard to listen. A day that had begun as a big adventure had taken a nasty turn, and she was trying not to think the worst.

By nine, Angelina was talked out and required no persuading to go to bed.

The kitchen fell quiet.

Brent picked up the envelope and held it in his hands, unwilling for a moment to proceed. When he finally removed the photographs from the envelope, he did so warily, as if he were letting a small animal out of a cage and wasn't sure if it would bite or not. Tina stood back from him, chewing nervously on a nail, disinclined to confront head-on what she knew to be unsavory.

Some of the photographs were blurrier than others, but there was no mistaking their pornographic nature. They showed two couples, their bodies enlaced in a variety of explicit sexual acts. Even though the faces were not always visible, the people were young and fit, and one of the women was even quite beautiful. These were not tired models, simulating the sad contortions of sex for a fee, Tina thought. Their passion was real, and when you could make out the faces, they were etched with ecstasy.

Tina had a sick feeling in her stomach.

Then, the realization hit. "My God, Brent," she said, incredulous. "That looks just like . . . that woman, that movie star . . . Jennifer Osborne."

She took the photographs from him and examined them more carefully. "I swear it is . . . I don't believe this . . . And isn't the man Christopher Knight? Tell me I'm seeing things." She handed the pictures back.

Brent didn't have to take a second look. He knew she was right. Anyone who'd been to the movies in the past ten years would have had no difficulty recognizing the stars. These were no look-alikes. They were the real people, doing the real thing.

A more shocking discovery was still to come: Jennifer Osborne was making love to another woman. The person with Christopher Knight was a man. Yet there were no orgy shots, no group gropes, nothing that could be explained as a party that had gotten out of hand. There weren't even any shots of the famous actor and actress together. All the photographs depicted same-sex couplings. Man with man, woman with woman. It was hard for Tina to know which was more disturbing—the identity of the people or the candor of their acts.

"How did you get these?" she managed to ask.

"I'm not sure."

"You have no idea where they came from? Are you telling me you just found them someplace?"

"No, of course not. I must have put them in the locker. I mean, I did. Obviously."

"Well, did someone give them to you? Pictures like these don't just turn up out of thin air. These are famous people, Brent."

"I know that." In his agitation, he was unable to come up with an explanation. Everyone knew Christopher Knight and Jennifer Osborne, so the fact that he had recognized them, too, didn't necessarily mean anything. His mind was muddled.

He couldn't put names to the other two people, nor could he tell where the pictures had been taken. They appeared to have been shot in plain daylight through a window. What could be seen of the bedroom—or bedrooms—was unremarkable. In one picture, a vase of exotic flowers stood on the bedside table. In another, the figures were completely blurred, but oddly enough, a ceiling fan was in focus. As with most pornography, the surroundings seemed irrelevant.

But this was more than pornography. The pictures had been snapped without the subjects' knowledge. Unaware of anything but their immediate pleasure, these people were being spied upon. Not only had their naked bodies been caught in a state of arousal, but the photographs conveyed the impression that their psyches had been ravaged as well.

Only one thing was clear to Brent. It had come to him as soon as he'd opened the envelope in the lobby of the theater, and it was why he'd resealed the package so hastily. And it came to him again here in the kitchen in

Queens. He knew who had taken these photographs. He didn't even have to ask himself how he knew, either.

He had pressed the shutter.

Tina gave out a long, troubled sigh. "Do you suppose this is why you were attacked in the park and what the threats are about? Somebody doesn't want this stuff to get out. Not that I blame them. I'd kill anyone who had shots like this of me. And I'm not even famous."

Brent walked away from the counter and tried to marshal his thoughts. He must have known about the lockers beforehand. That's why he'd gone to the theater—to hide the photographs there. He had no recollection of the play, because he hadn't stayed to watch it. He'd simply deposited the package in the locker and left. Which meant that Tina was right: somebody did want them from him.

"I know this is none of my business, Brent," she said. "But in a way, it sort of is, so I'm afraid I have to ask you this." She put the back of her hand to her mouth, as if she didn't like the words that she was about to blurt out. "By any chance, do you think you might have taken those pictures?"

"Me?"

"Is it possible, I mean?" She was looking him squarely in the eye.

He found himself looking back at her, his eyes round and unblinking, convinced that she would trust him in spite of appearances. "Do you think that's something I would do, Tina?"

"I can't say . . . What I mean is . . . no. Of course, not . . . Oh, shit, I don't know . . . I thought we were going to be able to straighten everything out today. It's just gotten more complicated, that's all."

"I can imagine what you're thinking. You must be wondering what I've dragged you into. I can't explain it, Tina. Not yet. So, if you want me to leave, I will. I appreciate the help you've given me. What would have happened to me otherwise? I don't know how to thank you for that. But I'll understand if you want me out of here. I can go right now . . ."

Tina let the offer sink in. Then she tossed her hands in the air. "Ah, don't listen to me. Paula H. Prude! So you've got a few dirty pictures. Big deal. I hate to think what Johnny has stashed away in his room . . . No, stay, Brent. We'll figure this out."

She sat back down at the kitchen table, rested her chin in the palm of her hand, and thought.

"Do you think these pictures are from some porno flick they made before they were famous? You're always reading about things like that. Didn't Sylvester Stallone make one?"

Both sets of eyes went to the video cassette on the counter.

"Well, there's always one way to find out, isn't there?" Tina said. "Let the games begin."

She popped it into the VCR in the living room. There was a brief blizzard of snow on the TV screen before the picture came on and the snow was replaced by an amorphous blue pattern that turned out to be water. Slowly, the camera panned up to reveal an empty white sand beach, fringed with palm trees, then turned back out to the ocean and tracked a couple of sailboats in the distance. The video appeared to be nothing more than a homemade travelogue about some tropical island.

That impression was not altered by what followed:

footage of rough junglelike terrain, dense with low-growing trees and vines that had been taken from the window of a moving car. Pink and purple hibiscus bushes flashed by. Now and then, the road opened onto a clearing and a tidy cinder block cottage, its tin roof painted fire-engine red or peacock green.

"What is this—Hawaii?" Tina wondered out loud.

Suddenly, the video cut to a small clapboard church, with gaily colored shutters propped open to take advantage of the breeze. Standing in the doorway, a large black man in a flowered shirt beamed at the camera and extended his arms in welcome. One of his front teeth was gold and caught the light. In the next sequences, shot inside the church, a casually dressed couple stood before a bamboo altar, holding hands. The black man seemed to be performing a ceremony.

"It's just somebody's wedding," Tina concluded, relieved that the video didn't depict more X-rated love-making.

The couple kissed and then turned sheepishly toward the camera and laughed. The preacher allowed himself to kiss the bride, then he, too, broke into an expansive laugh and shook both of the newlyweds' hands. The folksiness of the moment was unintentionally underscored by the art-less camerawork.

Whoever was recording the event pulled back, and a second couple came into view. They were casually dressed in shorts, exceptionally good-looking, and both had flowers in their hair. They seemed to be the witnesses, because another round of kisses and congratulatory handshakes ensued, then all four people clustered close together and made silly faces for the cameraman.

"Wait a second," Tina said. "Isn't that—"

"Yeah, it is," Brent interrupted. The witnesses were Jennifer Osborne and Christopher Knight, looking so radiant and relaxed that it was difficult to believe they were also the writhing figures in the black and white photographs. As the video continued with what amounted to innocuous vacation footage—more beach scenes, a picnic, a hike—Brent sat riveted to the television. He was trying to recall the secluded island, the beach, the church. Because another certainty had come to him: The photographs and the video had all been taken in the same place at the same time by the same person.

The tape ended and the blizzard of snow reappeared. Tina pressed the eject button. The video cassette popped out of the machine and the television screen reverted to a show already in progress.

Deborah Myers was looking directly at them.

". . . two of the biggest stars in Hollywood. They are powerful, they are self-assured, they are sexy. For one full hour, Christopher Knight and Jennifer Osborne talk about their careers, their marriage, and their biggest gamble yet—the controversial $100 million epic *In the Beginning*, in which they play Adam and Eve. We'll have a preview. Stay with us."

Tina gulped.

"You have our full attention," she said, sinking into the sofa next to Brent.

Two security guards were stationed by the elevator to turn back anybody who got off by mistake on the fifteenth floor and chanced to wander in the wrong direction. The interconnecting suites at the end of the corridor were officially occupied by "N. Hobart and party." But the hotel staff knew that that was the cover for Christopher Knight, Jennifer Osborne, and their friends. The one thing the Carlyle prided itself on—even more than the understated elegance and impeccable service—was the total privacy it guaranteed its famous guests.

Jennifer's mother and Christopher's assistant had been given rooms on a lower floor, although both of them had gathered soon after, along with Ned and Dolly Hobart, in the larger of the two suites. Geoffrey Reed had called almost immediately, wanting to make dinner arrangements, but Christopher had begged off, saying that they were exhausted from the long trip.

"Tell him we're going to have a pajama party and watch Deborah Myers," Jennifer had called out. Christopher had simply said something about making an early night of it. They would talk in the morning.

The management had provided the sumptuous buffet as a welcome. Jennifer and Dolly barely picked at the fruit and cheeses, but Eleanor Osborne, having fewer concerns about her figure, had shown correspondingly less constraint, along with a growing willingness to speak her mind.

All through the opening segments of the *Deborah Myers Special*, the plump woman had offered her running comments until Jennifer finally had to tell her mother to be quiet.

Now that the two-minute film clip of *In the Beginning* had come on the screen, the woman was keeping her tongue only with considerable effort. The question on everyone's mind was how the network censors would handle the nudity. Just as the camera was about to reach Jennifer's breasts, the focus went soft and fuzzy.

"The cowards!" roared Christopher. Ned joined in the laughter.

Dolly applauded gleefully. "If that doesn't sell tickets, I don't know what will."

Eleanor Osborne was unable to contain herself. "I think I have seen enough for one evening," she sputtered, standing up and brushing the crumbs off her lap.

"Sit down, Mother. It's almost over." It had become obvious to Jennifer that including her mother on this outing had been a mistake. She had hoped that the woman's presence at the premiere might help dispel some of the controversy. After all, if a middle-class matron like Eleanor Osborne found the film acceptable, others with similar backgrounds might not be so wary. Now, Jennifer concluded, it wasn't worth putting up with her mother's temperament and innuendos. She focused on the TV program again.

"So it looks as if Hollywood's first couple is about to become Hollywood's first family . . ."

Deborah Myers oozed sincerity, as if few announcements in recent history had brought her such pleasure. Then, she turned to the home viewers and thanked them all for watching, and managed to imply that their devotion, week after week, special after special, meant even more to her!

The credits rolled over outtakes of the stars, walking with Deborah along the beach at Malibu.

Jennifer caught Christopher's eye and knew they were thinking the same thing. They'd pulled it off. The program had a few choppy edits, but there hadn't really been a false moment. They both looked good—for that, they should probably send Deborah Myers's lighting man a case of champagne. Even better, they came across as real people, with a real marriage and real aspirations. And a kid on the way, too! That kind of publicity couldn't be bought.

Not yet over her pique, Eleanor Osborne felt obliged to make one more point. "I think you'll have a very different view of things once you are a mother, Jennifer."

"What do you mean?"

"Maybe you will think twice about prancing around in the buff. Have you thought about how you are going to feel, when your child sees that movie a few years from now? Or some friend of your child rents it at the video store?"

Jennifer let her mother rant on. Eleanor Osborne was enjoying having one up on her daughter, who had been strong-willed from the start and had grown up entirely too fast for her liking. Eleanor didn't know much about movies or stardom or Jennifer's friends, but she did know about being a mother. For the moment, she felt on high ground and in a position to instruct her daughter once again.

"No, I bet you haven't thought about it at all. You'll find out soon enough. A child changes your perspective on everything." With that, she announced that she would like to go to her room. Christopher's assistant, Jim, volunteered to accompany her.

Once Mrs. Osborne had gone, Ned observed, "What your mother doesn't realize is that this child is going to have the most unique perspective of all—with four parents."

"It's going to be *two*, Ned, not four," Jennifer reminded him.

"Two parents and two devoted *god*parents," Dolly said.

"That sounds great to me," concurred Christopher. "Let's start with that scenario and work out the rest as we go along."

Jennifer looked at her husband approvingly. "Chris has always been terribly good at improvisation."

"I have to be with you, darling. I almost hit the floor when you announced to Deborah Myers that you were pregnant. Honest! If you'd told me in advance, I could have prepared. We could have rehearsed."

"It just came to me on the spot. Besides, you were brilliant, as usual."

"Always living on the edge. My wife—I think I'll keep her." Christopher gave her a peck on the cheek and then ran his fingers through Ned's hair. "I think I'll keep you, too."

"Come on, hon," Jennifer said, pulling Dolly gently to her. "I know a cue when I hear it. Time to leave the boys alone."

Arms linked, the two women passed into the adjoining suite and the connecting door was shut tight.

29

The reception room could have been that of any success-ful East Side plastic surgeon, with its tasteful off-white sofas and the abstract paintings in mauve and gray. Nothing indicated the scurrilous mission of the Informer News Agency or the fact that, elevated as its offices were, some ten floors above Madison Avenue, spiritually speaking its heart dwelled in the gutter.

"Mr. Stevens?"

Brent looked up to see an immaculately coiffed woman in her thirties, wearing a sober business suit with a Hermes scarf draped artfully over one shoulder. She could have been the plastic surgeon's wife or one of the more successful examples of his handiwork.

"I'm Lisa Jacobson." The woman extended her hand forthrightly. "I was beginning to wonder if we were ever going to meet. Won't you come this way?"

Brent passed by the receptionist, who only minutes before had regarded him with some disdain when he had asked for "a person called Lisa." He had no last name to give her, and the receptionist wasn't predisposed toward supplying one. At Brent's insistence, she had spoken to someone on the intercom, cupping her hand over the mouthpiece so he couldn't hear what was being said, and Lisa Jacobson had materialized.

He followed her and her gently rippling scarf down the carpeted hall to an office with rich, mahogany furniture. He had been expecting stacks of yellowing newspapers, ashtrays overflowing with cigarettes, and maybe even a plastic Jesus on the wall, miraculously dripping blood. The understated elegance made him wonder if he had totally misconstrued the nature of the Informer News Agency.

She took a seat behind the desk and motioned for him to sit opposite her. "Can I get you anything to drink? Coffee? A soda," she said, the solicitous hostess.

"No, nothing, thanks."

"Well, then." She took a second to adjust her scarf and adopt a more businesslike air. "I must say I was a little disappointed when I didn't hear from you the other day. We thought we had reached a preliminary agreement. You did get our welcoming gift?"

He figured she meant the $1,000 and said he had.

"So you can understand why we expected you to show up here. That was the arrangement, wasn't it?"

"I believe it was."

"Is there any reason you chose not to come, Mr. Stevens? What seems to be the problem?" There was an edge of irritation to her voice. Lisa Jacobson's concern for social niceties ran only so deep.

"I was mugged. Hurt pretty badly. I've been in the hospital."

Her attitude changed instantly, and she was all solicitude again. "Oh, dear. I trust you're better now?"

"Improving every day, thank you.

"I'm so glad. What a nasty thing to happen to you. You must have a horrible opinion of New York."

"It's not so bad. I've met some nice people, too."

"That's very generous of you, Mr. Stevens." She made another adjustment to her scarf. "When I didn't hear from you, I assumed that perhaps you had—what shall I say?—misled us, that perhaps there were no pictures at all."

"No, the pictures are real."

"Not grainy or out of focus. You can recognize the people in them?"

"Yes."

"And the poses are every bit as . . . *intimate* . . . as you indicated to us?"

"Let's just say that you won't be disappointed."

"I hope not. Of course, we'll be the judge of that, won't we?"

"I suppose you will."

"Do you want to show them to me? You were so secretive before. 'Guaranteed front page,' you told me. 'A big scandal!' So what is this scandal?"

"Each of them is with someone else."

"Really? I assumed the shots were of them together."

"No."

"Are these other people famous, too?" Lisa tried not to sound too curious, but Brent sensed her mounting interest and intentionally ignored her question.

"So how does this work?" he asked.

"You prefer to keep me on tenterhooks? Very well. Have it your way." Lisa Jacobson leaned back in her chair, joined the tips of her fingers in a tent, and rocked back and forth gently. Sooner or later, the greed came out in all of them, and Brent Stevens was surely no exception. They played hard to get only for so long. It was just a matter of waiting them out.

"It's very simple, Mr. Stevens. You give us the pictures and we pay."

"How much?"

The corners of her mouth edged up ever so slightly into the beginnings of a knowing smirk. "That all depends. I have to see them first. If the quality is good, rest assured that we will make you an attractive offer. The price can go higher, if the story that goes along with the pictures is as scandalous as you imply. I presume we are talking about more than just a kiss on the cheek."

"The photos are pretty explicit."

"And Christopher Knight is totally naked?"

"Yes."

"That would be far more unique, of course, than Jennifer nude." Lisa unconsciously blew air over her top lip. "We'd be willing to go as high as five hundred thousand dollars. Assuming, of course, that everything you've been telling me is true."

"Okay. Fine, that's all I wanted to know." Brent stood up and prepared to leave.

"What do you mean, 'okay, fine?' I'm talking in general terms, you understand. The price can be adjusted, if need be . . . if circumstances merit."

"I thought that would be the case. Thank you, Miss Jacobson."

"Well, are you going tot let me see them or not?"

"I don't know." He started toward the door.

She jumped up, startled at the sudden turn the meeting had taken. "I hope you haven't shown them to anyone else? Exclusivity is crucial to us."

"I haven't shown them to anybody yet."

"In that case, consider the figure I quoted you a starting price."

"Ms. Jacobson, let's not waste each other's time. Just how high are you willing to go?"

"One million tops," she said, without missing a beat. "With their movie opening tomorrow night, we don't want to put this off much longer. You realize that, don't you? Timing makes these pictures all the more valuable to us . . . and to you, of course, Mr. Stevens."

"I'll be in touch," he said and left her office.

A minute later, wrapped in thought, he was walking rapidly down Madison Avenue.

He had an image of himself, facedown on the tile mosaic in Central Park, dead to the world, bleeding from one ear. And then he pictured the bullying man in the hospital, asking him if he'd learned his lesson yet, if he was going to cooperate now.

The images were beginning to make sense.

He knew he'd taken the photographs of Jennifer Osborne and Christopher Knight as soon as he had laid eyes on them. And Lisa Jacobson had just confirmed that they were worth a lot of money. If she said $1 million without flinching, the real price had to be even higher.

On the *Deborah Myers Special* last night, the stars had held hands and paraded their happy marriage before the viewing public. Deborah had bought right into it. But they were lying! The photographs could ruin them. And he was in the position to make it all happen. The idea that he controlled their fates made him feel light-headed.

Then he thought of the shabby house in Dover Plains and his mother's "estate," a shriveled-up checking account that had barely lasted out her final days. That was part of the picture, too.

He was reminded of the puzzles she laid out on the kitchen table and worked on for months at a time. She always hid the cover of the box away, refusing to consult it for helpful hints, which she considered a form of cheating. "I'll figure it out by myself," she insisted. Indeed, a piece here, a piece there, and the front of a picturesque English cottage would begin to take shape. Then she'd add a few more pieces and the cottage would turn into a store. And the store eventually became a butcher's shop.

What looked at first like fragments of bright flowers were, when joined together, carcasses of raw meat, hanging in the window.

Tina was sitting out on the stoop, still wearing her exercise gear, when he came down the street. Absorbed in her thoughts, she was hugging her knees, a wistful expression on her face.

For a moment, she looked completely defenseless to him, as people did when you caught them unawares, pondering their destinies, and he wondered where her strong will came from. Life had knocked her around enough from what she had said, and being the single parent of a rambunctious six-year-old daughter had to be difficult. Johnny was no blessing. Yet, resentment hadn't poisoned her. Her tongue was foul, but her heart wasn't. She still went out to people.

She had rescued him for no other reason than he was in trouble. Trusted him enough to bring him home, put him up, and help get his life together. Even when it appeared that his life might not be such a nice one, she had proceeded on the assumption that there were explanations. It wasn't so much that he was innocent until proven guilty, either. No, she seemed to operate with a different view of people, one that put them outside the usual categories of guilt and accountability.

Was it naïveté on her part? Or decency? Maybe she had just been so harshly judged in the past that she simply refused now to judge others.

Once Tina was aware of his approach, she waved, and he realized that she had been waiting for his return.

"So where have you been?

"I went to the *Informer*. I found Lisa."

"No kidding. *The* Lisa, Miss Bug-Up-Her-Butt?"

"Herself." He sat down next to her on the concrete stoop. "She offered me a million dollars for the pictures."

Tina's mouth opened wide. "You didn't show them to her, did you?"

"I didn't have to. I told her enough about them. I think the price would go higher if she actually saw them."

"I don't believe you, Brent."

"You better!" he boasted. "She was panting to make a deal when I left."

Tina shifted her position on the steps. "That's not what I meant." The enthusiasm she had shown upon his arrival drained out of her voice. "I don't believe you went there. I don't believe you discussed selling that garbage . . . So what's your price?"

Brent hastened to correct her impression. "Tina, I was just trying to find out a few things."

"What things!"

"If that's where I was going the morning you found me. If that's why Lisa kept telephoning? If that's what all this craziness is about . . . a million dollars is a pile of money. People do screwy things for a lot less. Somebody must be out of their mind that I've got those pictures . . . I don't exactly blame them."

Tina hugged her knees more tightly. "As soon as I saw the pictures, I figured that's what the trouble was about. I was *hoping* not, but that's me, the eternal optimist, always hoping for the best . . . Patsy H. Pollyanna, live and in person . . . One million dollars, huh? For a bunch of lousy pictures that belong in the trash. What a world!"

A motorcyclist varoomed down the street. They waited until the noise had faded before resuming the conversation.

"Well, there's something I have to tell you, too," Tina said. "I went into that apartment on the third floor of the Dakota."

"When? Why didn't you say so before?"

"I meant to. But with all the commotion here, the break-in, I forgot. Anyway, nothing came of it. I decided it was wasted effort. But as I was sitting here, thinking about those photographs, I remembered."

"What?"

"There was a picture on the guy's wall of him, Jennifer Osborne, and Christopher Knight. With their arms around one another. I just happened to notice it. He's got tons of photos on the wall."

"Who is this guy?"

"His name is Reed. I suppose it could just be a coincidence. Still, in the picture it looked like they were all pretty good friends."

"Reed, you say?"

"Yeah. Geoffrey Reed. Why? Does the name ring a bell?"

"It sounds familiar. I can't put a face to it, though."

She sat up, her curiosity pricked by his.

"Older man. Silver-haired. English accent. Dresses very well."

Brent struggled to conjure him up. The person he'd spotted in the window of the Dakota had whitish hair, but there was no telling what clothes he was wearing. And English? Did he know anybody from England?

She watched him process the information. More and more, she had the impression that the truth was on the tip of his tongue. At such moments, the pupils of his eyes actually seemed to get darker, the whites whiter. But then, for some reason, the truth would vanish, his face would go slack, and he would be back in that no-man's land of resignation and confusion.

Maybe the truth didn't disappear, though. Maybe it was there all along and Brent just couldn't bring himself to acknowledge it. She'd heard of cases like that. Suppressed memories was the term for it. People just struck things from their minds or rewrote parts of their lives they didn't like—which was the same thing, really. They ended up remembering only what they chose to remember, and the rest . . . well, gone, forgotten, never was. Was that what Brent was doing?

"Perhaps if I saw him . . . ," he said, aware he had let her down. "It was simpler when you didn't know anything about me, wasn't it?"

"It probably was."

"When *I* didn't know anything about me . . . I'll bet you're sorry you ever got into this."

"No . . . but I'll be sorry if you sell those pictures."

"I wish none of it was happening, Tina. It would have been better if things had turned out some other way."

Tina moved down a step so she could look him directly in the face. "Things turn out the way you make them turn out, Brent. No, listen to me. Sometimes it's easier to let things run their course. 'Oh, it's not my fault. I'm not the responsible one here.' Who knows that refrain better than me? I blame my mother. I blame that son of a bitch husband of mine all the time. I blame everybody but myself. When I first met you, I thought you were a good person. Maybe you weren't. Maybe you aren't now. What the hell kind of judge am I, anyway? But you can be. I know that. You have a choice, Brent. You may not want to make it, but it's still yours to make."

Midway down the street, a series of shrieks broke out. School had let out, and Angelina and her best friend, Megan, fueled by the fresh air, were jostling and pushing each other for possession of a small children's book. Behind them, Megan's mother walked wearily, muttering a perfunctory "girls, girls, girls" now and then, but otherwise making little attempt to adjudicate the dispute.

Spying her mother and Brent on the stoop, Angelina ran ahead. "Megan won't let me read *Dragons at Dawn*," she complained. "I lent her *Mummies in the Morning*, too. It's not fair."

Megan clutched the book possessively to her chest and broadcast her defense to the whole neighborhood, "It's my book, Angelina, not yours!"

"I'm afraid it's one of those days," sighed the child's mother, when she reached the stoop. "They're at each other again. Can you imagine what it would be if they didn't like each other? Okay, enough girls! I've been running all day and I'm in no mood for this. I was two minutes late, and when I got to the school yard, they were already fighting. You pick them up tomorrow, right, Tina?"

"Yeah. Try to relax tonight, hon."

"With all her energy? I've been seriously thinking of sedatives. Oh, for me, not her!" She gave her daughter a gentle push. "Come on, Megan sweetie. Time to go home."

"So," Tina said, after they'd left, "how was school?"

"Good." Angelina reached into her backpack, pulled out an envelope and offered it to Brent.

"What's this? Something you made in class?" he asked.

"No." The child squatted down and ran her finger along a crack in the concrete.

"Show me," Tina said eagerly, looking over Brent's shoulder and thinking of the cards that were already taped to the refrigerator door.

But it wasn't a card. It was a piece of writing paper. On it, someone had written a single sentence in large, block letters: "No one will be safe if you don't cooperate, not even Angelina."

Tina felt as if she had been hit between the shoulder blades. Her impulse was to grab the paper from Brent and tear it up into tiny pieces. She had to make an effort to control her shaking. For her daughter's sake, she tried to keep her voice casual. "Angelina, honey, where did you get this?"

The child continued to trace the crack in the walk with her fingertip.

"A man gave it to me."

"What man?"

"The man from the zoo."

"What do you mean? What man from the zoo?"

The child looked up ingenuously at her mother. "The man I *talked to* at the zoo. He gave it to me and told me to give it to Mr. Stevens."

"A man gave you this letter at the zoo the other day?"

"No, silly! Not the other day!" The child stood up and planted her hands firmly on her hips. "He gave it to me now. At the playground. While we were waiting for Megan's mother to come."

30

"The sick sonavabitches."

Once more, Johnny read the note that Angelina had brought home, tossed it on the kitchen counter, then, for emphasis, pounded the counter so violently that a dirty cup and saucer rattled in the sink. "What does it mean? 'No one is safe if you don't cooperate. Not even Angelina.' What the hell do they want? Who are these people?"

Johnny's anger was doing nothing to diminish the helplessness Tina felt. Although she didn't relish the idea of finding herself in danger, other people's bullying usually brought out her combative streak. But who was she supposed to bully back here? If she—or she and Brent—had been the target of the anonymous threat, she might have reacted with more feistiness. What paralyzed her was that the only person mentioned in the note was her daughter.

"Angelina claims that some man she met at the zoo gave it to her," she said. "I don't know who she is talking about. We didn't meet anyone at the zoo."

"She must have met someone. Notes like this don't come out of the blue," Johnny countered. "First somebody goes through the house. Now this! Maybe we're all on *Candid Camera* and no one's bothered to tell us yet."

"You're a riot, Johnny."

"Sorry, but this has something to do with one of us, and my best guess is that it's not Angelina. Or even you, Tina. So maybe you can tell us, Brent? What the hell is going on here?"

"It's gotta be the pictures," he answered.

"What pictures? What are you talking about?"

"See for yourself! You're old enough," Tina said, gesturing to the envelope on the kitchen table.

Johnny looked at his sister, then at Brent, as if he were waiting for further explanation. When none came, he picked up the envelope and pulled out the stack of eight-by-tens. The subject matter didn't register on him right away, and he flipped through the first few photographs in silence. Then he bellowed, "Jeez, what is this? This is disgusting!"

"Recognize anybody?" asked Tina.

"What's that crack supposed to mean? You think I know people who pose for this sort of crap?"

"I don't mean *know* personally. I mean, recognize. Don't you recognize who they are?"

Johnny examined the photographs more closely, his curiosity prevailing over his indignation, which was not all that strong to begin with. Slowly, his jaw went slack.

"Holy shit . . . Isn't this whatz-her-name? The Osborne broad? . . . Oh, no . . . Don't tell me . . . That's her husband. And I liked his movies, too . . . Where did you get these?"

"They were in a locker that Brent had the key to. We found them yesterday afternoon."

"You're one of them paparazzi guys? Is that it, Brent? You make a living catching famous people with their pants down? Oh, boy! That's really swell! How many times I got to ask you, Tina? When you gonna bring home somebody decent for a change?" Scornfully, he tossed the envelope on the table, then went to the refrigerator and took out a beer. He made a gulping sound as he drank. Then he wiped his mouth with the flat of his hand. "So now we know what the joker, who broke into the house, was looking for, don't we?"

"I think so," said Brent.

"Well, you sure have brought all kinds of good things into our lives, haven't you, buddy?"

"I'm sorry. I didn't even know about these pictures myself until yesterday."

"Tell me another one."

"He didn't, Johnny," Tina said. "He was as surprised as you were when he saw them."

"Well, maybe as a payment for all the shit you've put us through, you should give us those pictures and get the fuck out of here." Johnny started to reach for the envelope, but Tina stepped in front of him, blocking his hand.

"Are you out of your mind?"

"Get out of the way, Tina. Do you have any idea how much these pictures are worth? You see it on TV all the time. They pay half a million bucks for a blurry photo of some famous person's butt. I could retire on these. Don't you think Brent owes us for what he's put us through? You saved his hide. He's staying in our house. We deserve something out of this."

"You can't be serious," Tina objected, refusing to step aside.

"Couldn't be more serious. Whatever's going on here, I think our man Brent oughta cut us in on it. That's only fair. How about it?"

"So he should be a total scumbag and sell the pictures! Is that what you want?" A rush of indignation warmed Tina's cheeks, and she felt her old combativeness awakening.

Johnny backed away, muttering that "people have done worse things."

"Sure," she snapped. "They accost six-year-olds in school yards."

"So we make them pay for that, too."

"Oh, stop acting like Mr. Big Shot. If you want to ruin your own life, go ahead. You can ruin yours, too, Brent. Be my guest. But the thing you can't do, either of you, is ruin someone else's life. Mine or Angelina's or those actors'. I don't know a damn thing about those pictures or the people in them. I don't want to know anything. It's none of my business. I just want them out of our lives. So Brent can do whatever he has to do. But I've had my fill! You hear? *Basta!*"

With a flip of the wrist, she snapped her fingers, as if the two of them would disappear. She had learned the gesture from Ida, for whom it was always the final argument and the sign that no appeal would be permitted. Brent caught its meaning.

"Nothing more is going to happen to you or Angelina," he said as forcefully as he could. "I'll do something, I promise."

"What?" Her voice bristled with challenge.

"Something. I'll go see that guy in the Dakota. You said you thought he had a connection with the stars. Maybe he can help. Or at least put me in touch with somebody who can."

"Hold it," Johnny interrupted. "What guy in the Dakota?"

"His name is Reed. Geoffrey Reed," explained Tina. "I went by his apartment yesterday after Mrs. Shriver's. He's some high-society muckety-muck, who pals around with a lot of famous people. He seems to be friends with everybody, including the actors in those pictures. Anyway, Brent believes he knows him."

"Oh, so Brent *believes* he knows him, does he?" Johnny's skepticism rippled with irony. "Three days ago, he couldn't remember his own name. Well, I hope to hell he's got his wires straight this time."

"You're not exactly helping here!" Tina shot her brother a look. "We've got to start somewhere. Let's call him."

"But we don't have his phone number," Brent said.

Tina leaped up. "No, but I bet I know who does." She grabbed a notepad and pencil off the counter and checked her wristwatch. "He should still be there." She dashed into the living room and dialed the Princess phone. A momentary truce was called in the kitchen while Brent and Johnny listened to her.

"Thanks, you're a real doll!" she finally said, hanging up the phone. She didn't return right away. Instead, they heard her open a drawer, shuffle some papers, then emit a sharp whistle. "What do you know!"

A glint of triumph lit up her eyes as she stood in the kitchen door. "We're in luck. Joey was still on duty. He says he could get fired for doing this, but he gave me Geoffrey Reed's number. And guess what, Brent? You called it already. Yeah! The number is the same one that was on the slip of paper I found in your jacket at the hospital. You tried it the other morning, remember? I thought it sounded vaguely familiar. I just checked. See?"

She showed him the number on the piece of Mayflower stationery from their cache of evidence and then the number she'd just coaxed out of Joey. They matched.

Unimpressed, Johnny slumped up against the refrigerator. "So what's that prove?"

"A lot. Brent was trying to get in touch with Geoffrey Reed after he was mugged. At least, we're pretty sure he was. Joey says he was trying to get inside the building that morning. Well, Brent must have called Geoffrey Reed the day *before*, too. Why else would he have written the phone number on a piece of hotel stationery? And Geoffrey Reed is friends with the two stars in the dirty pictures. Jeez, Johnny, you don't have to be Grandma H. Moses to connect the dots. Geoffrey Reed is smack in the middle of all this."

"Okay, okay! So what's Brent going to do? March up to this guy's door and say what? 'I'm from Ballbuster Video, mister. Here's your X-rated home delivery!' "

"Hilarious, Johnny!"

"I'm being serious! If this Geoffrey Reed is just some rich schmuck who collects celebrities, how do you think he's going to react when Brent presents him with a package of filthy pictures?" He turned to Brent. "And if he is behind this, you'd be pretty stupid to walk into his apartment, unless you're willing to go to the hospital again. Or worse."

"So what are we supposed to do? Wait until Angelina gets further instructions?"

"Will you calm down, Tina." Johnny swigged down the rest of his beer. "Brent can see this guy, if he wants to. Okay? But not in his apartment. Arrange to see him in a public place, at least. Meet in a restaurant, where there are other people present. Look, I'll even go along in case there's any trouble."

Tina retrieved the phone from the living room, gave a tug to the extension cord, and passed the instrument to Brent. "Johnny's right. Go ahead, call. Just be careful what you say."

A voice came on the line after the third ring.

"Yes?"

"Geoffrey Reed, please."

"Speaking."

"This is Brent Stevens."

"Brent! . . . What a pleasant surprise. I was wondering if I was ever going to hear from you . . . Are you here in town?"

"Yes . . . I think we should talk, Geoffrey."

"Well, of course we should, my dear boy. Why don't you drop by the apartment for a drink? It would be lovely to see you. You remember where the apartment is, don't you?"

"I'd rather we meet someplace else. In a restaurant."

"Really?" Geoffrey Reed managed to elongate the two syllables so that they conveyed surprise and, more importantly, a measure of superiority at the same time. "I guess if that's what you want, it can be arranged. What did you have in mind?"

Brent covered the mouthpiece and whispered to Johnny, "What restaurant?"

"Um . . . Rockefeller Center . . . the outdoor café."

"The outdoor café at Rockefeller Center," Brent repeated into the receiver.

"Awfully noisy, don't you think? How about something cozier? The Cafe des Artistes in my neighborhood is always pleasant."

"No, Rockefeller Center is what I'd prefer."

"Very well, then, that's what it shall be. What time's good for you?"

"Tonight? Six o'clock?"

"Oh, dear me. The premiere is tonight. Or have you forgotten? I'm supposed to meet our friends at the Carlyle on the way to the movie theater . . . Of course, nothing would please me more than to see you beforehand, catch up on things, as it were . . . Can we make it a tad earlier?"

"Meet me there in an hour then."

"You're not giving me much notice."

"We've got a lot to talk about. Besides—" Brent ran his tongue over his lips, which felt dry and papery—"I think I am willing to cooperate now."

The phone went so quiet that all Brent could hear was his own breathing. He wasn't sure if Geoffrey Reed was still on the line. Then the cultured voice came back, smooth and in control.

"That's nice, Brent." Geoffrey Reed could have been talking about the weather. "I really can't tell you how delighted I am to hear from you. I'll see you shortly."

Brent handed the phone back to Tina. "It's done. He said he'll meet me there! There's only one problem."

"What's that?"

"I don't know if I'll recognize him."

"Of course, you will. I told you. Silver hair with a wave in it. Nice-looking man in his midfifties . . ."

When the description failed to elicit a reaction, she added more insistently, "About six feet tall. Quite fit, although he told me he's put on weight and is thinking of starting an exercise program . . . Expensive clothes . . . Brent, you said you know him! He knows you, doesn't he?"

"He seems to . . ."

Brent willed himself to see the man she was describing, but to little avail. The old sense of bewilderment was coming back and his face took on the strange blurry quality that Tina remembered from the hospital.

"Don't get upset," she said. "It doesn't matter. What if I come with you to Rockefeller Center? I can point him out. Johnny, I'm going into the city with Brent. You stay here with Angelina."

"And let the two of you handle this by yourselves? Fat chance. Not the way things have gone up to now. Someone's got to be there if it gets rough."

"Rough? In Rockefeller Center?"

"I'm coming anyway."

"Okay, but I'm not leaving the kid alone. I will never leave that child alone again, if it means I have to hire some guidos from Brooklyn to protect her." She marched to the foot of the stairs and called up, "Angelina, get down here."

Then she came back and announced authoritatively, "We're *all* going."

31

No matter what the season, tourists liked to gather around the edge of Rockefeller Plaza and stare down at the activity below. In the winter, when the plaza was transformed into an ice rink, they stared at skaters circling counterclockwise to canned music. In spring and summer, when the rink was supplanted by an outdoor café, they stared at diners eating overpriced Nicoise salads. Also to canned music.

What they were actually seeing on this particular day was a sea of bright yellow umbrellas, spelled by dabs of leafy green citrus trees in wooden planters. Here and there tops of heads were visible, but mostly what protruded from under the umbrellas were arms and hands. Waiters scurried back and forth industriously, like so many ants in white aprons.

At five minutes to five, the usual tourist throng was augmented by office workers from the neighboring buildings. People seemed happy to linger in the temperate weather, and Tina and Brent had to maneuver past several clusters of tourists to get to the front of the west wall of the plaza, where a huge bronze statue of Prometheus rose above a pool, spouting arches of water. Tina gripped

Angelina's hand tightly, and Johnny followed closely behind them.

From their vantage point, they had a clear view of the marble steps on the other side that descended to the café entrance on the lower level. Yet they blended in with the crowds. If anyone had bothered to look their way, the large manila envelope Brent was carrying marked him as just another accountant getting off work.

It was a good spot to watch and not be watched in return. Brent already felt the confusion of the last few days beginning to lift. Someone had gone to extraordinary lengths to find the photographs and prevent them from getting published. Geoffrey Reed was the obvious person. He was rich, powerful, a close friend of the stars. People like that stuck together. When Brent had jeopardized their privileged lives, they'd come after him. But that meant Geoffrey Reed could stop the madness, too.

"There he is!" Tina tugged at Brent's sleeve and pointed to a silver-haired man, who had paused at the top of the stairs. He had on a dark blue suit with a tie that matched his hair. After taking a quick look around, the man continued to the bottom of the steps, where he conferred briefly with a maître d'. With a beckoning gesture, the maître d' led him to a nearby table and pulled out the chair for him.

"Go on," Johnny said, nudging Brent gently. "I see where he is sitting. I won't let you out of my sight."

Brent tucked the manila envelope under his arm, circled the plaza, and a minute later, found himself facing the same maître d'. "I'm joining Mr. Reed."

"Very good, sir. He just arrived. This way, please."

At Brent's approach, Geoffrey slid back his chair, stood

up, and exclaimed, "My, my! Look who's here at long last—Mr. Brent Stevens, in all his glory!" He reached out and pumped Brent's hand vigorously.

In anyone else, the heartiness of the greeting would have been suspect. But Brent seemed to remember that a certain effusiveness was part of Geoffrey Reed's manner. He met people all the time, made a business of meeting people, was good at it. He always gave out that wide smile, so wide that it revealed his upper gums, as he was doing right now. And always the pumping handshake. Up close, Brent noticed how silvery the hair really was. The highlights looked almost artificial. His skin was tanned, unless it was makeup.

There was no question in his mind that this was the face he'd seen hovering in the Dakota window.

"How are you, old chap?" Geoffrey chimed, and the "old chap" came back to Brent, too, from how many meetings in the past? As he slipped the manila envelope onto an empty chair, Brent saw a flaring of interest in the man's eyes.

"I've been fine, Geoffrey. And you?"

Geoffrey Reed sat down again and motioned for Brent to follow suit. "I am certainly much better, now that you're here. Things have been . . . rather in a turmoil this week." He hailed a passing waiter. "The usual for you?"

Brent nodded, wondering what that was.

"Two gin and tonics, if you would, waiter. Bombay gin, if you've got it." He retrained his gaze on Brent. "Actually, I needn't tell you how relieved I am."

"I guess I have everyone pretty upset?"

"To put it mildly, yes."

"I was hoping we could settle everything calmly today. End this craziness."

"I see no reason why we can't. No reason at all. Two *reasonable* gentlemen like ourselves." Geoffrey Reed showed his upper gums again.

"I just want to do what's right," Brent insisted.

"I'm happy to hear that." He nodded his head slightly in the direction of the manila envelope. "Is that . . . ?"

"Yes, it is."

"May I?"

Brent handed him the envelope. Geoffrey pulled a few photos partially out, studied them impassively, then slid them back in. He placed the envelope beside him and drummed on it absently with his fingertips before continuing. "I don't think I've slept a wink all week. I thought for sure you'd gone to one of those dreadful tabloids by now."

"I did. Yesterday."

Geoffrey leaned forward, suddenly anxious. "For God's sake, you didn't show them anything, did you?"

"No. I . . . implied there might be some racy photos, that's all. I didn't say what they were."

"Thank heavens. Because if they ever got out, it would be over for us. For me, for you. For them. Photos like that would ruin their careers. You realize that, of course. You're not stupid. That's why you're here."

The waiter returned with a small dish of salted nuts and two gin and tonics, which he placed before them.

"Chin chin!" Geoffrey lifted his glass and clinked it against Brent's. "Here's to . . . how shall I put it? . . . a more harmonious future." Brent remembered that Geoffrey always said "chin chin"—not "cheers" or "bottoms up"—

and took a sip of his drink. It was awfully sweet. Gin and tonic couldn't really be his beverage of choice. He drank it anyway and waited for Geoffrey to fill him in.

"I spoke to Jennifer and Christopher this morning. They asked about you. They've been worried. They wanted to know if I'd heard from you yet. When you didn't show up for work, they got concerned. Their new assistant called you numerous times and left umpteen messages. Finally, he went over to your place and found it locked up. They're afraid something dreadful has happened to you."

Something dreadful did, Brent thought. He'd been beaten so badly he had lost all sense of himself for a while. Did Geoffrey know how terrifying it was to wake up in a void? He was tempted to recount what had happened, then changed his mind. It was better to let Geoffrey do the talking now. "What did you tell them?"

"I told them I had no idea where you were. Which was the truth, of course. Well, partly. I knew you were here. But now that you've surfaced, everything is back on track again." His fingers continued to drum automatically on the envelope. "I am even willing to admit that my first offer was, well, on the smallish side. But you know that, now that you've been to the tabloids."

"The *Informer* proposed five hundred thousand dollars as a starting figure. They'll go much higher." He watched Geoffrey's face closely for a reaction, but Geoffrey merely took a deep swig of his drink. Having the photos in his sight seemed to have relaxed him, and the gin and tonic was putting him in a mellow mood.

"I'm sure they will. That kind of money means nothing to them. Nothing at all."

"What do *you* propose doing?"

A little whoop of delight escaped from Geoffrey's mouth. "Getting right down to business, eh? You never were one for beating around the bush. What is your expression? 'Cut to the chase?' Is that what you'd like me to do?"

"Why not?"

"Dear Brent. A man of so few words! Unlike myself. Never mind. What I am about to say should please you. What I am proposing is an even split. Fifty-fifty. It should have been that way from the start, as you pointed out at my apartment the other night. Our original arrangement *was* unfair of me. I grossly undervalued your contribution. In my defense, let me say that I have been working for that poof for ten very long, very taxing years. For three of those years, no one knew who the hell he was or cared. Now that he's famous, he and that dyke he calls his wife want to discard me for some hotshot Hollywood press agent. They claim I don't know how to handle big stars. It's a whole different ball game now, they say. Horseshit!"

A final swig and he had polished off the contents of his glass. He allowed himself to savor the lemony sting of the drink, then resumed the account in a more confidential tone. "That's not the real reason, of course. They just don't want another poof around. They think nobody knows about them. But I do. Heavens, I have been on to Christopher for years. He thought he was keeping it a secret from me, but one can always tell. It takes one to know one. Isn't that what they say? I knew right from day one, when I caught him looking at the pool boy a split second longer than he ought to have. He can't help himself.

He responds to handsome men. Why do you think he hired you? For your driving skills?"

Geoffrey Reed's laughter wanted to be good-natured. Even though Brent had caused him some serious problems this week, he was fond of the boy. Basically always had been. He understood Brent's hunger and appreciated his detachment. A valuable combination. So when the opportunity had arisen, he'd placed him with the stars. It never hurt to have someone like that on the inside.

"Oh, don't sulk, Brent! I have no doubt you've been a perfectly adequate chauffeur. Jennifer and Christopher never complained to me, at any rate. I think they both rather like you. As I suspected they would. But that doesn't much matter anymore, does it? Now that you've demonstrated a far more valuable talent. You won't have to be their driver much longer."

"How much is that *talent* worth now?"

Geoffrey's hand closed instinctively over the envelope and he glanced at the surrounding tables. No one appeared to be taking notice of them.

"How shall I explain this? There will always be rumors about Jennifer and Christopher. Some past boyfriend or girlfriend, although I must say they have been fairly clever about their conduct. But photos are something else. Photos can't be denied. Christopher and Jennifer will pay handsomely to get them back. In fact, the way I envision it, they'll pay over and over, if they intend to remain the number one box office attraction in the world. I'd forget about the tabloids, Brent. We don't need them. All this will be much more lucrative if it remains in the immediate family."

Geoffrey sat there, digesting his triumph in advance.

"You know they offered me severance pay last week? Yes, they did. A hundred thousand dollars. Once their movie has opened. But we'll all stay the best of friends. Jennifer actually said that to me. 'The best of friends!' Well, I think not. They can shove their hundred thousand. How about five million dollars instead? More later, of course? If we play this little scheme right, there's no reason it can't last for years and years."

A certain euphoria had crept into Geoffrey's manner. His eyes had a liquid quality. In the changing light, his silver hair had acquired dark bluish tints, like a rich dowager's.

"And you're sure they'll pay?"

"Positive. They'll go to any lengths to cover their tracks. Why do you think that Ned and Dolly Hobart bothered to get married? That's nothing but a smoke screen. And a pretty effective one, too, I might add. Well, you were there. You saw the charade. Ned is his lover. Dolly is hers. Have been for years, as the photos make painfully obvious. But, you see, the press is so much less suspicious of a married couple! Two married couples, in this case! Sometimes, I daresay, the press can be actively stupid. If Jennifer has a child, their heterosexual credentials will be unassailable!"

Geoffrey signaled to the waiter for another round of drinks. "So, in answer to your question, yes, I'm sure. Mr. and Mrs. Christopher Knight will agree to any financial terms we propose. And you, my dear Brent, shall have your freedom. You will no longer have to be a chauffeur. Maybe you'll even get around to pursuing that acting career you used to talk about all the time. You can't keep putting it off forever, you know. Frankly, I always thought you had the looks for it. But remember, my dear, looks do fade eventually."

Somewhere deep inside, Brent felt the flicker of his old ambition. To be an actor. That was why he'd gone to California. That was the youthful dream. To be able to pretend he was somebody else and have other people believe him. How that prospect had enthralled him once. They said he did it well, too. Said he was a natural. Where was that? In L.A.?

No, L.A. was flooded with actors, would-be actors, has-been actors, do-anything-for-a-part actors. He had been one of them, one of the thousands who went no place fast, waiting tables, parking cars, scrambling at the end of every month to pay the rent. It was in Dover Plains that he was special, where people had singled him out with pride. Back in Dover Plains they had told him he would go far.

He had.

Until now, he hadn't realized how far.

"Well, you're right. I guess I always did want to act," he acknowledged. "Maybe it's time. I just have a couple of questions."

"Fire away." Relishing their new accord, Geoffrey Reed reached into his breast pocket for a Benson & Hedges.

"Were you responsible for the beating in the park?"

The hand stopped in midair. "Since we're leveling with each other . . . yes, I was . . . I'm terribly sorry about that. They were just supposed to scare you. I'm afraid they got carried away."

"Carried away? I landed in the hospital."

"That was not the intention, I assure you. I'll make it up to you. Try to understand the situation, though. I was fully prepared to pay you a fee for your work—a fee we both agreed on, I might point out. But then you began screaming at me from L.A. that it was not enough, not enough! No matter! I said I would discuss it with you when you came east. And I meant it."

The pause was intended to emphasize his sincerity.

"I had a presentiment our discussion would go nowhere. So I took a few precautions. When you stormed off, I panicked. What more can I say?"

Through an opening between the yellow umbrellas, Brent looked up at the people lined along the west side of the plaza and saw Tina. Next to her, Angelina's head barely cleared the top of the wall. He thought of how the child had wanted all the lights in the house turned on after the break-in and, later, of how she had brought home a vile note some creep had given her in the playground. They were sickening thoughts. Angelina wouldn't always be an innocent, but she was now, and she deserved to be one for as long as possible.

Angelina's hand shot up in the air. She had spotted him and was waving excitedly and bouncing up and down. Tina quickly grabbed the child's hand and restrained her, then bent down and whispered something in her ear. When she stood back up, she glanced anxiously in Brent's direction, but he couldn't tell if she saw him or not.

"What about threatening a six-year-old girl?" he said to Geoffrey. "Was that your idea, too?"

Geoffrey sighed. "I had to get your attention some-how. That note was . . . just a reminder, Brent. A reminder that we had a deal. You're the one who chose not to honor it. No hard feelings, dear boy. Anyway, I thought we'd decided to put everything behind us today. Fresh start?"

In his mind, Brent heard Tina talking to him, heard the flat New York accent that made everything she said seem so direct, so unequivocal. Geoffrey's suave tone was slippery. It made good sound distasteful and implied that right was vaguely foolish. His smugness and condescension confused the issues. What had Tina said? "If you want to ruin your own life, go ahead . . . be my guest . . . the thing you can't do is ruin someone else's. Mine or Angelina's or anyone else's."

Brent stood up and swept the envelope off the table. "Sorry, Geoffrey, I guess there are a few things I can't put behind me. The deal is off. You won't get a dime for these pictures. Not only that, when Christopher and Jennifer hear of this conversation, I wouldn't count on that severance check, either."

Geoffrey reached out and caught Brent by the sleeve. "Sit down, Brent. You're acting like a child. Let's not start this ridiculous squabbling all over again."

"I agree. Let's not. It's over." He shook free of Geoffrey's grip.

Anger flushed the older man's face. "If you walk out of here, I cannot guarantee your safety."

"Good-bye, Geoffrey."

As Brent turned to leave the café, Geoffrey nodded sharply to a gentleman seated under an umbrella several tables away. At the prearranged signal, Spiff promptly got up, buttoned his jacket, and headed briskly toward the entrance of the café.

Brent got there first. Looking back, he was reassured to see that Geoffrey was still busy settling the bill with the waiter. Off to the right, someone was making a commotion, pushing around chairs and jostling customers. He seemed to be headed in Brent's direction.

Brent started up the stairs, his leather soles making a sound like the swish-swish of sandpaper on the stone steps. Soon he was aware of another set of feet behind him, making the same swish-swishing sound. Trying not to panic, he picked up his pace.

So did the person following him.

From the sound, Brent judged that the distance between them was growing smaller.

At the top of the stairs, he hesitated for a moment, not sure which way to go.

"Brent! Over here!"

He heard his name, turned toward where the voice had come from, and broke into a run.

Only a few seconds later, Spiff also arrived at the head of the stairs. Spying Brent's retreating form, he was about to take off after him when all at once a body coming out of nowhere slammed into his chest. The wind went out of his lungs. With a furious windmilling of his arms, Spiff struggled to maintain his balance, then reeled backward, gasping for air. One of his hands flew out to the side and caught the railing on the stairs. His body swung around and hit hard against the stone wall. The impact left him stunned.

"Sorry about that, pal," Johnny muttered under his breath, allowing himself a surge of pride that he hadn't lost all his prowess as a star high school linebacker. Catching up to Brent, he explained, "Tina recognized him while you were sitting there in the restaurant. Now let's get the hell out of here."

Dodging tourists, they dashed up the gently inclined esplanade that led to Fifth Avenue, where Tina and Angelina were waiting.

On the steps, a crowd formed around Spiff. A couple of do-gooders volunteered their assistance, but most were content just to speculate on the cause of the accident.

"Sue," one man kept urging Spiff. "That's what I'd do. *Sue.*"

Humiliated to be the center of their attention, Spiff got up and tested his weight on one foot, then the other. No broken bones from what he could tell. His left elbow, which has cushioned his fall, was throbbing, though. What angered him most was the smudge on the leg of his pants. He brushed at it vigorously, but it wouldn't come off.

"You all in one piece?" asked the man who had been advising litigation.

"I'm fine. Beat it."

Encouraged by his scowl, the crowd began to melt away as Geoffrey came trotting up the stairs.

Spiff waited until the Englishman was at his side. Then he hissed, "That little mother-fucker! I'll kill him."

The flush had receded from Geoffrey's face and his features, so animated earlier, seemed tooled in leather. "That's just what you'll do, Spiff. I don't want Brent Stevens talking about this to anyone. Understand? I don't want Brent Stevens talking ever again."

32

"What happened?" Tina asked as soon as Johnny and Brent reached her side. "What did Geoffrey Reed say? Why didn't you give him the pictures?"

Brent glanced behind him and wondered how long it would be before the man on the stairs got to his feet.

"He's one of the scum-suckers."

Brent's answer brought her up short. She pulled Angelina out of the path of the passing pedestrians and put her arms around her protectively. "What do you mean? What went wrong?"

"Save the questions for later, will ya?" barked Johnny, his adrenaline still pumping. "Let's just keep moving." He bent over and scooped up his niece. "Okay, Angelina, time to play horsy." He swung the child over onto his back and hooked his arms under her legs. Once she was securely in place, he began sprinting up Fifth Avenue toward St. Patrick's Cathedral, which was a block away on the opposite side of the street.

Brent gripped the pictures with one hand. With the other, he took Tina's elbow, and they ran after Johnny. Angelina's laughter floated over their heads, light and silver, like blossoms blown off an apple tree by a spring

breeze. Her delight in riding on her uncle's back was magnified by the zigzagging course he was obliged to take on
the busy sidewalk. People heard the ripples of laughter,
looked up at her, and smiled.

Children had a way of making a game out of everything, Brent thought. For Angelina, there was no Geoffrey
Reed. No thug crashing down the marble stairs. No
obscene pictures. There was just this unexpected piggy-
back ride on a crowded city street and strangers deriving
happiness from her happiness.

Inside St. Patrick's Cathedral, an organ was sounding
stately chords. Groups of sight-seers milled about rever-
ently, their heads tilted back in contemplation of the
stained glass windows and the richly ornamented columns.
As soon as they entered, Johnny lowered Angelina gently
to the floor then, satisfied that no one had followed them,
slipped into the first empty pew. He gestured for Tina and
Brent to join them.

Angelina kicked her legs playfully while the adults
struggled to catch their breath.

Tina spoke first. "Explain what happened," she said to
Brent, between huffs. "Is Geoffrey Reed friends with the
stars? Did he know anything about the pictures?"

"He's the one who's blackmailing them, Tina. He's
their press agent. He put together this whole scheme to
extort millions of dollars from them. And I'm a part of it.
I've been part of it all along."

"How? I don't understand."

"Geoffrey Reed got me a job working for the stars. I go
by their house all the time. I even travel with them. That's
how I was able to take pictures of them."

"Why would you do something like that, Brent?"

"For money. He promised to pay me. He said he'd pay me a lot."

"I told you those pictures were worth a fortune," Johnny said, with a gloat. "So how much did he offer you?"

"Not enough. Nowhere near enough. Apparently, we had a fight about it the night I was attacked in the park. I wouldn't hand over the pictures to him then. Now he admits he was wrong. He says he'll give me more. More than the tabloid can pay me. He says we should keep this all in the family."

The excitement glittered in Brent's eyes. It was plain to Tina that the encounter with Geoffrey Reed hadn't ended the craziness at all. If anything, Brent was more keyed up than ever, drunk almost with the fortune that awaited him. "I thought you didn't have a family," she said sharply and looked away.

"Can you imagine it, Tina? He's talking millions and millions of dollars. He says the stars will do anything to keep those photos private."

"Well, I suppose they will," she said. "Who wouldn't? I mean, they must have the money. They can buy anything they want. So what are you going to do?" She trained her eyes on the altar at the other end of the nave. She didn't want to hear what he was going to say next. But more than that, she didn't want to see him as he said it.

He dropped his voice to a near hush. "I don't know what came over me. All the time Geoffrey Reed was explaining this to me, I kept hearing you. One of the first conversations we ever had. You told me you wished you could just erase parts of your life and start over. Remember?"

"Yeah, I did. So what?"

"Don't you see?" Brent reached over and turned her chin toward him, so that she had to look him in the eye. "I want that, too. This is my chance to do it. Start over."

"What are you telling me, Brent?"

"I've got to reach Christopher Knight and Jennifer Osborne. I've got to let them know what Geoffrey is doing. Someone's got to warn them he plans to blackmail them."

"They're going to believe you, a perfect stranger?"

"But that's just it. I'm not a stranger to them. *I drive their car!* They know me."

"And what about Geoffrey Reed? He's a wealthy, influential man. I've seen where he lives. He knows everybody, Brent. You're asking for more trouble. It'll be your word against his. Just get rid of the pictures, Brent. Destroy them. Wouldn't that be best?"

"If I destroy the pictures, it *is* my word against Geoffrey Reed's. But if they see the pictures with their own eyes, they'll have to believe me. What's the Carlyle?"

"A hotel," said Johnny.

"Where?"

"About twenty blocks north of here. Why?"

"Because Geoffrey Reed said he was meeting the stars at the Carlyle. If I can just see them, I can explain everything."

Johnny couldn't help scoffing. "You're telling us you're a lousy chauffeur and you're going to rescue a couple of movie stars? Don't you think they can take care of themselves? They got lawyers for that. They probably got a whole firm of lawyers on their payroll. So why bother?"

"Shut up, Johnny," said Tina.

"Be sensible, Brent. I hope you don't think they're going to thank you when you show up with a bunch of obscene pictures. They'll have you arrested on the spot. So don't do the perverts any favors. What did they ever do for you, except let you drive them fancy places, I guess, and hold the car door for them! Shit, they probably make you wear a uniform, too!"

"But I'm not doing this for them. It's for me. If I can't make good on this, my life will never be worth anything. There are lots of things in my past I'm not proud of. Lots of things I'm just finding out about. Things I haven't even told you about, Tina. And I don't know how I'm going to make them right. But this is one thing I *can* fix. And if I fix one thing, maybe I can fix some of the others, too."

"You're talking pure bullshit," said Johnny.

"Am I, Tina? Is this bullshit to you?"

Tina was at a loss for words. How could she have been so wrong? The excitement in Brent's eyes had nothing to do with money. She'd misread it. He was elated about something entirely different. He wasn't one of the bastards Johnny was always accusing her of dragging home. He was a good guy, as she had believed all along. It hadn't been wishful thinking on her part.

A weight slipped from her shoulders, and for an instant she felt so light and giddy she almost burst out laughing.

"Let me just put it this way," she said. "We're wasting precious time sitting around here yammering! Come on, Angelina. On your feet, you guys. We're going to the Carlyle."

"Oh no you're not," objected Johnny. "Brent and I will handle this, if we have to. You and Angelina are going home."

"And run into that goon? Like hell we are. We're sticking together. What did Geoffrey Reed say? That this should stay in the family? Well, we're all family here. Isn't that right, Brent?"

The smile that broke across his face made him, she thought, look like a ten-year-old.

At the door of the cathedral, she hung back and let the two men pass before her. "Stay with your uncle," she said to Angelina. "I'll be right along."

She turned back and gazed up at the vaulted ceiling.

"Norna, it's your granddaughter here. Miss Smarty-pants. I was just thinking of the times we used to take meals down to the bums on Grand Avenue and how scared I used to get. You told me there was nothing to be frightened of, that you'd keep an eye on me. And you were right. Well, we're about to make another delivery today. Not exactly food. Something else. I'd just as soon not go into the details, if you don't mind. But it's pretty important all the same that we get this package into the hands of the right people. The point is, I probably never would have gotten mixed up in any of this, if it hadn't been for you and those plates of spaghetti and meatballs. And, well, I'm scared again. For Brent, more than me. So what I'm asking is, do you think you could manage to keep an eye out for him this time? I'd really appreciate it, Norna . . ."

She dipped her fingers in the font of holy water by the door, crossed herself hastily, and slipped outside without waiting for Ida's reply.

Jennifer Osborne scrutinized herself in the mirror, satisfied that after forty-five minutes at the makeup table, she looked as if she were wearing no makeup whatsoever. The press had always described her as a natural beauty, an illusion that required an increasing effort to perpetuate. There was an irony in that, if she chose to dwell on it. She chose not to.

"What do you think, Dolly?" she asked, giving her head a shake so that her blonde hair fell loosely about her shoulders.

"Only that you are the sexiest woman alive," Dolly replied.

"You're looking fairly smashing yourself. Give me a hand with the dress, will you?" The Todd Oldham gown left her shoulders and a generous portion of her back exposed.

A few minutes later, the door connecting the two suites cracked open. Then Christopher popped in his head and said, "Knock, knock. May I come in? Magic time is approaching."

From the start of his career, "magic time" had been his mantra. Unfailingly, before each take on the set, he'd mumble it to himself. It functioned as a kind of wake-up call to his imagination, a reminder that he was leaving the world of reality for the world of make-believe, although sometimes he wondered which was which. Lately, he had begun uttering the mantra whenever he had to appear in public and assume the stance and attitude of the movie star. Which, he reasoned, was as much a role as any he played before the camera.

Ned entered the room right behind him. Both of them wore tailored tuxedos with shawl collars that emphasized the broadness of their shoulders. The red ribbons on their lapels, signifying AIDS awareness, had been a standard component of evening dress for years.

"If anyone wants my opinion," announced Dolly, "I think we all look fabulous. That includes you, Mr. Hobart."

"Thank you, Mrs. Hobart. I do my best to keep up appearances."

"Don't we all!" Dolly linked her arm in Ned's. "Just remember, if any photographers aim their cameras our way tonight, try to look adoringly at me, not Chris."

"I haven't let you down yet, have I?" At the door, Ned turned back to their friends and said, "We'll meet you two downstairs. Break a leg tonight."

Christopher and Jennifer listened to their voices trail down the hall. Then he came over to her and placed his hands gently on her shoulders.

"Nervous?"

"The usual jitters, that's all. Okay, more than the usual. I'm scared as hell. This is a big one, isn't it?"

"It's a good movie. We have a lot to be proud of."

"I know that. It's just that I wish we didn't have to go through this part of it. I wish we didn't have to bother with premieres and photo shoots and the ridiculous heart-to-hearts with Deborah Myers."

"They serve a purpose."

"Tell me. Sometimes, though, I'd like to dispense with the whole charade. Just make our movies and go home afterward, put our feet up and watch television like everybody else in the world."

"No, you wouldn't, Jennifer. You don't wish anything of the sort, and you know it. You like seeing your picture on the cover of *Vogue* and being shuttled around in limousines and having the public recognize you. You've worked all your life for it."

She raised a wrist to her forehead in a gesture of mock agony and said, "Ah, the price of fame!"

Christopher laughed. "Oh, fame is not as bad as it's cracked up to be, if you use it right. Most people don't. It's like a wall between us and them, and it can offer great protection. You can hide behind the wall. As long as you appear at the gates now and then, that is, and wave at the nice people on the other side. That's all we're doing tonight. Appearing at the gates. Letting people think that life isn't so different on our side."

"Well, as long as no one decides to storm the gates!" Jennifer reached up and ran her finger over his lips. "You've always made our lives sound so much simpler than they are. Maybe that's what I love about you. I'm too complicated."

"We're actors, remember? Actors act. Besides, everybody plays some sort of role in his life. We happen to play more than most. We should. We're good at it."

"Are you happy, Chris?"

"In quite a philosophical mood tonight, aren't we? Yes, I'm happy. I get to do the work I want. I'm surrounded by people I love, and I'm married to my best friend. Why do you ask?"

"Just needed to know. I'm glad you feel that way." She kissed him lightly on the cheek. "I do, too."

There was a rapping at the door. Christopher opened it to find his assistant standing in the hall. "The limousines are here, sir. If you'd like, I've arranged with security to take you down the service elevator, so you can avoid the front door. Oh, yes, Geoffrey Reed arrived a few moments ago. I told him that you'd join him in the car."

"Very well. We'll be right there."

"One other thing. Apparently a few protesters have gathered outside the theater. There may be some chanting and cat-calls tonight. It shouldn't be a problem."

"Have they?.... Well, the only bad publicity is no publicity."

"What was that you were just saying about the nice people at the gates, darling," chided Jennifer.

"Dear Jennifer. I have only two words for you."

"What are they?"

"Magic time!"

The oval lobby of the Hotel Carlyle was small and discreet—its only concessions to conspicuous luxury being a highly polished marble floor and a profligate floral arrangement by one of New York's pricier florists, which commanded its own pedestal.

The reception desk was purposefully uncluttered, free of even so much as a bell to summon a bellboy. (A gentle nod from the head receptionist did that.) The impression earnestly fostered by the management was that the clientele was staying in a private apartment building, not a hotel, and that customers were considered residents, not transient guests. Whenever possible, they were addressed respectfully by their last names and told how good it was to see them back again, a greeting occasionally lavished on those arriving for the first time.

It hadn't taken more than a cursory glance, however, for the head receptionist to conclude that the slightly rag-tag group before him—three causally dressed adults and a young girl in fuchsia leggings—had never been in the Carlyle before. In truth, the young girl wasn't standing. She was spinning exuberantly across the marble foyer by way of demonstrating to anyone who cared to watch something she called "the leg dance."

"If you don't mind, madam," the receptionist said to Tina. "Your child!"

"Oh, yeah. Sorry. Angelina, get over here."

The receptionist turned a frosty gaze on Brent. "Yes?"

"I'm trying to get in touch with Christopher Knight and Jennifer Osborne."

"I'm sorry. We have no one staying here under those names."

"I was told they were here. Are you sure? This is very important."

"Positive." The receptionist opened a ledger, bound in Moroccan leather, ran his eyes over several pages, then looked back up at Brent. "We have no record of an Osborne or a Knight. Is there anything else I can do for you?"

"I realize it's your policy not to say when famous people are at the hotel. I understand the reasons for that. But I work for Mr. Knight and Ms. Osborne. They know me. Could you just let them know that Brent Stevens is in the lobby?"

"Really, sir. How many times must I repeat it?" If the receptionist's manner had been icy before, it was arctic now. "How am I supposed to give a message to someone who isn't registered at the hotel?"

Tina pulled Brent aside and asked, "Do you think we've come to the wrong place?"

Brent brushed off the question and approached the receptionist again. "Look, I don't even have to see them. Okay? I would just like to leave this envelope for them."

"You expect me to take an envelope for someone who isn't a guest? Please!"

"In case they check in, then. Will you do that for me?"

"I assure you they *won't* be checking in. Now I'm really going to have to ask you to leave." He nodded ever so slightly and a burly security guard suddenly materialized in the lobby. "Mr. Johnston, would you please escort these people to the door?" With that, the receptionist promptly turned his back on them.

"Hey, relax, guy," Johnny said to the guard. "I think we can find our way by ourselves." In deference to Johnny's bulk, the guard backed off but continued to watch, stone-faced, until they'd passed through the revolving door.

"Why is it people get so high and mighty in this city, as soon as you put them behind a counter. Ever notice? Even if it's a coffee shop!" Tina was in a huff. "Angelina, don't dance in the street. Get back here. You think the stars might be staying someplace else? Like the Plaza? I hear it's gotten awfully touristy these days?"

"Geoffrey Reed said the Carlyle. That receptionist is just protecting them. There's got to be some way of reaching them."

"How about the telephone?"

"The operator wouldn't put the call through."

"We could camp out on the sidewalk until they come out?" said Johnny, who was beginning to wonder if they hadn't embarked on a wild goose chase. "They aren't going to stay holed up all night."

Her energy flagging, Angelina leaned up against Tina. "I want to go home, Mom. Can we?"

"Not yet, Honey."

"Why not?"

"Because Brent has to deliver this package to the movie stars we saw on television last night."

"Where are they?"

"Well, we think they are staying at this hotel. But they're not here right now."

"Where did they go?" The child clasped her arms around her mother's waist and let her legs go slack.

"Don't pull on me, Angelina."

"They must be someplace, Mom!"

"Well, they are. We just don't know where, honey."

The answer clicked into Brent's mind. "The premiere, that's where! Thank you, Angelina. It doesn't matter if they're staying here or not. They've got to go to the premiere tonight. I can contact them there."

"Brent, it will be a mob scene."

"All I have to do is catch their attention as they're entering the theater. They always stop and pose for the photographers and wave to the crowd. They'll recognize me, if they see me. I can hand them the package. It'll only take a couple of seconds."

"And say what to them? Don't people scream their heads off at those things? How are you going to talk to them?"

"Why don't you write them a letter!" cracked Johnny.

"Very funny! When did you start doing stand-up, Johnny?" Tina shot her brother a reproving look. "Why don't you try and help?"

"No, that *is* a good idea," replied Brent. "I can slip a note in with the pictures, explaining that this is all Geoffrey Reed's doing and that I'm putting a stop to it. Do you have anything I can write with?"

Vigorously, Tina stirred the contents of her purse. A ballpoint pen rose to the surface.

"Here you are. Let me see if I've got a piece of

paper . . . What's this? . . . Telephone bill? Huh, I thought I paid it . . . Life Savers . . . Tampax . . . shit, I don't seem to have any more of my business cards. Can't you just use the back of one of the pictures?"

"I'll have to."

While Brent scribbled his message to the movie stars, Johnny stepped out into Madison Avenue and flagged down a cab.

33

Metal barricades prevented cars from turning off Seventh Avenue onto Fifty-fourth Street, where the Ziegfeld Theater was located, but to make sure, two burly policemen, positioned in front of the barricades, waved the traffic south with a continuous wheeling motion of their arms. Despite their efforts, every minute or so a cab or a delivery van would attempt to turn left anyway, and a shouting match would ensue. It was a typical New York confrontation—the driver expressing disbelief that a public thoroughfare was actually closed to his vehicle; the cops expressing disbelief that anyone would be so stupid as to try to enter a blocked-off street. The only vehicles allowed to pass were the limousines carrying dignitaries and guests to the premiere of *In the Beginning*. However loudly they complained, the Pakistani cabbies or the work crew from EeeZee Carpet Cleaners didn't qualify and were briskly directed to move on.

The people on foot were another matter. Although they were being successfully channeled onto the sidewalks for the time being, their numbers were swelling rapidly. Only about half of them had planned on being there. The other half were passers-by, wondering what was going on and stopping to take a look. That was how it usually went in Manhattan, where curiosity was endemic: A crowd simply guaranteed a bigger crowd. Most of the time it made for a carnival atmosphere, some good-natured screaming when Stallone or Schwarzenegger stepped out of the limo, and flashes of chalky white brilliance, like strokes of heat lightening, as the paparazzi went into action. But a half hour later, after the stars had disappeared into the theater, the crowd melted away, leaving behind only a few hardcore autograph seekers and a lot of trash in the street.

The mood tonight was less fun loving. What added a strident note and gave an undercurrrent of edginess to the event were the protesters. Some had already gathered in small groups, their arms linked in solidarity, but others seemed to be on their own and wandered through the crowd, proselytizing anyone who would listen. Many carried homemade signs, reading SHAME ON YOU, CHRISTOPHER AND JENNIFER! DO NOT TAKE THE LORD'S NAME IN VAIN, and in a nod to Reverend Greenway's recent campaign, TAKE THE GENITALS OUT OF GENESIS. On one banner, made from an old bedsheet, the word *Hollywood* had been crossed out with a large *X*. Underneath, golden script proclaimed the supremacy of *HOLYwood*.

Not far down Fifth-fourth Street, a ragtag choir, draped in silver robes, was singing "Amazing Grace," obliging the crowds to pass on either side of it. Confident that they were an island of piety in a sea of iniquity, the singers ignored the occasional taunt and looked for souls to save instead. At the sight of a television crew, their fervor doubled and they broke out the synchronized hand gestures.

The cab carrying Brent, Tina, and Angelina in the

backseat—Johnny in the front—traveled south on Fifth Avenue until it reached Fifty-ninth Street, where it swung west, then followed the southern edge of Central Park to Seventh Avenue, where it swung south once again. With each block, the traffic grew thicker, building inevitably toward gridlock. At the intersection of Fifty-seventh Street and Seventh, it finally came to a dead halt. Horns snarled angrily as the stoplight changed from red to green and back to red without effecting the slightest movement.

"It'll be quicker to walk," said Johnny. He handed the driver a ten-dollar bill as the three passengers in the back slipped out and threaded their way to the curb through the maze of stalled vehicles. On the sidewalk, people seemingly fated to collide managed, usually at the last second, to step out of one another's way without breaking pace. Tina grasped Angelina's hand so firmly the child squealed, "Mom, you're hurting me."

"Sorry, sweetheart."

"Why is everybody always squeezing my hand so hard?"

"Everybody must think you're pretty special."

As they rounded the corner onto Fifty-fourth Street, Tina's spirits fell. The crowd on the avenue was nothing compared to the throngs that had massed midway down the block before the Ziegfeld Theater. Teams of patrolmen, unable to keep people moving, were now content merely to keep them out of the street. And there on the sidewalk, smack in front of them, a choir had just begun to warble "We Shall Overcome" at top pitch.

"Holy Moses! Is the Pope supposed to be coming to this shindig?" she said. "What do we do now?" She looked at Brent to see if he shared her amazement.

"I've got to get nearer somehow," he said, his grip on the photographs tightening. "If they can't see me, how can I hand them this package? You can go home if you want to. This is no place for Angelina. I've got to stay and give it a try."

"Of course you do," she said, offended that Brent would think she was giving up so easily. "We all do." She appealed to her brother for advice. "What do you suggest, Johnny?"

"A tank."

"When did you start getting so hilarious? Jerry H. Seinfeld himself!" she snapped. "You're supposed to be helping."

"Dynamite, then? There aren't too many other ways you're going to get through a crowd like this."

He wasn't exaggerating. The premiere had been organized to produce the most excitement, which meant the most protracted screaming, which meant, in turn, that having the stars enter the Ziegfeld by the front doors had been ruled out days earlier. Such an entrance would have required them to walk only a couple dozen feet at most, hardly enough time to generate the requisite pandemonium. Since the side doors of the theater opened onto a spacious plaza, it had been pressed into use instead. Bleachers had been put up and a red carpet had been laid from the curb to the middle of the plaza. There, it angled sharply to the left and led to a microphone and podium by the side doors.

Near the podium, an area had been cordoned off for members of the press and the television cameramen, who would have the best view of Christopher Knight and Jennifer Osborne as they emerged from their limousine, walked the length of the carpet, paused to wave at their fans, then came over to the officials who were to greet them. Virtually under the reporters' noses, there would be handshakes, kissing, more waving at the crowd, and if the stars were so disposed, a few off-the-cuff remarks. Since the L-shaped trajectory would be lined with delirious fans, the thinking went, the cheering by this point would be deafening.

No one thought it would be like running the gauntlet, because, when the plans were formulated, no one took into account the protesters.

The police lifted the barricade for a glossy black limousine, which purred down Fifty-fourth Street.

"It's Meredith Murphy," someone called out. The information spread throughout the crowd, and someone else said, "Who the hell is she?" Meredith Murphy had, in fact, enjoyed several seasons of popularity on a television sitcom set in a Laundromat. As Cain's wife in *In the Beginning*, she was hoping to establish a beachhead in feature films.

"Yo, Meredith!" cried out a teenage boy, who wore his baseball cap backward in the prevailing fashion. He rapped on the hood of the limousine and laughed loudly. By the time the limousine reached the Ziegfeld and Meredith Murphy stepped onto the red carpet, reports of her identity had preceded her. There was some scattered applause, but more startling, especially to the actress, who was expecting an appreciative welcome, were the chants that arose.

"Don't go in, Meredith. Don't go in, Meredith."

They weren't coming from one isolated group, either. The pockets of discontent seemed to be sprinkled everywhere. The actress, initially disoriented, waved as if nothing were out of the ordinary, then hurried along the carpet, her lips in a frozen smile. As she reached the door and prepared to go inside, the chants from the bleachers turned to jeers.

"Shame on you!"

"God sees what you're doing."

Brent and Tina heard the jeering, too, and wondered what had prompted it. Tina stood on her toes and craned her neck. "Can you see anything?"

"Not much. Some redheaded actress."

A second limousine passed the police barricade and inched toward the Ziegfeld. In the next few minutes, Brent knew, the pace of the arrivals would pick up. It was already quarter to seven. Christopher Knight and Jennifer Osborne would make their appearance by seven, and he was still stuck far back in the crowd. At this rate, he'd never make it to the front in time.

Tina shot Johnny another of her What now? appeals.

"Okay, okay," he replied, getting the message. "I think you better follow me."

Folding his arms in front of his chest, like a plow, he waded into the mass of bodies. His bulkiness counted for a lot, but so did his determination to advance against whatever obstacles were in his path. Like an ice floe cracking under the onslaught of an icebreaker, the crowd split apart. Johnny moved deftly forward along the fault lines.

"What the fuck you doin', buddy?" a young man shouted at him, but when he saw the resolve on Johnny's face, he backed off.

"Coming through" was the only explanation Johnny bothered to give anyone, and he barked it out gruffly, as if he were a sheriff with a bullhorn. People were pushed, jostled, elbowed or simply leaned on until they lost their balance and moved (or fell) aside.

"Walk on your own feet, dammit."

"Coming through!"

"Where's the goddam fire?"

"You hear me? *Coming through!*"

Tina followed on Johnny's heels, then Angelina, who clung to the back of Tina's belt. Brent brought up the rear. As soon as they passed, the crowd closed in quickly behind them. Retreat was out of the question. The only choice was to plow onward.

Little by little, Johnny prevailed. By five minutes to seven, he had brought his caravan within view of the metal barricades that separated the fans from the arriving stars.

The television comedian Melvin Foster—instantly recognizable by his trademark horn-rimmed glasses, if not by the tuxedo he had donned for the premiere—fluttered at the edge of the red carpet, his jaw slack with astonishment.

"Don't go in, Mel," the protesters chanted. "Don't go in."

Melvin Foster's jaw dropped even more.

Deborah Myers figured that she had to have attended five hundred movie premieres in her lifetime. Minimum. At this point, who was counting? Whatever the number, it felt like a million. *Primary Colors, The Horse Whisperer, In the Beginning*—the films changed, but the basic ritual never did. She could have negotiated the red carpet in her sleep by now.

But knew she wouldn't.

She had her end of the bargain to uphold. Christopher Knight and Jennifer Osborne had accommodated her with a special moment, so it was now incumbent upon her to appear thrilled by their premiere. Not that appearing thrilled required great effort. Very little was required, actually. She would hesitate as she got out of the limousine, open her eyes wider than usual, as if dazzled and disoriented by all she beheld, then blink several times in a row to drive the impression home.

She called it her Dorothy in Oz look.

It seemed to counter any negative thoughts she might be thinking, and it read well on camera. Just freeze, open eyes, and blink-blink-blink. If she did that three or four times, she'd be home free. Sometimes it didn't hurt to throw in a little gasp, just before she blinked. But she liked to reserve the gasp for really big occasions.

As her limousine inched along, Deborah took a small compact out of her purse and flipped it open. Once her mascara had smudged without her realizing it, and in the next day's newspaper photos she'd looked like Dorothy on a Bender. Ever since, the last-minute check had become an automatic reflex.

The compact mirror revealed no smudges, no cracks, no waxy buildup. Just one damned good paint job, if she did say so herself. Her confidence restored and feeling good, Deborah Myers settled back in her seat.

Maybe she would give Jennifer and Christopher the benefit of a gasp, after all.

Spiff had always liked large crowds. More precisely, he liked being in the middle of a large crowd when everybody's attention was drawn to the fireworks exploding overhead or to the falling ball that ushered in the New Year.

Everybody *else's* attention.

Spiff watched the *people* watching the fireworks or the falling ball. It made him feel almost invisible, as if he were a peeping tom, huddled in dense foliage. He could stare at the young girl next to him, look her right in the eye, knowing he was just a blur in her peripheral vision, and she wouldn't notice him. No one would.

Like now. The arrival of a minor starlet with red hair had captured everybody's attention, as if she were Marilyn or Sophia or somebody really glamorous. Hell, she wasn't even that pretty, Spiff thought. Her chin was too sharp, and that smile was as phony as Monopoly dough, but that didn't seem to prevent people from applauding enthusiastically. Well, not everybody, true. Some people were shouting at her, telling her to stay out of the theater. The point was, she had the attention of the crowd for the moment, and that allowed him to scan the faces around him freely.

That's what Geoffrey Reed wanted him to do—keep an eye out for Brent Stevens in the event "the little prick"— those were his exact words—showed up at the premiere and tried to make contact with the stars. Spiff thought it more likely that Brent had gone back to the brick house in Queens, where that little girl and her mother lived. But you never knew. And there was no arguing with Geoffrey when he was upset.

Anyway, Spiff would go to Queens later tonight and check out the neighborhood one more time. It offered real possibilities. He didn't like the idea of harming the kid. She was a cute kid. Her mother wasn't half bad, either. But as long as Brent insisted on keeping the photos, what alternatives were there? You did what you had to do. Right now, what he had to do was stay alert.

Spiff felt the bodies pressing up against him and enjoyed the sensation of detachment that came over him. He was all alone and feeling . . . well, not blue, that was for sure! Feeling good. Feeling invisible! Sounded like the makings of a song to him.

"One of those country western ballads," he said, with a chuckle. He was talking to himself again.

Spiff slipped his hand into his pants pocket to reassure himself that his Kershaw Talon was still there. Of course it was. Where else would it be? Still, in a crowd like this, there were bound to be pickpockets. With so many people on top of one another, how much skill would it take to separate a few wallets from their owners?

"Oops! Excuse me, sir. Didn't mean to push!" and it was done!

Without removing the knife from his pocket, Spiff turned it over in his hand several times.

Jennifer and Christopher were accustomed to the frenzy that their appearances provoked. It was part of the game. They showed up. The fans screamed. They feigned surprise. The fans screamed all the louder. But it was organized frenzy, and nobody was really fooled by it. Half the time, it was the same bunch of screamers who turned out, whether to see a visiting head of state or a minor rock singer. It didn't seem to make a whole lot of difference to them.

This wasn't the usual crowd, Jennifer thought as she peered out the tinted limousine window. "A few protesters, my foot!" she said. "It's Kent State out there."

"You're exaggerating, Jennifer."

"Think so? Look."

Much as Christopher hated to admit it, she was right. The placards that usually greeted them bore adoring messages: WE LOVE YOU, CHRISTOPHER. BE MY SHINING KNIGHT! There certainly weren't many of those tonight. Geoffrey Reed had fallen down on the job again! The only signs Christopher could see were angry and spiteful. One, proclaiming that "BLASPHEMERS BURN IN HELL!" was being brandished by a woman who could have been his grade-school teacher back in Iowa. She had on a shapeless tan sweater and thick glasses. Everything about her was mousy and prim, except for the snarl that twisted her thin lips.

As the limousine passed, she stepped off the curb, ran up to the window, and spat on it.

Christopher pulled back into the protective depths of the limousine. "She must mean us, Jennifer. How's it feel to be a blasphemer?"

"Mother was right. People don't like it when you fool around with their God."

"We're not fooling around with anything. We made a serious movie. Don't you think people should see it first before they shout it down?"

"They'll be seeing it in a few minutes. Maybe they're just getting an early start," Jennifer noted tartly.

The limousine came to a halt, the motor idling silently, while the car in front of theirs unloaded its passengers—Ned and Dolly Hobart, Geoffrey Reed, and Jennifer's mother. The Hobarts appeared vaguely amused by the scene, but Eleanor Osborne's worst fears were coming true. Her clenched teeth testified to her conviction that she had landed in the kingdom of barbarians. She checked the metal barriers and hoped they would contain the human tide.

"Shame! Shame! Shame!"

The rhythmic chant went up from a group immediately to her right, so she concluded it was meant for her and flushed with embarrassment. Without waiting for Geoffrey Reed to escort her, she hastened down the carpet toward the lobby of the theater. As she went by, a fan announced authoritatively, "That's Ginger Rogers."

"No, it isn't," countered another voice with no less certainty. "Ginger Rogers croaked years ago. It's Shelly Winters." The fan reached out over the barricade to touch her. "We love you, Shelley."

Eleanor Osborne kept her eyes straight ahead and wondered if she really looked that awful.

Geoffrey Reed hung back at the curb. Jennifer's mother would have to fend for herself. He had more urgent concerns. Christopher and Jennifer were in the next limousine, and he intended to keep his eyes on them until they were inside the movie house and the lights had gone out. Not that they would be all that tempted to mingle with these fanatics. Premieres were chaotic enough in Geoffrey's experience, but this one was turning into a madhouse.

Brent had begun to think that Johnny had pulled it off. They were close to the metal barricades that blocked the sidewalk on the north side of the street. Although several rows of people were still in front of them, he could actually see the plush red carpet now and beyond it, another set of barricades and more people on bleachers. The corridor between the two groups, he estimated, was twenty-five, maybe thirty feet wide. While that was enough to hold the overzealous fans at bay, it wasn't so wide that Jennifer and Christopher wouldn't hear him when he called out their names.

If they were in a good mood, they would enter the theater in a leisurely fashion, chatting up a few people along the way. Even if they didn't, all Brent needed was a few seconds to get their attention. A glance his way would be sufficient. He'd hand them the envelope, which he now clutched to his chest, tell them how important it was, and warn them not to let it out of their sight. The message inside would explain more, when they got the chance to read it. But the important thing was that the incriminating pictures would be in their possession. No one else would have them.

As Johnny edged them even nearer to the barrier, Brent found his optimism growing. Then he felt a stab of cold in his lower back. A strange burning coldness he had never felt before. Hot and cold at the same time.

A voice whispered in his ear, "Don't move."

The burning sensation became more acute.

"Hear me? Just give me the envelope and you won't get hurt." Brent realized that something sharp had penetrated his shirt and broken his skin. He tried to twist his head and see who was holding him from behind, but he was pinned in place by the bodies to either side of him.

"I am warning you. Don't say anything or you will have a very large hole in your back." Spiff gave a slight twist to the knife, causing Brent to cry out in pain. The cry was swallowed up in the general noise of the crowd, which was working itself into a fever pitch. The stars they had come out to see were arriving at last. Fans and protesters alike were mindful of little else.

The limousine glided to a stop. Then, the chauffeur got out. The cheering started before he'd even opened the back door.

Brent gritted his teeth and told himself not to relinquish the photos. He'd come too far to give up. Johnny and Tina were still pushing forward, angling for a better view, but any second now, one of them would turn back and understand what was happening. He pressed the package hard to his chest, determined to ignore the burning coldness in his back. Sweat trickled down his neck. Yet he was shivering.

Christopher Knight was the first to emerge from the limousine. A roar swept over the crowd, like a hot wind. Catcalls mingled with the cheers and whoops of approval. Then Jennifer Osborne slithered out of the long vehicle and joined her husband. He put his arm around her waist, and they stood there, every inch the fabled movie stars. They were smaller than they looked on the screen, but their glow charged the air. They didn't have to do anything; just standing was sufficient. Even the protesters, who were supposed to be above such considerations, were momentarily struck by the power of their presence.

"Magic time, darling," Christopher mumbled through his smile.

"Magic time, yourself."

The actor brought Jennifer's palm up to his lips and kissed it, as he'd done on the *Deborah Myers Special.* Several teenage girls hanging over a barricade could no longer contain themselves and let out shrieks of ecstasy.

A stout middle-aged man shook his fist over his head and bellowed, "Jesus died for you. God's only begotten Son gave his life for your sins. You are crucifying Him all over again!" If Jennifer and Christopher heard the sermon, they gave no indication. Serene and assured, they moved down the carpet, cognizant of the Instamatics and videocams pointed in their direction, turning slowly to the right, then to the left, allowing for as many different shots as possible. But never posing. No, just letting the fans verify that the dream creatures they worshipped on the screen were made of flesh and blood. We haven't tricked you, they seemed to be saying. Makeup and lighting have nothing to do with us. Reality is no different from illusion.

"I've seen *The Forgotten Summer* fourteen times," shouted a woman, red-faced with excitement.

"Hi, Chris! Hey, Jen!"

Pens and pieces of paper were thrust eagerly at them. "Could I have your autograph for my daughter." "Look over here!" And riding shrilly above the entreaties, the confession of a wounded male heart, "I loooooove you, Jennifer."

With every step the stars took, the comments grew louder and bolder. Everyone was yelling at once, feeding the tumult, pressing against the barriers in order to get nearer, because who knew when or if the stars would ever pass this way again.

So neither Johnny nor Tina heard Brent when he cried, "Help!" But then it wasn't a cry so much as a gurgle, like someone choking on a thick liquid.

Brent had the sensation of wetness spreading at the base of his spine and knew that it was blood. He wouldn't be able to hold on to the package much longer. Couldn't anybody see what was happening to him?

Please, look at me! he wanted to shout, but his voice had no power and his tongue was heavy in his mouth.

Then he realized that someone *was* looking. Angelina had turned around to see if he was still following. Her eyes were big and round, expanding saucers of surprise. Did she sense his pain? His panic? She was only a child. How could a child know such things?

"Take . . . the . . . package." He mouthed the words slowly, exaggerating them, hoping that she would at least be able to read his lips. With all his remaining strength, he drove his elbows deep into Spiff's stomach. As he did, the package tumbled to the ground. He managed to kick it with his left foot, moving it closer to the child.

Angelina hesitated only a second, then bent down and snatched it off the sidewalk.

Spiff watched with disbelief. The child was tugging furiously at the sleeve of a woman to get her attention. Wedged behind Brent, he was unable to do anything to prevent it. Rage coursed through him. "Don't say I didn't warn you," he growled and shoved the knife into Brent's flesh.

Tina turned just in time to catch the grimace of pain that distorted Brent's face.

"Oh my God. What's wrong, Brent?" she said. He seemed to have taken ill and his body was slumping toward the ground. Somebody behind him was propping him up. She looked closer. It was . . . him! The man from the hospital, the one who, only a few hours before, had been sitting in the outdoor café. He had managed to find them. She yanked Angelina behind her, shielding the child with her body.

"Johnny! Quick!" she cried. "The goon is back. Brent's in serious shit."

Johnny spun around and an instant later dove for Spiff.

*   *   *

307

Geoffrey Reed had to hand it to Jennifer and Christopher. Cool as cucumbers, both of them. You never would have thought that while half of New York was applauding them madly, the other half was calling for their condemnation. They could have been at a garden party, sipping tea and discussing the weather. Later he would hear it from them. Jennifer would bitch about the nasty placards, and Christopher would complain that the affair had been botched from the very start. Control freaks, one worse than the other. But some things couldn't be controlled. Surely, they had to know that.

If they didn't, they would soon.

This crowd was particularly volatile, Geoffrey conceded. That Greenway preacher had whipped his followers into a nice little fundamentalist frenzy. And all over a movie. What century were these people living in? Then he thought of the pictures that Brent had taken. If a little nudity on the screen could cause a ruckus like this, imagine what would happen if those photographs ever got out. Tonight would seem like a picnic. A church picnic.

The notion momentarily amused him.

Still, he wished that Jennifer and Christopher would hurry it up. Nothing was to be gained by stretching out this ritual. He knew exactly what was going on in their minds. Dallying was their way of denying the reality of the situation. He'd seen the stars look right through people at chichi parties, and that's what they were doing here on a larger scale—looking through the protesters, refusing to hear the chanting, seeing only what they wanted. They probably had convinced themselves it was one big love-in.

A scuffle of some sort had broken out on the sidewalk, to boot! Probably a couple of rabid fans, jostling for position. Maybe an atheist beating up on a Baptist! That would be nice! Geoffrey couldn't tell what the flare-up was about, but he figured the cops would take care of it, if it didn't stop soon. Or maybe they wouldn't. The cops couldn't be everywhere at once. Geoffrey was grateful to be on his side of the barrier, away from the hoi polloi. Rank had a few prerogatives. Not getting knocked black and blue by a bunch of screaming idiots seemed to be the chief one at present.

At least the stars had reached the entrance. There would be some official greeting next, and Jennifer would be given a bouquet of roses—Geoffrey had thought that far ahead. The paparazzi behind the velvet rope would all go nuts. And then, with a little luck, they could go inside, sit down, and get this damn movie over.

His eyes went back to the scuffle, which seemed to have grown more violent. It was a couple of men. One appeared to have the other in a bear hug. Too many bodies surrounded them for Geoffrey to determine much more. Then he caught a glimpse of one of the men's faces. He stepped closer to the barricade. Surely he was mistaken.

For a second, he thought he'd seen Brent Stevens.

"Repent now. Before it's too late. Repent and save your soul from hell."

Jennifer told herself that the worst would be over in a few more minutes. Premieres were taxing enough, but the protesters weren't making this one any easier with their absurd pronouncements. Did they really expect her to fall on her knees and rend her Todd Oldham? Fortunately, the microphone was in the possession of a local official, who was asking everybody to give "a big New York welcome to our special guests, America's royalty, Christopher Knight and Jennifer Osborne."

For a while, the big New York welcome eclipsed the calls for repentance. Jennifer smiled and waved yet again. That was all she did at these affairs. Her lips were numb from smiling. And roses of all things! What was she supposed to do with a bouquet of roses? Roses were for beauty queens. Or brides. She contemplated pitching them into the crowd but restrained herself.

How did Christopher do it? He managed to look as if he were actively enjoying himself. The trouble was, if you let down for a fraction of an instant, if you showed so much as a flash of irritation or disgust, a photographer was bound to record the moment. And that would be the picture that would show up in the tabloids, along with some story to the effect that Jennifer Osborne was having a nervous breakdown. Or her marriage was on the skids. It was simpler to smile.

So she smiled.

And was all set to go into the Ziegfeld Theater, when she spotted a little girl slip between the barricades and approach her. She couldn't have been more than six or seven and had wistful eyes. She was carrying something in front of her, like an offering. Jennifer had learned from experience not to accept gifts from fans—it was usually just junk, anyway—but the paparazzi were right there. How would it look if she turned her back on a child? This was one tribute she had better accept.

"For me?" she asked. The child gazed up at her and nodded. "How sweet!" Jennifer took the envelope, then knelt down and gave the girl a kiss on the cheek. As she expected, the photographers went into a frenzy. Flashbulbs exploded and expensive cameras buzzed like angry hornets.

"You are very pretty," Angelina said.

"What a lovely thing to say. Christopher, darling, come meet my new friend. She's brought us a present."

Christopher crouched beside his wife. "Who do we have here? What's your name, sweetheart?"

"Angelina."

"Thank you, Angelina," he said, giving the child a pat on the head. Jennifer looked adoringly at her husband. The buzzing of the cameras intensified. They held the pose.

Where had that little girl come from? Geoffrey wondered peevishly. It wasn't anything he'd planned. In his experience, children and animals were public relations catastrophes waiting to happen, even if the media did go wild for them. There was never any controlling what they would do or say.

The girl looked familiar to him, though. From a TV commercial perhaps? She had to be one of those precocious child actresses, whose pushy stage mothers were always conniving to get their daughters noticed any way they could.

It took a moment for the truth to dawn on him. He *did* know the child. He'd seen her just the other day in the park with Brent Stevens. So Brent Stevens *was* here in the crowd! He'd shown up at the premiere, just as Geoffrey feared he would. But why had he brought that little girl with him?

Geoffrey told himself to stay calm. It didn't matter why. The stars hadn't seen Brent and there was no chance they would now. That was all that mattered. The ceremonies were almost over. Just a minute more. Once Jennifer and Christopher obliged the paparazzi with a few more poses, they'd go inside, where they would be out of sight and out of reach.

A wave of panic washed over him.

The envelope! That was the gift in the child's hands. The envelope with the pictures inside. The one Brent had brought with him to the café. The little girl had given it to Jennifer. He had to get it back immediately.

Again, a voice in his head counseled him to remain cool. The stars wouldn't open it right away. Not in public. Not now. Once inside the theater, they would toss it to some flunky and not pay it another thought. The film was uppermost in their minds. The envelope meant nothing to them. All Geoffrey had to do was offer to take it off Jennifer's hands, tell her he'd put it away for safekeeping, if need be. She would give it to him! She might even tell him to throw it away!

And Brent thought he was being so clever! He couldn't have done Geoffrey a bigger favor, if he'd wanted to.

Savoring the irony, Geoffrey started toward the stars, his eyes riveted on the envelope.

If he'd glanced to the right, he would have seen Spiff and Johnny, locked together in a clinch, like two punch-drunk boxers while the crowd strained to pull away and give them room. But the photographs had eluded Geoffrey too long for him to think of anything else.

He didn't see Brent thrust out a hand in Tina's direction, his fingers coated with blood and bright as any stop sign. Or see Tina clap a hand over her own mouth in horror, before reaching out and taking hold of the slippery red fingers, as if she would never let go of them again.

Geoffrey was so fixated on the envelope, lest it slip away again, that he might have been a man hypnotized. As it was, he barely heard Tina when she screamed with all the lung power of a lifelong New Yorker, "He's got a knife. Watch out, Johnny! THE MAN'S GOT A KNIFE!"

Her warning was like a spark falling on gunpowder.

Starting with the people nearest Johnny and Spiff, the hysteria rippled outward in circular waves. People absorbed it like a contagion from the person in front of them and passed it on. Someone had the sudden urge to flee. Then someone else. But they were packed too tightly together and all they succeeded in doing was to hurtle up against one another.

The police might have been able to bring the pandemonium under control, had they reacted more quickly. But no less starstruck than the next person, they were slow to move. The pressure of the crowd built inexorably until there was only one way for the surge of bodies to go.

The metal barrier toppled over, catching Geoffrey at the legs and knocking him sideways to the ground. His skull hit the sidewalk with a dull thump, and he was blinded by a shower of fireworks. It couldn't be fireworks, he thought. It had to be the paparazzi with their cameras. But the incandescence was inside his head. He understood that he had fallen hard and the breath had gone out of him.

He struggled to pull himself into a seated position, but his legs were pinned under the metal barrier and people were trampling over it. Each time he raised himself up, he felt their weight driving him back down onto the concrete. If only someone would stop and lift it off him, he would be all right. The pictures. Had to get the pictures. Couldn't see the stars anymore. Inside the theater now. Little girl gone, too. Everybody screaming and running. Feet dangerously near to his head.

A heel caught him in the face—causing the fireworks to blaze up briefly. Then a heavyset man tripped and plummeted forward with a desperate shout. Unable to break his fall, he landed with all his weight on the barricade, and several of Geoffrey's ribs snapped like twigs.

"The wages of sin are death." "Vengeance is mine saith the Lord." "His kingdom is nigh."

What was he imagining now? What ridiculousness was this? The movie! Of course, he was watching the movie. Christopher and Jennifer's movie. No, he wasn't. His mind was wandering. Mustn't forget the envelope. With the pictures. Little girl knows where it is. Have to find her. Have to stand up first. Can't. Can't feel anything. Growing darker by the second. No point calling out. Too much noise. Surroundings just a blur.

As abruptly as if someone had thrown a switch in Geoffrey Reed's head, everything went to black.

34

Protests Disrupt Movie Premiere
One Dead, Many Injured in Violence
By Chris Becker
Herald Staff Writer

The star-studded premiere of *In the Beginning* was tragically marred last night when protests against the multimillion-dollar motion picture epic turned ugly, igniting panic in the large crowd gathered in front of the Zeigfeld Theater. The melee claimed one victim. As many as ten others suffered minor injuries, according to police reports.

The victim, Geoffrey Reed, known as the "press agent to the stars," was caught in the stampede and was apparently trampled to death. Doctors at Lenox Hill Hospital, where he was taken for treatment, said that he died of internal injuries.

Reed was attending the gala premiere with Christopher Knight and Jennifer Osborne, the stars of the film and his best-known clients. As soon as rioting broke out, the actors were quickly ushered inside the theater. Neither was harmed, although both were reportedly shaken by events.

In the Beginning, which is based on the Book of Genesis in the Bible, has been the target of conservative political and religious groups, which object to its sexual content and nudity. Many in the last night's crowd had shown up to applaud Knight and Osborne, America's most popular husband/wife acting team. A highly vocal minority, however, were there to express their dissatisfaction with a film they claim is blasphemous. They carried placards and taunted the celebrities as they arrived for the black-tie screening.

Police were unable to pinpoint the exact cause of the rioting. But from interviews with several eyewitnesses, the *Herald* has ascertained that one of the protesters carried a knife and threatened to attack Osborne. The unidentified assailant disappeared into the crowd before police could arrest him.

Sources told the *Herald* that Osborne was reluctant to attend the premiere, but that Reed had convinced her that it was necessary for the film's success. (The *Herald* has also learned that the glamorous blonde actress has received death threats in the past.) From the start, last night's mood was a volatile one, with clashes breaking out periodically between fans and protesters.

Comedian Mel Foster, TV starlet Meredith Murphy, anchorwoman Deborah Myers, and veteran actress Shelley Winters were among those whose appearance stirred strong reactions in the crowd. But it was the arrival of Osborne and Knight, who are rarely seen in public, that triggered the pandemonium. "People just seemed pretty excited and enthusiastic, and the next thing, they were out of control," said police chief Murray Huberman, who promised a thorough investigation of the incident.

Reverend Paul Greenway, the Boston minister who has called for a nationwide boycott of *In the Beginning*, said last night that he was "deeply distressed" by the rioting and that he would "pray for the friends and family of Mr. Reed." The violence, he added, did not surprise him, and he termed the film "the sort of provocation that is bound to have tragic consequences like these."

Typical of the fans, many of whom had waited for up to three hours to catch a glimpse of their idols, was Joanne Giovanelli, a secretary from Brooklyn. A distressed Giovanelli gave this account of Reed's death: "He arrived with Christopher Knight and Jennifer Osborne and you could tell he was very concerned for their safety. When the crowd started to panic, I saw him run to protect them. Before he could reach them, he was knocked over by a barrier, and he got pinned to the ground. By then, it was total hysteria."

The screening of *In the Beginning* took place with a forty-five minute delay. However, the stars did not show up at the lavish post-premiere party, held at the St. Regis Hotel.

Through a spokesperson, Knight and Osborne released a statement expressing their shock and grief. "Geoffrey Reed was one of our closest and most trusted colleagues," it read. "He was part of our family and we are deeply saddened by his death. This is a loss from which we will not recover soon."

The spokesperson said that the stars intend to dedicate *In the Beginning* to his memory.

From the reviews of *In the Beginning*:

"Above all, *In the Beginning* is a new beginning for Christopher Knight and Jennifer Osborne. It's not just their bodies they're baring here, but their souls as well. At a time when most sexuality onscreen is ambiguous, they represent a welcome throwback to an earlier era in Hollywood filmmaking, the era of manly men and womanly women. Their honesty triumphs."

—*New York Times*

"Christopher Knight and Jennifer Osborne convey the sort of raw sexuality that blisters movies screens, enrages prudes, and gets boys of all ages hot and bothered."

—*Playboy*

"Two thumbs up and a big hallelujah!"

—Siskel and Ebert

"Lush Trash." (A–)

—*Entertainment Weekly*

"The $100 million epic, lensed in the Tunisian desert, has already attracted widespread criticism from the right, but the combination of star power, familiar story line, and naked flesh should make for boffo grosses worldwide."

—*Variety*

35

The letter *I*—bright red in color, tilting slightly to the right—shimmered in front of his eyes. He blinked several times and the shimmering came to a stop.

Next to the letter was a heart, also outlined in red, and next to the red heart was another capital letter: *U*.

The strange code was etched on a wall only a few feet away from him. How curious, he thought. Beneath the letters and the heart, he could make out a name, "Angelina." What did it all mean?

Tina saw the flickering of Brent's eyelids. "That poster was Angelina's idea," she said. "She wanted it to be the first thing you saw when you woke up. She told me it would make you happy and you'd get better faster that way. How do kids know these things?"

She was sitting on the edge of the bed, holding his hand. "How are you feeling?"

"Okay, I guess," he said, groggily. His tongue was thick, and he felt drugged. "Where am I?"

"You'll never believe it! Roosevelt Hospital. Again! One of the nurses actually remembered you from the last time. You've become a celebrity around here."

"I have?" Brent started to sit up in the bed, but a sharp pain shot through his side, stopping him. He winced.

"I don't think you're supposed to move too much."

"Don't worry." With his fingers, he delicately probed his side and discovered the thick bandage under his hospital gown. He immediately looked to Tina for reassurance.

"It's not serious," she said. "You're gonna be fine. I almost passed out myself when I saw all the blood last night, but the doctors said it wasn't as bad as it appeared. You were lucky. The knife didn't hit any internal organs."

He took in the room, trying to make sense of it. The bed next to him was empty. A window gave onto an air shaft, but they had to be on a low floor, because he couldn't see the sun or tell what the weather was. He shook his head. "I don't remember—"

"Oh, don't say that!" Tina's heart skipped a beat at the thought that it was starting up again. Just when Brent had begun to return to normal, too. She knew what that bewildered look meant. The shock of the stabbing had traumatized him. His mind had gone blank.

She put her hands on his shoulders and stared him hard in the eye, fighting the temptation to shake him. "What's my name?" she said firmly. "Come on, Brent, tell me. What is my name?"

He looked at her, puzzled.

"I'm serious. Can you remember my name?"

His eyes widened with surprise. "Of course I can, *Tina*. Your name's Tina."

"That's a good sign. Now do you remember the premiere? Think! The goon with the knife? Everybody going crazy afterward?"

"What are you talking about? Why wouldn't I? Yes, I remember fighting the crowds and the stars waving and Angelina taking the photographs from me and then tugging on your sleeve . . . What's wrong with you, Tina?"

"Me? Nothing." Suddenly embarrassed, she let go of his shoulders and sat back. "I was just, you know, checking."

"Checking? . . . Oh, I get it. You thought I'd forgotten who I was again." Despite the pain it caused him in his side, he managed to laugh. "No, what I meant was I don't remember coming *here*. I don't remember *this room.*"

"Well, you wouldn't. When we got here, they took you right into the operating room and sewed you up. Then they gave you something to knock you out, so you'd sleep. By the time they transferred you to this room, you were out of it."

She blew out a long stream of air and flopped backward on the bed. "Whew! Don't do that to me again, Brent Stevens. That's the second scare you've given me in less than twelve hours. I don't know how many more I can take. I'm not a young woman."

There was light rapping at the door and a nurse swept into the room. "How are we feeling this morning?"

"Fine," Brent answered.

"Well, you've got some nice color back in your cheeks." She stuck a thermometer in Brent's mouth and automatically reached for his wrist in order to take his pulse. "You think you might stay with us this time? You see what happens when you try to run away before we're finished with you. You get sent right back." She chuckled.

"I don't imagine I'll be going anywhere this morning."

"I'll let the doctor know. He'll be glad to hear it, I'm sure." The nurse made some notations on her clipboard and left, still chuckling to herself.

As Tina reclaimed her position on the edge of the bed, Brent slowly pulled himself into a seated position so that his face was level with hers. "How's Angelina?"

"She did better than any of us. She thinks of it as a big adventure. When all hell broke loose, I saw that actress, Jennifer Osborne, take her inside the theater to get her away from the crowd. A security guard watched over her until things calmed down. She even got to see some of the movie. I had a hard time talking my way into the theater, but when Angelina waved at me, they let me in. She couldn't wait to get home and tell her friend Megan all about it."

"Did they catch the guy with the knife?"

"Not yet. I've never seen anyone run so fast, when I yelled. Poof! He was gone."

"I'm sorry I put you through all that madness. It's not right. I've got a lot to make up to you."

"No, you don't." Tina gave one of her self-effacing shrugs. "Anybody would have done as much."

"No, anybody wouldn't. *You* did. Thank you."

"Well, somebody had to, right? Me or the next guy."

"Tina, did you hear me? I said, 'Thank you.' Just say, 'You're welcome.' That's all. You've got to let people show you their gratitude. You gotta let *me* express my gratitude. You saved my life. Twice. I don't know what I can do in return. But I got to be able to tell you what it means to me."

"Words aren't necessary, Brent. Long time ago, I learned how to read between the lines."

"For my sake, you've still got to let me say it," he insisted. "It's important. When I saw those pictures in the locker, I knew right away I was the one who had taken them. I didn't tell you because I was afraid. Yeah, afraid and ashamed of what you'd think of me. I figured you'd want me out of your life and I didn't want to go. I've never felt that way before . . . Do you think I'm a terrible person?"

Tina chose her words carefully. "Well, I guess I look at it this way. I didn't know the person who took those pictures. I never met him. The person I met was the one who didn't want to add more trash to the heap. Isn't that how Jennifer Osborne expressed it on TV? The person I met put his life in danger, so those pictures wouldn't wind up in the wrong hands. Most anybody would have to respect that."

Brent sank back into the pillow until he'd gathered the strength for what he had to say next. Then he raised his head. "I hope that this isn't the end for us, Tina. I want to lead a different life now. I don't know what it will be yet. But I'm going to try. I'd like you to be part of it somehow."

She thought back to when she'd first seen him in front of the Dakota. It had been only—what? a week ago. So much had happened to them since then. That was life in the city for you—all sorts of people bumping up against one another, going through unexpected adventures together, then drifting on to the next unpredictable encounter with someone else. Or maybe that was life everywhere.

Everything that was so vivid to her right now was bound to fade with time, leaving just the outlines, and eventually, the outlines would fade, too. That's the way it happened, unless you made an effort to remember. You had to work hard to hold on to memories. Like people, they could slip away from you before you realized it.

She took only a second to decide.

"If that's what you really want, Brent, I think it's what I want, too."

"Thank you, Tina," he said quietly.

She bit her tongue. "You're welcome, Brent."

There was a clatter of people in the hallway, and the nurse stuck her head through the door. She was slightly flustered and out of breath, as if she'd just sprinted up a flight of stairs. "Oh, good, you're still awake. You've got some visitors. I told them I had to check on you first." She turned to the people in the hall. "It's okay. He's awake. You can go in and see him now."

She stepped aside to allow Jennifer Osborne and Christopher Knight to enter the room. The actor was wearing jeans and a navy cashmere sweater. His wife had on a suede jacket and her dark glasses. They were pushed up on her head and held her blonde hair back. Even though they were dressed to blend in with the crowd, their natural grace set them apart.

"Hello, Brent," Jennifer said, her voice barely a hush. Christopher's greeting was more assertive. "Hi there, buddy. How are you managing?"

Tina sprang up from the bed. The presence of the stars in Brent's hospital room would hardly have startled her more had they dropped from the acoustical tile ceiling. "I'll leave you all alone," she stammered, reaching for her dance bag, which she had inadvertently kicked under the bed in her excitement.

"No, you don't have to go," said Brent, grabbing her

324

arm. "This is my friend Tina. Tina, this is Christopher Knight and Jennifer Osborne."

Tina shook their hands. "I recognized you right away from your pictures . . . er, your movies. I'm pleased to meet you both."

"So how is the patient doing?" asked Christopher. "That was a little more than we bargained for last night, any of us. You, too, huh?"

"The doctors say it could have been worse."

"We're hoping he'll be able to go home in a couple of days," Tina volunteered.

"Home to L.A.?" Jennifer raised her eyebrows.

"I don't know yet," Brent replied. "I'm not sure where home is anymore. I was just trying to figure that out. How did you know I was here?"

Christopher exchanged a hasty look with Jennifer. "I called the number you gave us," he said. "The one inside the envelope. The man who answered told me that you were here."

"That must have been my brother, Johnny," Tina said.

"We wanted to see you before we went back to Los Angeles," Jennifer explained. "Make sure everything was okay."

"So you got the envelope?" Brent asked.

There was an awkward pause. Tina thought she saw a flash of discomfort register on the stars' faces, but when she looked again, it was gone. Their composure had returned, if it had ever deserted them.

"Yes, we did," Christopher said. "We were . . . a little stunned."

"I guess you would be," Brent said. "That's everything, by the way. There's nothing else, in case you were worried."

"Well, yes, I suppose we were," Christopher admitted. "You can understand. But we were worried about you, too."

"Thanks."

"And we're both grateful for what you did. Aren't we, Jennifer?"

He slipped his arm around Jennifer's waist and she looked up at him. The light from the overhead fixture made her eyes glisten and accentuated the translucence of her skin. "Of course, we are, darling. Very grateful."

"If you would like to recuperate in a hotel here in New York, we'd be happy to take care of that," Christopher went on. "A room at the Plaza with a view of the park? What do you say?"

"It would be our way of expressing our appreciation. You went to great lengths for us last night," Jennifer said. Tina wondered for a second if the actress wasn't blinking back tears.

"Thank you. But that's not necessary. I don't want anything from you. Having you come by this morning is enough. I didn't expect it, really. Anyway, it's Tina's little girl, Angelina, you should be thanking."

"Angelina," whispered the actress. "Such a lovely name. Little angel! That's how I'll think of her."

"Yeah, well, they can be little devils, too," Tina cracked. "But I guess you'll be finding that out for yourself before long."

"I guess we will." Jennifer allowed herself a brief smile. "If you won't accept anything, Brent, let us send something to Angelina for being such a brave girl."

"Whatever you give Angelina is fine by me."

"Just don't make it anything I have to assemble," Tina requested.

"Not to worry."

Christopher took his wife by the elbow. "Come on, Jen. We should probably let Brent get some rest now."

"Yes, dear," she replied. "It was good to see you, Brent. Stay in touch." She leaned over the bed, picked up his hand, then pressed his palm to her lips. "Lovely meeting you, Tina."

"What do you know!" whistled Tina after the stars had departed. "Mr. and Mrs. Hollywood. At the foot of your bed."

"Yeah, magic time!"

"What do you mean?"

"Oh, nothing."

Brent took her hand and they sat for a while, before he broke the silence. "I don't think I will go back to L.A. It's not the right place for me. I got pretty mixed up there. All the famous people and the mansions and the money."

"It happens," Tina said philosophically. "Know what Ida believed? In the end, you're not going to be judged by how big your house is or how much money you earned, but by how many people you made smile. Yeah! That's why she'd go down to Grand Avenue . . . To see all those toothless smiles."

"I'd like to go to Grand Avenue."

"I'll take you there."

Silence settled over the hospital room again. Brent's eyelids drooped and then closed altogether. Tina sensed he was drifting off to sleep. The visits had been tiring. As she slipped her hand out of his and started to tuck the covers around his neck, he spoke up. His voice was fuzzy and warm, and he scarcely moved his lips.

"The day you took me to the airport, remember, Tina?"

"Yeah, remember what?"

"You said you envied me. You said there were parts of your life you'd like to forget. Like I had. 'Who wouldn't want to make a fresh start?' you said."

"Well, I guess I did. So?"

The corners of his mouth turned up contentedly. "So now it begins."

Acknowledgments

Our thanks to Mitchell Ivers, Gail Hochman, Jozie Emmerich, Pat Lutz, Mary Pope Osborne and Bill Thomas. They know what they did. So do we and we're grateful.